What they're saying about Jim Michael Hansen's
SHADOW LAWS

"I ripped through the pages so quickly that I had numerous paper cuts at the end of the reading. There are so many twists, turns, and nail bites going on that you better make sure that you have a few hours to set aside to read this book. Once started, I guarantee that you will not be able to put it down. Hansen continues the tradition started with *Night Laws* and is destined to be crowned the new king of the thriller."

—Aldo T. Calcagno, CRIMESPREE MAGAZINE

www.crimespreemag.com

"Writing at a breakneck pace with characters and action that leap off the pages, *Shadow Laws* will make you laugh with joy one minute, and tremble with fear the next. This is what excellent storytelling's all about. Having read tons of crime fiction when I was young, this story really brought me back to the genre in a whole new—and refreshing—way."

—Byron Merritt, FWOMP BOOK REVIEW, www.fwomp.com

"This is the second crime thriller I have read by this author. The first, *Night Laws*, was superb and this new one is even better. ... There are so many twists, turns, and gotcha's in this story that it keeps the reader guessing and surprised all the way to the end ... We rated this author's second book five hearts of heart-stopping action."

—Bob Speer, Editor, HEARTLAND REVIEWS

www.heartlandreviews.com

"Without a *shadow* of a doubt, Hansen knows murder."

—Paul Anik, I LOVE A MYSTERY

www.illoveamysterynewsletter.com

"I believed that Jim Michael Hansen did a good job with his first novel, *Night Laws*, and I expected to feel the same satisfaction from this second book. But I have to say *Shadow Laws* blew my socks off!"

—Kathy Martin, IN THE LIBRARY REVIEWS
www.inthelibraryreviews.net

"A nail-biter, pager-turner read, one that has all the elements that simply must be there for a top-notch murder mystery. Draw the shades, leave the lights on and double lock the doors as you settle back for a bone-chilling adventure. Outstanding and exceptional! Highly recommended!"

—Shirley Johnson, Senior Reviewer, MIDWEST BOOK REVIEW
www.midwestbookreview.com

"Wow. This is how, in short, I would describe *Shadow Laws*, the second in the line of hard-hitting *Laws* series by attorney Jim Michael Hansen… A page-turner of a read that is, mildly put, spectacular… The suspense in the novel is spine chilling… A fine, fine read and a highly recommended buy."

—Nayaran Radhakrishnan, NEW MYSTERY READER MAGAZINE
www.newmysteryreader.com

"Jim Michael Hansen does not make anything easy. His novels contain more spirals than a corkscrew. From the first page, the reader finds him or herself sucked into an unfamiliar area, but that same town becomes vividly real. You can almost smell the victims' fear. Jim Hansen is a master at creating powerful suspense."

—Tracy Farnsworth, ROUNDTABLE REVIEWS
www.roundtablereviews.com

"A very fast moving, exciting, suspense-filled crime thriller… Jim Michael Hansen has a wonderfully unique writing ability that delves deep within the thoughts of the mind of a killer and has brought out the terror that lies underneath. He has come up with yet another thriller that will pull the reader right into the spine-tingling story... It is on-the-edge-of-the-seat excitement that will leave you, the reader, shivering."

—Wanda Maynard, SIMEGEN REVIEWS, www.simegen.com

"Hansen's story surges with action like a screaming Ferrari with no brakes. His plot captivates and terrifies, while the characters vault from the page—alive and kicking—dueling with sizzling dialogue. Throughout the tale, Hansen's razor wit snicks and slices with wry cunning, giving the reader a complex, intriguing and satisfying ride."

—Mark Bouton, author of *Max Conquers the Cosmos* and
Cracks in the Rainbow, www.markbouton.com

"From the opening scene to the wrap up, *Shadow Laws* is one edgy thriller. Edgy characters, edgy plot, skillful storytelling—a page-turner for sure. The opening scene grabs you immediately and the pacing keeps you turning pages all the way to the end. Definitely a recommended read!"

—L.B. Cobb, author of *Splendor Bay* and *Promises Town*
www.LBCobb.com

"Chills will crawl over your skin and up your spine as you join Detective Bryson Coventry in his latest case... A fast-paced, well-plotted tale by very talented author Jim Michael Hansen... Danger lurks on each page. Highly recommended."

—Anne K. Edwards, author of *Death on Delivery* and
Journey into Terror, www.mysteryfiction.net

"Chiller thriller."

—Geraldine Evans, author of the *Rafferty & Llewellyn* series and the
Cassey & Catt series, www.geraldineevans.com

"Jim Hansen has again captured the evil that men do and created a detective's criminal nightmare."

—Lt. Jon Priest, Homicide Unit, Denver Police Department
Criminal Investigation Expert Consultant for Court TV

"In Jim Hansen's latest legal thriller, *Shadow Laws*, he does it all: vividly evokes a setting, Denver, from its sleazy Colfax Avenue bars to its slick Cherry Creek mansions; brings to life a quirky bunch of characters; and twists a plot so capably that the reader hasn't a chance to put the book down until it's finished."

—Ann Ripley, author of the *Louise Eldridge* gardening mysteries

"Jim Hansen's books just get stronger and stronger. *Shadow Laws* is part police procedural, part legal thriller, and completely satisfying."

—Mark Terry, author of *Dirty Deeds* and *The Devil's Pitchfork*
www.mark-terry.com

"A taut, crisply written psychological thriller, steamy as homicide cop, Bryson Coventry's sun-baked streets of Denver. *Shadow Laws* has everything you could want in a suspense novel—intriguing complex characters, a gripping tension-filled plot, fast-paced action and a villain so menacing we are reminded on every page how unsafe is this world in which we live. Jim Michael Hansen has given his fans another winner."

—Nancy Tesler, author of the *Carrie Carline*
Other Deadly Things series, www.nancytesler.com

"As with *Night Laws*, this is the thriller equivalent of comfort food."

—Russel D. McLean, CRIME SCENE SCOTLAND
www.crimescenescotland.com

ALSO BY JIM MICHAEL HANSEN

NIGHT LAWS
ISBN 0-9769243-0-7
Trade Paperback $13.95

Denver homicide detective Bryson Coventry is on the hunt for a vicious killer who has warned attorney Kelly Parks, Esq., that she is on his murder list. Something from the beautiful young lawyer's past has come back to haunt her, something involving the dark secrets of Denver's largest law firm. With the elusive killer ever one step away, Kelly Parks frantically searches for answers, not only to save her life but also to find out whether she unwittingly participated in a murder herself.

What they're saying about Jim Michael Hansen's
NIGHT LAWS

"Talk about a Rocky Mountain High…"
            —Jack Quick, BOOKBITCH, www.bookbitch.com

"Hansen's got what it takes to make your heart pound."
            —Angie Cimarolli, BOOK PLEASURES, www.bookpleasures.com

"*Night Laws* is fast paced and well plotted… While comparisons will be made with Turow, Grisham and Connelly, Hansen is a new voice on the legal/thriller scene. I recommend you check out this debut book, but be warned…you are not going to be able to put it down."

—Aldo T. Calcagno, CRIMESPREE MAGAZINE
www.crimespreemag.com

"Jim has managed not only to put together a believable and strongly created cast of characters, but the plot that they dance so nimble along would stand up against Hitchcock in a psychological standoff."

—Naomi DeBruyn, LINEAR REFLECTIONS
www.linearreflections.com

"Jim Michael Hansen works every angle that a thriller should have…leaving you in a heap of reading ecstasy. *Night Laws*, in my humble opinion, is a Masterpiece…"

—Shirley Johnson, Senior Reviewer,
MIDWEST BOOK REVIEW, www.midwestbookreview.com

"This is a tightly written, titillating contemporary mystery and it leaves you with a feeling that this could really be true… Enjoy discovering how it all turns out in this erotic, noir legal suspense thriller that is guaranteed to entertain readers and especially those who like a John Grisham type thriller!"

—Cheryl McCann, Editor, REVIEW BOOKS
www.review-books.com

"Fans of shows like *24* will love *Night Laws*, the first book in the *Laws* series about Denver Bryson Coventry of Denver… The plot moves at a breakneck speed… There is never a dull scene or a slack moment…"

—Linnea Dodson, REVIEWING THE EVIDENCE
www.reviewingtheevidence.com

"Jim Hansen has the ability to move readers from the edge of their seats and back multiple times while keeping the reader absorbed, turning pages wanting to learn more. The characters are well drawn; and the novel is an intense, fulfilling read."

—Karen L. MacLeod, SIMEGEN REVIEWS, www.simegen.com

"Jim Hansen has crafted a tough and hardbitten legal thriller, compelling and intricately plotted by an author who clearly knows his terrain."

—Baron R. Birtcher, author of *Roadhouse Blues*, *Ruby Tuesday* and *Angles Fall*, www.baronbirtcher.com

"Jim Hansen's *Night Laws* delivers a suspenseful storyline with a strong dose of action that will hold the reader's attention until the very last page; a welcome throwback to the classic crime noir genre."

—Tony M. Cheatham, author of *Round Up* and *Father's Footsteps*, www.tonymcheatham.com

"This high altitude, high suspense tale of mystery and intrigue takes you up the high rise and into the sanctuary of one of America's top law firms in search of a murderer that will leave you dying to know more."

—Eric L. Harry, author of *Arc Light*, *Society of the Mind*, *Protect and Defend*, and *Invasion*, www.eharry.com

"A chilling story well told. The pace never slows in this noir thriller, taking readers on a stark trail of fear."

—Carolyn G. Hart, author of the Death on Demand series and the Henrie O series, www.carolynhart.com

"If you're a John Grisham fan, you'll really enjoy Jim Michael Hansen's novels."

—Joan Hall Hovey, author of *Nowhere to Hide*, *Chill Waters* and *Listen to the Shadows*, www.joanhallhovey.com

COMING NEXT

[UNTITLED] LAWS
ISBN 978-0-9769243-6-4
(2007)

Women who mysteriously disappeared several months ago
are found in shallow graves near one another, each killed in a
distinct, brutal manner. As Bryson Coventry's frantic investigation takes him on a wild ride from the highbrow boardrooms of
Denver's largest law firms to the bed of a suspect, he discovers
that the killing is far from over and that answers come with a
heavy price.

SHADOW LAWS

A NOVEL

Jim Michael Hansen

DARK SKY PUBLISHING, INC.
GOLDEN, CO 80401

Dark Sky Publishing, Inc.
Golden, CO 80401
www.darkskypublishing.com

Copyright © 2007 by Jim Michael Hansen
www.jimhansenbooks.com
www.jimhansenlawfirm.com

ISBN-10: 0-9769243-4-X
ISBN-13: 978-0-9769243-4-0

Library Of Congress Control Number: 2005911022

Cover photography / Getty Images

10 9 8 7 6 5 4 3 2 1

Made in the USA

DEDICATED TO
EILEEN

Acknowledgements

The author gratefully thanks and acknowledges the generosity, encouragement and contributions of the following fantastic people, without whom the *Laws* novels would be nothing more than dusty paper stuffed in a old desk drawer:

Paul Anik, Baron R. Birtcher, Rebecca Blackmer, Kathy Boswell, Mark Bouton, Aldo T. Calcagno, Tony M. Cheatham, Angie Cimarolli, L.B. Cobb, James A. Cox, Lisa D'Angelo, Naomi DeBruyn, Linnea Dodson, Anne K. Edwards, Geraldine Evans, Tracy Farnsworth, Sgt. Mike Fetrow, Denise Fleischer, Barbara Franchi, Norman P. Goldman, Eric L. Harry, Carolyn G. Hart, Emily Hois, Joan Hall Hovey, Shirley Priscella Johnson, Jon Jordan, Harriet Klausner, J.A. Konrath, Cathy Langer, Katherine Shand Larkin, Andrei V. Lefebvre, Sarah Lovett, Karen L. MacLeod, Kathy Martin, Wanda Maynard, Cheryl McCann, Russel D. McLean, Evan McNamara, Byron Merritt, K. Preston Oade, Jr., Stephanie Padilla, Sally Powers, Lt. Jon Priest, Nayaran Radhakrishnan, Patricia A. Rasey, Ann Ripley, Shelley Singer, Bob Spear, Mark Terry, Nancy Tesler, Safiya Tremayne and Laurraine Tutihasi; and

My many friends at Barnes & Noble, Borders, and countless other fine bookstores throughout the country; and

The many people I have had the pleasure to meet at my author events; and, most importantly,

My readers.

Chapter One

Last Month - June 15
Wednesday Night

THE YOUNG WOMAN SHIFTED the half-empty cup of Zinfandel to her left hand, set the cruise control of the car at 105, and dimmed the dashboard lights until the gauges disappeared entirely. With the interior of the vehicle now in total darkness, the black desert nightscape took on an even greater surrealistic edge as the headlights punched through it.

Outside, the dotted white lines of the two-lane road blurred together like cartoon frames and looked like one long string of white. The automobile drifted over the line and she brought it back, shifting her body in search of a more comfortable position.

"Mark your map," she said, "because we're officially in the middle of nowhere."

The man in the passenger seat chuckled, then said: "There goes another one."

"Another what?"

"Squashed rattlesnake," he said. Then he laughed as if he'd just heard a joke.

"What?" she questioned, curious.

He shook his head. "I mean, talk about your basic bad luck. Here you are, a rattlesnake, out here in the middle of the desert, and you come to a road. It's probably the only road you'll ever see in your entire reptilian life. You go to cross it. It's going to take you—what?—thirty seconds, maybe? You're ten seconds into it and then—wham!—the only car within twenty miles flattens your ass."

She pictured it and chuckled. "Just not your day," she said.

"Apparently not."

The road ran flat and straight, occasionally rising or falling with the curvature of the desert floor but not bending an inch to the right or the left. The car purred, unchallenged, and even at this speed seemed to still be half asleep.

She brought the cup of wine to her mouth and drained it, feeling the alcohol drop warm and tingly into her stomach.

"It is weird though," he added. "There you are, one minute everything's perfect, and the next you're totally screwed. And you really didn't do anything, except travel through time for a few seconds, just like you've done a gazillion times before."

She considered it. "There's a difference between just traveling through time for a few seconds, and traveling through time *stupidly* for a few seconds. A huge difference."

"Example," he said.

"Take that rattlesnake," she said. "All he had to do was look around a little before he slithered his little ass onto the asphalt."

"Look around for what?"

"What do you mean, for what?—for cars."

He laughed. "For cars? Rattlesnakes don't even have brains. They don't even know that cars exist."

She smiled. "Yeah, well, they have enough brains to know they need to be looking around for *stuff*, all kinds of stuff, is what I'm saying." She handed him the empty cup. "More, s'il vous plait."

"I love it when you talk dirty."

The man swallowed what was left in the beer can, his third, and then powered down the passenger window. The desert air immediately rushed into the vehicle, loud and hot and furious, punctuating their speed. He flung the can into the darkness and powered the glass back up as fast as he could.

"Goddamn hurricane out there," he said.

Then he twisted around to the back seat, managed to get the top of the cooler up, and pulled out another can of Bud Light for himself, plus the bottle of Zinfandel. Both were ice cold. He poured what was left of the wine bottle into her cup, filling it to the brim, handed it to her, and then powered the window back down just far enough to throw the bottle out.

She took it. "Merci beaucoup."

They popped in a CD and settled into the ride while the desert rolled by outside, seriously stunning in a video-arcade-game kind of way. Small bushes dotted the landscape, a tribute to Darwinism at its best. Somehow they managed to not only find a way to live out here, but actually thrive.

"You know, you get out here, in a place like this, and it's like the rest of the world doesn't even exist," she said. "I mean, look around. I'll bet it looked the same exact way a thousand years ago. No people, no buildings, no nothing."

The man chuckled.

"What?"

"Just the contrast," he said. "Here, absolutely nothing. A hundred miles from here, more lights than some entire galaxies."

"Can't wait," she said.

He nodded. "I just hope this actually happens," he said.

"It will." She exhaled. "It has to."

HE ROLLED A JOINT and they passed it back and forth until it was gone.

Then he rolled another.

She knew that the smell would hang in her clothes and probably be noticed when they checked into the hotel later this evening but really didn't give a shit.

The wine felt good in her gut but the pot would take her to the next level. She could get higher than she was and still have more than enough control to keep the vehicle pointed in a straight line. It wasn't like they were in the middle of a New York rush hour.

The desert floor rose and fell more now. At times, when the road crested, the vehicle actually lifted as it flew over the crown, making her lighter in her seat.

Time passed and the miles clicked off. Songs came and went. Some they listened to twice, others they couldn't skip over fast enough.

Then the man had his hand on her leg, just above her knee. "Let's see what we have up here," he said, inching it up teasingly.

She bit her lower lip and spread her muscular legs ever so slightly. He hiked up her skimpy cotton skirt, exposing her panties, and ran one finger up and down the inside of her golden thigh.

"Say, *Take my panties off,*" he told her.

She said it, lifting her ass off the seat as she did.

He slipped them off, briefly waved them like a victory flag, and then tossed them into the back. Then he put a hand on each knee and spread her legs apart as far as they would go. She let him, then left them there.

He went back to running a finger ever so teasingly up and down the inside of her thigh. Then finally, after an eternity, he touched her where it counted, with that magic rhythm of his.

The road went on, perfectly straight.

The heat built up between her thighs and her hips gyrated with a mind of their own, getting the most from his contact.

They crested a hill. Then . . .

Shit!

They were on the wrong side of the road.

Headlights came directly at them.

Another car.

There was no time to get back in their lane.

They were going to crash head-on.

She clenched the steering wheel with all her might and stared at the lights. Then, just before impact, she shut her eyes as tight as they would go and screamed . . .

Chapter Two

Day One - July 11
Tuesday Morning

WITH A MORNING BRAIN THAT STILL WASN'T ready for the
world, Taylor Sutton, Esq., unlocked the door of her dark three-
room law office, stepped inside and flicked on the lights. The
familiar décor greeted her like an old friend, a décor described
by some as more befitting a sleazy private eye from an old
black-and-white TV show—cheap gray metal filing cabinets, a
scratched pine desk with about two thousand coffee cup rings,
and mismatched furniture that looked like leftovers from rainy-
day flea markets.

She wore a sleeveless green cotton shirt, shorts, white socks
and white tennis shoes. She also wore a bra, but it was a thin
flimsy thing, just enough for some push-up and cupping. She
wasn't in the mood for discomfort today, not to mention it was
supposed to be over a hundred again. Not your typical attorney
attire, granted. But life is too short to not be comfortable. If
someone wanted a stuffed shirt or a pinstriped suit sitting behind the desk, they could take their business down the street.

She really didn't care.

Of course she had real clothes, a whole closet full, right behind that door over there—all conservative with an expensive hang, more than acceptable for a 29-year-old attorney.

Books covered the east wall from floor to ceiling, many of them law books, but just as many hardbacks and paperbacks. Every book ever written by James Michener, Ayn Rand and John Steinbeck was there somewhere, plus just about every hardback mystery or thriller to hit the *NY Times* Bestsellers List in the last ten years.

There were no diplomas or awards on the walls; they were all safe and sound in boxes at home, in the basement or garage somewhere. But there were lots of newspaper headlines and articles with her name displayed under glass, albeit in mismatched plastic frames.

She kicked off her tennis shoes and walked over to the coffee machine in her socks. The carpet felt good under her feet. She jiggled the cord to get machine working, and then booted up the computers and printers while it gurgled.

Outside, Denver started to wake up.

HER OFFICE WAS A SECOND-FLOOR WALKUP, above a souvenir shop on the 16th Street Mall in the heart of downtown, not far from the Paramount Café. Shuttle busses ran up and down the street and lots of people were already downtown and on the move. The shuttles were electric now and the smell of diesel didn't hang in the air anymore. That made the city less city-like, somehow.

She set the alarm clock fifteen minutes early this morning, as usual, so she could spend some time with the vibrator before crawling out of bed. That usually kept her hormones in check until noon. But this morning she fell back asleep and missed the whole thing.

Her thoughts strayed to getting drunk and laid.

AT EIGHT O'CLOCK SHARP, her appointment—longtime friend Nick Trotter, Esq., the infamous criminal lawyer himself— arrived right on time. He wore a summer-weight Brooks Brothers suit and had his hair in the usual ponytail. He hugged her, handed her a cardboard sign—Will Litigate for Food—and headed over to the coffee machine, looking over his shoulder to get her reaction.

"Thought you might need that," he said.

She held it at arms length and studied it.

"The lettering needs to be bigger," she said.

He chuckled.

"You need to be able to read it from thirty feet, through a dirty windshield," she added.

He pondered it, and agreed. "You're way too much of a free spirit for your own good, you know that I hope."

"Yeah, but I don't give a shit."

"I rest my case."

TWO MINUTES LATER SHE ENDED UP BEHIND HER DESK, and he in a chair, with an unusually serious look on his face.

"Listen," he said, "let me tell you why I wanted to see you. By the way, I'm coming to you as a client, not a friend, so turn the meter on and open a file."

She started to wave him off but he pushed a check for $10,000 across the desk. "That's a retainer," he said.

"Nick, you're insulting me."

"This is for me," he interrupted. "I need this to be formal."

She left the check where it was and studied him.

"What's going on?" she asked.

He shifted around and for a moment she thought he was actually going to get up and leave. But he didn't. Instead, he cleared his throat and said: "It's pretty simple, really. About two years ago, someone by the name of Mr. Northwest mailed me $5,000 in cash, out of the blue, as a retainer apparently, with a note that he'd be calling me later."

She picked up a pencil and started jotting down notes.

"Lucky you."

He chuckled. "Yeah, so I thought. Anyway, time goes on, and then one day I get a call from the mysterious Mr. Northwest. It was mostly light chitchat. In hindsight, he was feeling me out."

"Oh yeah? About what?"

"Confidentiality, I think."

"Confidentiality?"

Nick nodded. "He was trying to figure out if I was the kind of guy who knows how to keep a client's secret a secret." He slurped the coffee and retreated in thought. "I must have passed the test, because the calls started coming quicker and lasting longer. It was becoming more and more apparent that he just wanted someone he could brag to in a confidential setting."

"Brag to about what?"

Nick shrugged. "Nothing specific. He was always careful to not give me details. But things were weird enough that I started to tape the conversations." He pulled a CD out of his briefcase and pushed it across the desk. "I copied them for you, about forty of them."

Taylor picked it up and twisted it in her hand.

"To this day I don't know who he is," Nick told her. "I don't know his name—other than Mr. Northwest, which is no doubt a fake. I don't know his address or phone number or anything else."

"So you have a client and don't know who he is," Taylor said. "That's interesting."

"That's my question," Nick said. "Do I have a client or not? I've never taken a cent of the money he sent; it's still sitting in a trust account. I've never formally given him any legal advice, and I don't know who he is."

"But you've talked to him forty times?"

"Roughly."

"So what's the issue Nick, exactly?"

He twisted a pencil in his fingers. "I want a legal opinion from you as to whether these telephone conversations are within the attorney-client privilege."

"Because?"

He hesitated. "Because if they're not, then I'll know that I have the option to turn them over to the police, if I decide to."

Taylor couldn't help but laugh.

"Nick, this is me. Stop feeding me bullshit. First of all, you know damn well these conversations are privileged, whether or not you formally take this guy on as a client or not. Just communicating in this type of manner is enough to invoke the privilege, particularly after you took money from the guy. Second, you'd be the last person on the face of the earth to ever give the cops anything." She leaned towards him. "So stop wasting my time and tell me what's going on."

He chuckled, with a nervous edge.

"Okay, here's the deal. I want to have these phone conversations in someone else's file besides mine. Giving them to you and requesting a legal opinion is one way to do that without breaking the privilege."

She nodded. That was true. He could give them to her because she was as bound to honor the privilege of the communications as he was. She couldn't show them to anyone any more than he could, even though technically speaking Mr. Northwest wasn't her client, Nick was.

"What's so important about having these in someone else's file?" she asked.

"The truth?"

"No, give me lies and deceit like everyone else."

He grinned, then grew serious. "Someone tried to run me off the road Saturday night and my gut tells me it was Mr. Northwest. So, I want someone else to know what's going on, and to have the phone conversations, in case something happens to me."

She pondered it.

Nick wasn't a man who exaggerated.

Or scared easily.

"Have you tried to track him?" she asked.

Nick shook his head. "Not really. I mean, I've always been curious, but not curious enough to throw time at it."

She picked up a book of matches, lit one, waved it out and threw it in the ashtray—a nervous habit she'd had since age twenty, when she quit smoking after four years.

The sweet smell of sulfur hung in the air.

"Tell me about getting run off the road," she said.

He had a hesitant look, as if reaching for it, then said: "Saturday night, about ten o'clock. I'm driving on Santa Fe, way down south, halfway to Castle Rock, when someone in a pickup truck starts playing cat and mouse with me, pulling up alongside, getting on my tail, that kind of thing."

"Any damage?"

"No actual contact," Nick said. "But only because I kept evading him. Then, after a couple of minutes, he just dropped behind, turned around and vanished."

"Weird."

She looked down at the CD and back at him.

"So what do you want from me?" she asked. "Other than to hang on to the CD?"

Nick leaned forward. "Find out who he is," he said.

She studied him. "That's not what I do, Nick. You'd be light years ahead with a P.I."

He frowned. "First of all, I'm not so sure that I could even legally give privileged information to an investigator, since he'd be working *against* the client, not for him. It seems doubtful that the attorney work-product doctrine would apply. But even if it did, I still want you to handle this."

"Yeah, well, you're making a mistake."

"Maybe, but it's my mistake to make."

She studied him. "How much money do you want to throw at this, exactly?"

He looked her straight in the eyes. "Whatever it takes. This guy's going to kill me. I can feel it."

She cocked her head, lit another match and blew it out.

Smoke snaked towards the ceiling.

"Why?"

He shrugged and looked genuinely puzzled. "I don't have a goddamn clue."

CLAUDIA MARTINEZ, TAYLOR'S PERSONAL ASSISTANT and

army of one, got the news about the Nick Trotter case as soon as she reported for work, before she could even sit down and put her purse in the drawer. As Taylor laid out the details, the young assistant's forehead got tighter and tighter. "I'd stay away from him if I was you," she said in that thick Columbian accent of hers. "And you know why."

Chapter Three

Day One - July 11
Tuesday Morning

DOWNTOWN DENVER ALREADY RADIATED heat, even this early in the morning, warning of yet another blistering July day. Lieutenant Bryson Coventry—the 34-year-old head of Denver's Homicide Unit—took off his sport coat, too hot to care if his weapon scared anyone. He walked down the 16th Street Mall deeper into the frying pan, concentrating on trying to find the place he was supposed to meet Jena Vernon. She was the last person he expected to get a call from this morning, anxious to meet him as soon as possible.

Two minutes later he entered an Einstein Bros, spotting her almost immediately at a corner table, waving him over. Most people along the Front Range knew her as the Channel 8 TV roving reporter, the charismatic blond with the big green eyes who was always smack dab in the middle of the mess. Coventry knew her from the old high school days in Fort Collins, when she was the ticklish tomboy down the street, three years younger than him.

"Bryson," she said, hugging him straight on with that famous full body squeeze. She looked expensive and professional, decked out in a summer suit with a crisp white blouse and an inescapable emerald necklace that probably cost more than Coventry's first car.

He spotted two cups of coffee on the table, meaning one was his. He sat down, picked it up and took a sip. Some type of chocolate flavor, piping hot.

"Stirred, not shaken," Jena said.

"Perfect," he said. "Thanks."

"I'm on a short leash, so I don't have time for chitchat," Jena said, getting a serious tone in her voice. "Here's the reason you're here. Last week, Monday I think, the station received this weird letter in the mail."

She handed him an envelope.

It was addressed to the TV station's general manager. It had no return address. Inside was a piece of paper. It said: *Next visit: Weekend of July 7th.* Both the envelope and letter were computer printed. Neither had any handwriting or marks.

The weekend of the 7th was this past weekend.

He looked at her, confused.

"Now get ready for the weirder part," she said. "This showed up in this morning's mail." She handed him a second envelope, mailed yesterday, Monday, according to the postmark. Inside there was one piece of paper, a Xerox copy of a driver's license—the driver's license of one Ashley Conner to be exact. He studied the document and saw the photograph of a young woman with a timid look, neither pretty nor ugly. She had the plain vanilla appearance of a person you could watch for two hours in a movie at night and then not recognize the next morning if she stopped you on the street and slapped you in the face with a hotdog. According to the woman's license, she was nineteen years old.

Coventry felt a knot in his stomach.

Jena waited for him to process the information and said: "We did some snooping around this morning to see if we could find out who this Ashley Conner is, to figure out if this is just some kind of a prank. She's not in the phonebook. So we had someone swing by the address on her driver's license. It turned out to be a crappy little apartment building off Broadway. The mailbox has her name on it all right, but no one answered when we knocked. That's when we decided that the police should have this information. Since I know you, I volunteered to be the messenger."

"Thanks," he said.

She hesitated, then said: "Bryson, I'm hoping that this turns out to be a great big nothing. But if this is the opening act of some publicity-crazed maniac, and you want to give me an inside track on the story, that would be fine with me."

He frowned. "Let's not jump the gun."

"I'm just saying *if*," she said, standing and hugging him. "I got to run."

"Wait."

"What?"

"Did any other TV stations get letters like this, do you know?"

She shrugged. "We don't exactly sleep with each other."

He raised an eyebrow: "So who do you sleep with?"

She looked at him over her shoulder as she walked off: "Why, are you applying for the job?"

"What's the pay?" he asked. He intended that to be the last of the discussion and fully expected her to keep walking. But instead she came back, leaned in close and whispered in his ear: "The pay is very, very good. Send your application in."

Chapter Four

Day One - July 11
Tuesday Morning

THIRTY MINUTES LATER COVENTRY FOUND HIMSELF on
the south side of the city, circling the neighborhood around
Ashley Conner's apartment building, finally finding a place to
park on Broadway in front of a bondage paraphernalia shop. He
walked up the street past a tattoo parlor, a vacant building with a
full-length crack in the glass, and a Chinese takeout place. Then
he turned west down the first street he came to and kicked a
box down the middle of the sidewalk until he came to the
woman's building.

The elevator had a cardboard sign duct taped on it that said
Broke, which was all the same to Coventry because he wouldn't
have stepped inside it to escape a T-Rex attack. So he hiked up
the dim-lighted cinderblock stairwell to the fourth floor.

When he came to apartment 406—Ashley Conner's place—
he put his ear to the door and listened for signs of movement,
heard none, then rapped on the door.

No one answered.

He tried the doorknob and found it locked.

Damn it.

He knocked again.

Come on, be home; don't be dead on me, I don't have the time.

Suddenly the door behind him opened. When he turned he found a woman standing there, a woman so striking that it took him a moment to realize that she was major pissed-off and ready to smack him upside his head.

"Get the hell out of here before I call the cops," she said. By the look on her face she most definitely meant business. Coventry backed up and held his hands up in surrender, then pulled a business card out of his wallet and handed it to her.

"Here's the number," he said.

He studied her as she read it. She had a dark exotic Island Girl edge, with hair down her back, thick and black, looking as if she had washed it, let it hang until it dried, and then raked it out with her fingers. She wore a pink T-shirt barely long enough to cover her ass; no pants or socks, just legs. Her body was strong and toned and taller than most. She looked to be around twenty-eight or twenty-nine. She should be sipping Margaritas in a South Beach bar and fighting off men instead of hiding her life away in a rat-hole like this.

No ring on her finger.

"You're with homicide?" she questioned. She had a soft English accent, very sexy.

"Yes."

"Is Ashley dead?"

He shifted his weight to his left foot. "Not that I know of," he said, which was true.

"So what do you want with her?"

Coventry shrugged. "I just want to be sure she's okay."

"Why wouldn't she be?"

"No reason, I'm just checking," he said. "You don't happen to know where she is, do you?"

She shook her head. "School, I'd assume. She goes to art school, the Art Students League, down on Grant Street."

Coventry found himself focusing on a smell.

It came from the woman's apartment.

"Sorry," he apologized, "I thought I smelled coffee."

"You did."

"Oh."

"Does that mean you want some?"

He shrugged. "I wouldn't want to intrude."

"What if it wasn't an intrusion?"

"Then I wouldn't mind intruding."

INSIDE THE WOMAN'S APARTMENT, Coventry sat down on a couch that could have used a few more springs. The place was clean and organized, but frugal. He could duplicate everything in there for five hundred dollars and still have change left over for a Big Mac.

While she set about making a fresh pot, he stepped into the hallway for a minute to call Detective Shalifa Netherwood, the newest member of the Homicide Unit—a young African American woman who Coventry stole from Vice Unit almost a year ago. After filling her in, he asked if she could find out whether Ashley Conner was scheduled to attend class this morning and, if so, whether she had shown up. He also wanted her to call the other TV stations and find out if they received envelopes similar to Jena Vernon's.

Back inside, the woman told him her name.

Darien Jade.

He liked it.

Darien Jade.

For a brief moment he pictured them together, at a nice air-conditioned restaurant, laughing and getting tipsy, with a long night still ahead.

Her apartment faced east and was already heating up, in spite of the open windows and the fan. He couldn't imagine what it would be like at four this afternoon when the asphalt got sticky.

She handed him a cup of coffee, black.

"Sorry, no cream or sugar," she said. "Money's a little tight."

He took a sip. It was hot and actually pretty good. "Thanks. I'm going to need a lot of this today."

She sat on the couch next to him and crossed her legs. "Your eyes are two different colors," she said. "One's blue and one's green. I've never seen that before."

Coventry shrugged. "One of my many flaws," he said.

She smiled briefly and then grew serious. "So what's going on with Ashley?"

Coventry pondered the question.

"All I can tell you is we have some information that's suspicious. That doesn't mean that she isn't perfectly fine, though. When did you see her last?"

Darien retreated in thought.

"Saturday afternoon, about four-thirty, I guess. Just before she went to work." She sipped coffee and added: "Ashley is only a hundred pounds, dripping wet. She's the smallest, sweetest, most demure, innocent thing you've ever seen in your life. If something happened to her, I can't say that I'm totally surprised. She's the world's perfect victim."

Coventry cocked his head. "What do you mean by that?"

"Let me show you." The woman put her cup down and

walked over to the kitchen cabinets, which were cheap pine painted a putrid olive green. She said, "Turn your face for a minute, because I have to reach up in the cabinet and I'm not wearing anything under this T-shirt."

"Okay," he said, turning his head towards the windows.

"Close your eyes, too."

He did.

Hinges squeaked. "Okay, you can open them."

He did.

"You didn't peek, did you?" she questioned.

He shook his head. "No, but I have to warn you, I used up all my willpower for the entire day. Now I have to cross the street if I get too close to a donut shop and it's all your fault."

She laughed, sat back down and handed him two photographs. "This is Ashley," she said. "You can just look at her and tell that she'll do anything you want. She's nineteen with the heart of an eight-year-old."

Coventry had to admit; she did have an innocent look.

"Guys can smell women like her," she said. "She doesn't give people problems." She sipped her coffee. "I thought you were one of those creeps who comes around to see her."

"What do you mean by that?"

"Let me put it this way," the woman said. "Ashley's not a prostitute or anything, but she runs into guys here and there and they can tell she needs money. So they show up at her door, smiling and polite, with cash in hand, looking for a little company." She looked sympathetic. "The girl has to eat, just like the rest of us."

Coventry nodded.

"I'll bet I've chased three or four guys off in the last couple of weeks."

"So, she's trying to get by on her own? No parents or anything?"

"As far as I can tell, every penny she gets, she gets herself."

SUDDENLY HIS CELL PHONE RANG. Shalifa Netherwood told him that Ashley Conner was in fact scheduled for an eight o'clock class this morning but hadn't shown up; or for yesterday's classes, either. Also, both of the other local TV stations had in fact received similar letters.

"Clear your schedule for the indefinite future," he told her.

She laughed.

"I'm serious," he said, which was true. "Oh, and call the radio stations and see if they got anything."

He hung up and told Darien that Ashley missed class.

The concern on her face was real. "Art is that girl's life. She never misses class, even when she's sick."

Coventry stood up, walked over to the window, and looked down, getting a birds-eye view of some old man rifling through an overfilled dumpster.

The sound of running water came from the bathroom. He must have been distracted by it, because Darien said: "That's the toilet. It runs."

Coventry headed that way. "Let's have a look." The rubber valve in the bottom was old and brittle and didn't fit tight anymore. It would have to be replaced. Also, the chain from the handle to the valve was broke, meaning you had to reach into the water and pull the valve up by hand to flush. He reconnected the separated chain links with a paperclip and at least got the handle working again.

All the while they talked about Ashley Conner. Most of the

young woman's life was spent either at art school or at the Mile High Eatery, a restaurant in lower downtown where she worked as a waitress, straight down Broadway by bus.

"You don't have the key to Ashley's apartment, by chance, do you?"

No she didn't.

He headed for the door. "Thanks for the coffee. I'll be back this afternoon sometime. Are you going to be around?"

"I can be, if you want."

"Good. I'll probably have some more questions for you."

She nodded. "Sure. Whatever you want."

Coventry started through the door and then turned around. "Say, would you mind if I took those two pictures of Ashley with me?"

Two minutes later he was in his truck with the air conditioner on full blast, heading down to the office to work up a search warrant for Ashley Conner's apartment.

She was dead or dying.

He could feel it.

She wasn't the last one, either.

That was even clearer.

Chapter Five

Day One - July 11
Tuesday Noon

NATHAN WICKERSHAM SAT AT A WOBBLY TABLE in a rat-on-a-stick restaurant called Mama's, picking at a stale lunch salad, with the corner of his mouth turned up ever so slightly.

The one and only waitress scurried about, lugging chipped plates full of crappy food from the kitchen to lowlife customers who looked like they were more than ready to argue about whether a 25-cent tip was fair enough.

He didn't pay any attention to her. She took his order, brought him a glass of water, delivered his order, refilled his glass, walked by his table again and again, and asked a number of times if everything was okay. Through all that, he hardly glanced at her. From his table, he had an unobstructed view of Ashley Conner's apartment building, and that's where he focused his attention.

He wore a blue cotton shirt, clean pressed jeans, and New Balance running shoes—size 11 EEE—that he stumbled across on sale last month. The shoes, while sold for "running," would-n't get a second glance from any serious runner. They had good padding and were fairly light, but they'd cost you at least an extra second or two in the quarter mile, if you were actually stupid enough to use them for such a purpose. Wickersham just wore them for walking or light jogging.

The quarter mile had always been his best distance. He was just a tad too slow off the line for the hundred-yard dash and didn't quite have enough strength to keep a knees-up sprint going for a full half mile. The quarter mile, however, was his. Even in high school he could whip it out in 52.8 seconds. Today, he could still close it in the 53s, with proper warm-up and a solid day of rest beforehand. Not world class by any means, but more respectable than 99.9 percent of the population.

It always surprised people that he could run that fast. That's probably because most runners had no upper body to speak of. His chest and arms, on the other hand, were the kind you find on a rock climber, rippled and strong beyond their mass, without an ounce of fat. Back in his heyday, he could crank out fifty legitimate pull-ups any day of the week. Today, he could still get forty. They were painful, make no doubt about that, but he could get them.

He was one of the only people he knew who could do a one-armed pull-up. You grab the bar with one hand, hang so that your arm is completely straight, and then get your chin up above the bar without using the other arm or swinging your legs.

It sounds easy.

It's not.

He can do it with either arm.

AS EXCEPTIONAL AS HIS BODY WAS, it wasn't his crowning genetic achievement. That award would have to go to his intellect. He graduated from Harvard in just three years, fifth in his class, with a double major, Mathematics and Physics. From there he went straight to Yale, picking up master's degrees in both subjects; then on to Berkeley for his Ph.D.s. All his education, of course, was under a full scholarship.

The Ph.D. in Mathematics was tricky, even for him. You have to think of something new, something no one has ever thought of before. That means you either have to take an existing mathematical universe—like Topography or Real Analysis—and extend it, or you have to take two different mathematical universes, and bridge them. He came up with a triple thesis, bridging two mathematical universes and then finding a way to extend both of them, leveraging from the bridge.

Every mathematician in the world learned his name.

The Ph.D. in physics, of course, was a lot easier. With a whole physical world out there to grab, he could come up with topics for physics dissertations *ad nauseam* if he had to.

Of course, all that was before his life went to shit.

HE FINISHED EATING and the waitress took his plate. Unfortunately, it looked like he'd been wasting his time. There simply wasn't any action at Ashley Conner's apartment building.

The waitress brought his check; with tax, it came to $5.35.

Then it happened.

A Channel 5 News van came down Broadway and started to slow down as it approached Ashley Conner's street.

Bingo!

Wickersham flagged down the waitress, handed her a ten, told her to keep the change and then walked out the door.

The heat hit him immediately.

It was supposed to get over a hundred degrees today and

had to be every bit of that right now.

He headed straight for the Camry, walking as fast as he could without arousing suspicion. He had left the windows cracked, but the interior still had to be at least a hundred and twenty degrees when he opened the door. From the glove box, he grabbed a pair of black-rimmed glasses, a fake moustache and a baseball cap, and put them all on. From the backseat, he grabbed a notebook and a pen. Then he shut the door and headed straight to Ashley Conner's apartment building, getting there just about the same time that the TV crew had organized themselves and were walking up to the building.

He nodded to them and fell into step.

"You guys here about the letters?" he asked.

The man carrying the camera, a big red-haired fellow with a history of beer in the gut, looked at him. "Yeah. You?"

"Yeah, same," Wickersham said.

They came to an elevator but a cardboard sign said it was broke, so they headed over to the stairway.

A well-dressed woman barked the orders. Wickersham recognized her as Alicia Beach, a TV reporter with a greatly exaggerated opinion of her relevance to the universe.

The cameraman looked at him. "Who you with?"

"Freelance," Wickersham said. "Hope this is really something, I could use the money."

"No telling," the cameraman said.

They walked up the stairs in silence, concentrating on the climb, with Alicia Beach's made-for-TV face leading the pack. It was cooler in the stairwell than outside, but not by much.

When they finally arrived on the fourth floor, everyone was sweating. The woman, Beach, took a few moments to powder her face and get her breath back while the cameraman set up,

41

pointing the lens at the door with the 406 on it.

Wickersham stood there looking as nonchalant as he could, fighting to keep the excitement from busting through.

When everything was finally set up, the reporter knocked on the door while the camera rolled.

No one answered.

She knocked again.

Nothing.

"Okay," she finally said, stepping back, "cut. No one's home."

AT THAT MOMENT THE DOOR from the stairwell opened and two figures entered the hallway, a man who carried a sport coat draped over his forearm, and an African American woman.

Both wore weapons.

Wickersham knew the man—Bryson Coventry—only too well from the TV, but had only been this close to him once before, and that was by accident. Coventry was a fair height, about six-two, with a solid build that looked like it had been downright chiseled at one point. His face looked like something that belonged on a magazine cover. Thick brown hair flopped down over his forehead, which he combed back with his fingers, only to have it flop down again. He had a no-nonsense air to him. And his eyes—there was something wrong with his eyes, no, not *wrong*, but unusual.

Wickersham wasn't sure, one way or the other, if he could take Coventry in a bare-knuckles, life-or-death fistfight. It would be close. Wickersham would be faster and just as strong if not stronger. But Coventry had a slight height advantage and a definite weight advantage. He wasn't a runner, though, that much was obvious.

The African American woman, on the other hand, had all the earmarks of a sprinter. Even though she wore a loose suit, Wickersham could sense the power in her thighs and ass and stomach by the way she walked. She wore no makeup and didn't really need any. She looked to be about twenty-four or twenty-five and had a street-wise air to her.

Wickersham shifted behind the cameraman as the two figures approached.

Before anyone could say anything more than the usual meet-and-greet, Coventry had his arm around the shoulders of Alicia Beach, escorting her towards the end of the hall, saying, "Let me talk to you in private for a minute."

Wickersham hated the way the reporter went with him so willingly. Coventry's life always came to him way too easily. But that would change.

Wickersham knew what they were talking about.

Coventry was trying to keep a lid on the publicity.

It would never work.

Maybe short term, but not in the end.

Everyone else hung behind, complaining about the heat, while Coventry and the reporter spoke in low voices at the end of the hall. When they finally walked back towards the group, the reporter told everyone, "We're done here. Let's go."

Wickersham went with them, to all intents and purposes just one more person from their group. Coventry and the African American woman were already entering the apartment of Ashley Conner, using a key, before Wickersham made it to the stairwell.

He started down, smiling inside.

The game had begun.

As he walked down the stairs, someone climbed up—a

woman carrying a bag of groceries. Wickersham covered his face as she went by, but peeked enough to tell that she was absolutely stunning. She wore abbreviated, cutoff jean shorts that showcased the most incredible legs he had ever seen. He couldn't help but look back up at her after she passed.

The cameraman did too; then he looked at Wickersham with a *Wow* expression on his face, as if saying he'd have no trouble eating her for breakfast, lunch and dinner. Wickersham nodded to him in one hundred percent agreement.

Wow indeed.

She would most definitely be fun to spend some quality time with.

Tingling inside, he walked back to the Camry, powered down the windows and turned the air conditioner on full blast. Then he headed into traffic, intent on getting back to see how his little catch, Ashley Conner, was doing.

Get yourself ready, he told her.

Chapter Six

EASING HIS WEARY BODY onto the hard plastic seat of the RTD bus, Bryson Coventry realized as soon as he touched down that someone might sit behind him, not at this stop but at the next one, or the one after that.

Damn it.

If he wasn't so tired, if the workday wasn't already going on seventeen hours and counting, he probably would have been smart enough to take the rear seat right away. Now he had to pry himself up and move back, a pain but worth it.

There, that was better.

Just before the doors swished shut, a small African American man, about forty, ducked in, wandered to the back and took the seat across the aisle. Coventry nodded at him, yawned, and studied the magic-marker graffiti on the seat in front of him.

"I lost my job today," the man said.

Coventry looked over. "Well that sucks."

The man nodded. "Got three kids," he added.

Coventry didn't quite know what to say. Then he pulled out one of his business cards and wrote a name and number on the back. "Call this guy," he said. "Tell him I sent you. That's my name on the front."

The man turned the card over. "Bryson Coventry," he said. "Right."

"I've heard that name somewhere."

Coventry looked at him. "Not from the obituaries, I hope."

The man chuckled. "No, somewhere else."

"Long as it's not the obituaries," Coventry said.

AT THE NEXT STOP the African American man hugged Coventry, said thanks, and got off. Coventry exhaled and stared out the window, breathing diesel fumes and watching Broadway unfold as they headed farther out of downtown.

This is the same bus that Ashley Conner would have taken to go home when her waitress shift at the Mile High Eatery ended at 10 p.m. on Saturday. He wanted to follow her footsteps firsthand, see where she would have gotten off, and what the walk looked like at night from the stop to her apartment.

BEFORE THEY SEARCHED Ashley Conner's apartment this afternoon, Coventry had a pretty good idea what it would look like. It turned out that he wasn't far off; a mattress on the floor, a sink harboring two-week-old dishes, paintbrushes face down in old pickle jars half filled with turpentine, canvases and drawings in progress, an alarm-clock radio, etcetera. A *Monet* calendar thumb-tacked to the wall told them little, other than when her finals were. Nor did they find a diary or address book. The important fact was that there were no signs of a struggle or any indicia of abduction. If someone took Ashley Conner by force, it didn't happen inside her apartment.

The interviews at the Art Students League didn't help as much as he hoped. The teachers and other students portrayed Ashley Conner as a shy, semi-talented student who kept to herself and never missed class. Her locker busted at the seams with supplies, clothes, books and other articles of equal non-interest. She attended all her classes on Friday but didn't show up to any this week, unusual for her. She didn't have a best friend that anyone knew of and no one really knew much about her past, other than she supposedly lost both parents when she was little.

THEN THERE WAS THE INTERVIEW OF BELLA Richardson, the owner of the Mile High Eatery on Champa Street. She turned out to be one of those persons who speaks too loud and stands too close.

Ashley Conner worked as a waitress on the evening shift, from five to ten, Tuesdays through Saturdays. She did in fact show up on Saturday and worked her full shift, leaving at her usual time—a few minutes after ten—for the bus stop, right across the street. She appeared to be in her normal mood and showed no evidence of being upset or stressed. No one weird came into the restaurant Saturday night that Bella could remember, adding, however, "Give me a break. I don't exactly run up to everyone who comes in here and scan 'em with a weird-o-meter."

The city rolled by.

In the downtown area, Broadway saw its fair share of upbeat city life, but then entered a more peripheral zone once it got south of 6th Avenue. There the buildings shrunk, the streets became more dangerous and the trash kicked up. That's where

Coventry got off the bus, three blocks before Ashley Conner's street.

That's where she would have gotten off.

HE BACKED AWAY FROM A PLUME of diesel as the bus pulled away, then walked south with heavy legs and tired eyes, seriously needing the day to end. There were lights around, but not many. Up ahead, two women stepped out of a bar and walked in front of him, holding hands and bumping into one another like lovers.

The bar had the words Soft Sell stenciled on the door.

Curious, he opened it, and found himself immediately inundated with the heavy smell of smoke and alcohol, which triggered memories of the days when he lived to get laid. Several faces turned in his direction, all women. Music played, something energetic that he had never heard before. Lots of women mingled at a bar and tons more danced in the back. The only guy in sight was behind the bar, reminding Coventry of one of the Village People, the one with the black leather.

"Come back when you get tits," someone shouted.

Drunken laughter.

Coventry waved, as if in apology, then stepped back into the night.

The two women were thirty or forty steps in front of him now, coming up to a side street. Coventry expected them to turn down it, to a car, but they crossed instead and continued walking straight, stopping briefly to kiss and grope. He followed, now two blocks from Ashley Conner's street.

Fifty yards later something unexpected happened.

Shadow Laws

HE FOUND HIMSELF WALKING past a dark alley sandwiched between two buildings. He didn't even see it until he was right there. Looking into it, he couldn't see a thing. Someone could be in there not more than twenty feet away and he wouldn't even know it.

He started in, slowing, feeling his way, with litter and refuse brushing against his feet. He couldn't see much looking ahead, but when he turned around and looked back towards the street he could see that the space was wide enough for a car. It kept going for about a hundred and fifty feet and then dead-ended at another alley that came in from a side street.

He came back to Broadway just in time to see the two women entering another building about a block up the street. A small group of other women were strolling down the street towards him.

He kept walking and found the building the two women turned into. It turned out to be a place called Sophia, a bar, another bar filled with women to be exact. A half block farther up, just past Ashley Conner's street, there was yet another one: Voulez Vous. By the light of day, he wouldn't have noticed any of them.

HE WALKED BACK TO THE ALLEY, took twenty steps inside, then stopped and turned back towards the street. Tonight was Tuesday and there wasn't much foot traffic, but last Saturday night there would have been lots of woman bar hopping up and down this three-block stretch of the universe.

If you wanted to abduct a pretty little lady, all you had to do was pull your car in here and point it towards the back. You

49

wait for a single to come along—say Ashley Conner—get her into the alley, and bingo, you're in business.

Back on Broadway, Coventry looked around for any signs of surveillance cameras that could have recorded comings or goings from the alley. He saw none.

HE WASN'T SURE EXACTLY WHY, but he headed over to Ashley Conner's apartment building and walked up to the fourth floor. He rapped on the woman's door, hoping against hope that she would just open it up and be there, safe and sound, and he could go home and curse himself for wasting time.

Instead, no one answered.

He rapped again, just in case.

Silence.

He used her key—the one obtained from the building's owner after they obtained the search warrant this afternoon—to open the door, and then stepped inside to see if there was any evidence that she had returned. The place was exactly as they had left it. The digital numbers on an alarm clock said 11:02.

He flopped down in her bed, just to rest his eyes for a few seconds.

It felt so damn good.

He was sound asleep when someone knocked on the door.

Chapter Seven

Day One - July 11
Tuesday Afternoon

———————————

TAYLOR SUTTON SPENT MOST OF THE AFTERNOON at a class-certification hearing in federal court. When it was over, she took the elevator down to the first floor of the fancy marble courthouse and stopped in the lady's room. There she stripped off her pantyhose, skirt and black leather shoes and swapped them for cotton shorts, ankle socks and tennis shoes that she pulled out of her oversized briefcase. That was much better. Then she hoofed it back to her office.

Claudia Martinez, dressed better than Taylor, looked up from her computer when she walked in. "How'd it go?" she asked.

"Let's put it this way," Taylor said, pulling the blouse out of her shorts and unbuttoning it. "Three big-shot corporate lawyers from New York are about to have a very long plane ride home. It's hotter than hell out there. When is it going to rain?"

She got the blouse off, slipped into a T-shirt, and then hung the top on a hanger, a familiar ritual.

"I did what you asked and have one word for you," Claudia said.

Taylor looked at her, sensing seriousness in her tone. "And what might that be?"

"Creepy."

"The CD?" Taylor questioned.

"Oh, yeah. The CD."

"How creepy?"

"The guy's a killer," Claudia said. "I can see why Nick Trotter's looking over his shoulder. Maybe Nick's actually legit on this whole thing."

"The guy admits killing?"

"No, he never comes right out and admits it, and doesn't mention any names or specific details or anything like that, but when you listen to enough of these conversations and put them together, he's a killer. There's no question in my mind." She picked a pen off her desk and rolled it in her fingers. "Women, young women. That's his passion."

Taylor weighed the words.

"That's your transcript," Claudia said, handing her a manila file folder. "As near as I can make things out. Enjoy."

THAT EVENING AFTER SUPPER, Taylor Sutton drove her 1986 Porsche 911 up Highway 74 into Bear Creek Canyon, twisting through the mountains next to the river with the Targa top off, ending up in a parking space under an aspen tree five or six blocks down from the Little Bear Tavern. She didn't apologize for the Porsche. She had a number of clients who expected her to pull up in something nice. Plus she loved the way the headlights jutted out like torpedoes. It was a lot better looking than the newer models, in her opinion.

She slipped in the CD and followed along with the transcript, lighting matches and throwing them out the window onto the asphalt. Thirty minutes later she couldn't sit in the car anymore, her body just wouldn't let her. The man was a killer all right. But Taylor hadn't found a single clue on how to track him, at least not yet.

Or why he might want to kill Nick Trotter.

Assuming he did.

It was dark now and people had been pouring into the Little Bear ever since she got there, most of them arriving on Harleys. She put the Targa top back on the car, locked it and headed in that direction, wearing shorts and a tank top. A block away she could already hear the band and the hollering.

She fluffed her hair and put a spring in her step.

There was only one thing she needed more than to get drunk right now.

And that was to get laid.

Chapter Eight

Tuesday Night

ASHLEY CONNER MIGHT DIE TONIGHT.

She might not.

That was the beauty of the thing, not being in control.

Right now Nathan Wickersham could only concentrate on the moment. With the headlight of the Kawasaki dirt bike off, and the night blacker than black, he couldn't help but grin and wonder if he wasn't just a little bit crazy as he flew across the pitch-black field in third gear. The motorcycle twitched and bucked like a thing possessed, bouncing off the unseen earth and rocks and vegetation, but it couldn't throw his feet off the pegs or wrench the handlebars out of his grip.

The custom muffler did its job just fine, keeping the engine as quiet as a coffin.

He kept the knobby front tire pointed in a beeline towards the one and only visible light, a two-hundred watt floodlight perched on top of a prefabricated metal building at the other end of his property, more than a mile away.

Finally getting there, he pulled the bike along the side of the building, killed the engine, deactivated the building's security system, and walked around to the front. His quad muscles burned from the ride, not used to the rapid up and down movement. He opened the Master padlock, rolled the overhead door up and flicked on the lights. Inside, just where it should be, sat his getaway car should he ever need it, a 6-cylinder Audi with lots of horses under the hood and 7,500 miles on the odometer.

HE ROLLED THE OVERHEAD DOOR DOWN and started the inspection process, now a weekly ritual.

The vehicle's battery connects to a small trickle charger permanently mounted under the hood, with a plug that disconnects just under the front bumper. He unplugged it from the extension cord, slipped inside the car, pulled the key out from under the front seat, and turned the ignition. The engine fired right up—perfect—and he shut it down almost immediately, not needing the carbon monoxide.

Then he opened the trunk and unzipped the largest suitcase. It held several changes of clothes, leather shoes, tennis shoes, bathroom essentials, three colors of hair dye, two boxes of brown and green contact lenses, a couple of different colored wigs and moustaches, and other necessities. With everything there and as it should be, he zipped it back up and set it on the ground.

Then he turned to a second suitcase, a smaller one, filled with non-perishable food items and water, enough to keep him alive for a full week. Finding everything in place, he set it on the ground.

Good.

Then he turned his attention to the gun case. The shotgun, rifle and handgun—all legal—were inside, together with enough ammunition to get out of any predicament he could envision.

He set it on the ground.

From under the spare tire he pulled out a small black canvas bag and verified that everything was still there: two alias passports, three alias driver's licenses, $25,000 cash, blank checks, a small black book containing the banking information for his accounts in the Caymans, the Bahamas and Mexico City.

Okay, good.

No problems there either.

He put everything back, reconnected the battery charger, locked up, and then walked the two-hundred-yard stretch of gravel driveway from the building to the road—County Road 5—just to be sure there were no obstructions and that the chain across the entrance hadn't been removed.

Okay.

Good.

With everything in order he headed back across the field on the Kawasaki, to the other end of his 350 acres, where the house sat.

A HUNDRED FEET BEHIND HIS HOUSE stood a large prefabricated metal building containing four thousand square feet of footprint that he called the barn. He pulled the dirt bike inside, parked it in its usual place and topped off the tank with 91-octane gas.

As long as he was there, he decided to take a quick look around. The Ford van had been white when he bought it. He painted it black, soundproofed the windowless back compartment and modified the door so that it couldn't be opened from the inside, unless you knew the trick. He also installed eyehooks in the four corners of the floor, to attach handcuffs in case the need arose. Painting the vehicle black had been a brilliant idea. In case the cops ever got lucky enough to know to look for a black van, this one wouldn't pull up if they did a records search.

A toggle switch under the dash operated the two small lights for the rear license plate. When he was doing something he shouldn't, he could turn the lights off. Then, back on the road later, he could turn them on and be legal again. He liked that little setup so much that he installed it on all his vehicles.

He limited use of the van strictly to abductions and body drops. There weren't a lot of neighbors around, but he didn't want even them to know he had a van if he could help it. He only brought it out after dark.

Next to the van sat the hardtop Jeep Wrangler. It could have a value if he needed to escape in the winter, or drive directly into the miles of land that surrounded his property.

Next to that was the white Ford F-150 pickup truck, 8 cylinders, automatic, regular cab, short bed, four-wheel drive. All the vehicles were parked perpendicular, facing the opposite side of the structure, so they could be pulled out at any time without having to move another one.

He kept the Camry, his daily driver, parked next to the house.

All the vehicles were registered in the names of separate dummy corporations. So if the cops ever got lucky enough to get a license plate number, they'd still need a considerable amount of research and time before they had any chance of tracing the car to him.

There'd be another gap tracing him to the property, which was also titled in the name of yet another corporation.

With everything in the world exactly as it should be, he

walked to the house, humming, and let his thoughts turn to Ashley Conner.

Later this evening, very soon in fact, he would visit her. Tonight, however, things would be a lot different than the previous three nights.

Tonight she would play the game.

He grinned, just thinking about it.

FOR SOME REASON, A GLASS OF COLD wine seemed to be just the thing. He headed for the kitchen, pulled a fresh bottle out of the built-in wine cooler in the center island, and set it on the granite countertop next to the remote.

Seeing the remote made him realize he needed music. He picked it up and pointed it towards a wall of electronics in the adjacent room. Seconds later the familiar sounds of the Beach Boys spilled from a sound system that cost him one-point-two wheelbarrows full of money. He uncorked the bottle of wine and poured it into a crystal glass, smiling. The money had been worth it; the music couldn't have been more clear and vibrant if the band had set up right there in his house.

He held the glass up and spun around on the tile floor, as if dancing with a partner. The movement filled his head with flashes of expensive stainless steel appliances, distressed maple cabinets and contemporary light fixtures.

Ashley Conner had never seen this part of the house and never would.

When he got her home Saturday night, she was still unconscious in the back of the van. Nevertheless, out of an abundance of caution, he put a leather hood over her head and cuffed her hands behind her back before removing her. Then he carried her into the house and straight to the dungeon, amazed at how light she was. She didn't wake up for another two hours after that.

WICKERSHAM DESIGNED AND BUILT the dungeon with his own two hands, over a period of two years. At times, he wouldn't work on it for months, having almost no interest in it. Other times he seemed frantic to finish, working fourteen-hour days one after the other.

The house itself was a 5,000 square-foot contemporary stucco ranch with a walkout basement that had ten-foot ceilings. The dungeon occupied the back half of the lower level, hidden silently behind a normal looking recreation room replete with an entertainment center, wet bar and a pool table.

Dungeon was admittedly too strong of a word. True, the space was encased in concrete-filled, rebar-enforced cinderblock walls and soundproofing material galore. But from the inside, it looked more like a nice finished suite, albeit windowless. The main room was downright huge, taking up more than a thousand square feet. It had light-brown carpeting, drywall, oak trim and recessed lights. A queen-size mattress sat on the floor at the far end, near the bathroom. Scattered throughout the rest of the space were the devices; the Saint Andrew's Cross, the rack, the chair, the stocks, etc. Eyebolts for attaching chains and ropes were strategically placed in dozens of places in the floor, ceiling and walls.

The entry to the space is through a solid steel door. There's a second steel door, at the other end of the room, which leads to a small cinderblock room with ceiling hooks, the Punishment Room. Once someone was strung up in there, and the door was shut, they couldn't see or hear a thing. That's where they went if they were stupid enough to damage or deface the main room or the bathroom.

WICKERSHAM PUNCHED ANOTHER BUTTON on the remote control and a 50" flat-panel TV turned on in the adjacent room, displaying Ashley Conner.

She paced back and forth in front of the bed. She wore a steel cuff on each ankle. A heavy tempered chain was padlocked to her right ankle, followed by four feet or so of slack chain, which was then padlocked to her other ankle, followed by another ten or fifteen feet of chain which was padlocked to an eyebolt in the floor. The chain was long enough so that she could access the bathroom, the bed, the refrigerator and the sink without hindrance.

When she first regained consciousness Saturday night, he chained her naked in the Punishment Room with her arms stretched high above her head. He slammed the door and left her there for the better part of an hour, just so she understood.

It must have worked.

So far, she hadn't tried to do anything stupid like let the sink run over with water, tip over the refrigerator, break the lights or trash the walls.

She was a good girl.

Young.

Sweet.

Demure.

The wine crystal now empty, he refilled it and toasted himself.

The time had come to pay his first serious visit to Ashley

Conner. He rounded up the plastic bag, duct tape and dice, then headed downstairs.

Chapter Nine

Day Two - July 12
Wednesday Morning

WHEN BRYSON COVENTRY WOKE Wednesday morning, it
took him a few moments to realize he was on Darien Jade's
couch, the one that could have used a few more springs. The
sounds of early morning traffic sifted through the windows and
a faint orange light washed the room. He remembered Darien
knocking on Ashley Conner's door last night to see why light
was coming from under the door, then finding him asleep and
insisting that he spend the night at her place.

His watch said 5:45 a.m.

Good. He hadn't overslept; he still had a full day to devote
to Ashley Conner.

He stood up, stretched, peeked in Darien's bedroom, found
her sleeping naked on top of the sheets, watched her for a few
seconds, and then headed for the shower.

The hot water came up to temperature surprisingly quickly.
He stepped inside, one of those old bathtub-shower combinations with pink tile walls, pulled the shower curtain closed and
lathered his hair with the one and only shampoo in sight, a
cheap generic bottle of baby shampoo.

Three minutes later he was out, drying his hair with the towel just enough to stop the dripping. He found Darien at the breakfast table eating Cheerios with nonfat milk while the coffee pot gurgled.

"Thanks for last night," she said.

He raised an eyebrow. "What do you mean?"

"Being a gentleman, not making any advances."

"Oh, that." He put a concerned look on his face. "Just don't tell anyone. I have a reputation to maintain."

She chuckled. "If anyone asks, I'll say you rode me until I couldn't walk straight."

He nodded. "That'll work."

She walked past him to the bathroom. "Put that visual away."

He chuckled.

Busted.

HE EXPECTED HER TO BE A HALF HOUR at least. Instead, she was out in about ten minutes, wearing no makeup, dressed in a black T-shirt and jean shorts. Her hair hung wet and straight down her back, soaking the shirt and dripping onto the floor.

Right there, looking just like that, she was the sexiest thing he had ever seen.

"You just let it drip dry?" he asked.

She headed for the coffee and nodded. "Yeah, why?"

"Most women fuss," he said.

"I don't."

"No. Apparently not."

"Life's too short to spend in the bathroom."

Coventry cocked his head. "So where do you spend your

time?"

She looked at him, and for a second seemed to be defensive. Then she relaxed and said, "Around."

THEY BRUSHED THEIR TEETH—Coventry using his index finger—and stepped outside, cups of coffee in hand. Two minutes later they were in the alley that Coventry stumbled across last night, to see what they could see by the light of day.

"What are we looking for?" Darien questioned.

Coventry shrugged. "It's like a good song. You know it when you see it."

"Personally I've never seen a song."

"You know what I mean."

A few minutes later she said, "Hey, over here."

Coventry walked over and found her squatting down by a water bottle with ASL lettering.

"That's Ashley's," Darien told him. "ASL stands for Art Students League. She carried that thing everywhere."

Coventry left it in place and used his cell phone to call the Crime Unit. Darien Jade, bless her heart, went back to the apartment and returned five minutes later carrying the entire pot of coffee, which they drank until the van showed up. Paul Kubiak—one of the department's best—stepped out. Coventry brought him up to speed and helped seal off the alley as Darien Jade waited on the sidewalk.

Lookey-Lews walked past, slowing down and pointing their faces in to see what all the fuss was about.

"Saw a '56 T-bird on the way over here," Kubiak told him, scratching that big old potbelly of his. "Must be a show somewhere today."

"What color?"

"Red," Kubiak said. "The color was right, but if I was going to own a baby-bird, it would be a '57. I never could get used to the continental kit on the '56."

"Makes them look ass heavy," Coventry said.

"Exactly," Kubiak agreed. "And you can't have a '55 either, with that goofy electrical system they put in 'em. So that only leaves you with the '57."

"That's the keeper," Coventry said.

"Not that I wouldn't take a '55 or '56, if someone gave it to me," Kubiak said.

Coventry had already walked the entire alley, with Darien's assistance, and hadn't found anything else of relevance, besides the water bottle. At least Kubiak would be able to photograph it in place, bag it for fingerprints, and make field sketches to memorialize where it had been found.

"When we're done here," Coventry said, "we'll head over to Ashley Conner's apartment and get some fingerprints to compare to the water bottle."

PROCESSING THE SCENE CONSUMED the rest of the morning and Coventry didn't get to headquarters until shortly before noon. His desk was over by the windows next to a snake plant that had grown halfway to the ceiling in spite of—or maybe because of—everyone's best efforts to drown it with coffee and pop.

As the head of the Homicide Unit, he had every right to occupy the office down the hall, which was a real office with real walls and a real door, viewed by most as the symbol of having arrived. He actually sat in there for three miserable days once before the walls closed in on him and he reclaimed his desk back on the floor.

"I couldn't think without the chaos," he told everyone, which had more truth to it than he liked to admit.

As soon as he sat down his phone rang.

It was James, one of the co-owners of the Carr-Border Gallery, a reputable establishment of fine art with a solid following and a Cherry Creek address. James was a good guy who could schmooze with the best of them.

"Hey, Picasso," James said, "One thing. No, two things, actually. One, we need some more work."

"Really?"

"Yeah. I got tired of looking at your old stuff and sold it."

Wow.

That was encouraging.

Coventry started to dabble in oils only a couple of years ago but found quickly that he had a knack for *plein air* landscapes. He managed to place his work in the Carr-Border Gallery and actually even found a check in his mail every once in a while. They told people he was an *up and coming talent*.

"How many do you need?"

"As many as you can fit in your truck."

Coventry considered it. He had some eight-by-tens at home that weren't quite commercial yet but probably could be with the right tweaking. If he could get one full evening to himself he could probably get all of them up to standards.

"I'll see what I can do," he said.

"Don't see, do," James said. "Second thing, the Abenshall-Nyster Gallery from Santa Fe called me a couple of days ago. They want to talk to you about hanging your work."

Coventry scratched his head. "Are they any good?"

James laughed. "You really need to start reading Southwest Art or something. Quality-wise, they're ten times what this place is, all day long. You'll be hanging next to the best."

"So what do you think?"

"That's not even a discussion point. Most people paint their whole lives and never end up in a gallery like that," James told him.

"But I can't even keep you stocked."

"My suggestion is, in that case—and I hate to say it—but switch over to them," James said. "Maybe send me some of your C or B-minus stuff at some point down the road if you start to get prolific."

Coventry didn't even have to think about it.

"Tell them I appreciate the opportunity, but don't have enough work for two galleries at the moment. Anything else?"

"You mean, other than the fact that you're nuts?"

He chuckled. "Yeah, other than that."

"No. That's it."

DETECTIVE SHALIFA NETHERWOOD CAME OVER and sat down as soon as he hung up, looking like a cat had dragged her around all morning.

Coventry said, "You're looking lovely."

She scrunched her face. "I got some news for you, *Infatuation Man*," she said. "This woman you're suddenly so interested in—Darien Jade—doesn't exist."

Coventry raised an eyebrow. "She doesn't?"

"Not that I can tell," she said. "She has no social security number, no driver's license, no bank accounts, no credit history, no nothing. INS hasn't heard of her either."

He twisted a pencil in his hand.

"You checked?"

She nodded. "Someone has to take care of you, Bryson. Obviously you're not interested in the job."

Coventry considered it. "So she's using a false name, is what you're saying."

"At the very least."

"Hmm." He tossed the pencil on the desk. "What's your availability today?"

She rolled her eyes. "I'm a thousand light years behind on everything."

He chuckled. "Good, because I need you full time on the Ashley Conner case."

"On *everything*," she repeated.

He shrugged. "Hand things off."

"To who?" She gave him a mean look. "Besides, Ashley Conner isn't even a case. She's a driver's license in an envelope. For all we know she's partying with a boyfriend in Central City and they're laughing their asses off about the clever little prank they came up with."

Coventry waited until the expression on her face softened, then said: "The first thing I need you to do is a nationwide search to find out if anyone has sent envelopes like this to TV stations in any other cities."

She looked stressed.

"I'll let you have the snake plant," he added.

She ignored the comment, then retreated in thought as if trying to figure out how to rearrange everything. "You just seriously wrecked my life, for the record."

He leaned across the desk and squeezed her hand. "I owe you one."

"You owe me *ten*."

"Three."

"Seven."

"Five."

"Okay, five then. And don't forget."

"Have I ever?"

"Don't even go there," she said. "By the way, all the envelopes that we got from the TV and radio stations are in forensics getting printed."

Coventry nodded in appreciation. "Thanks."

"We won't get anything out of it," she added.

He was already up and walking out of the room. "I know, but we still have to document it," he said over his shoulder.

HE WAS SCHEDULED TO TESTIFY in Denver District Court at an evidentiary hearing that was supposed to start at 1:00 and last about an hour. As usual, they ended up cooling their heels in the hallway waiting for the case to get called to the docket, and once it did it ran all the way until 5 p.m. Ten seconds after the defense rested the trial court ruled from the bench in favor of the People. They won but it took all afternoon to do it.

Coventry picked up a meal from Wendy's, carried it back to headquarters, eating fries on the way, and pounded out overdue paperwork alone in the room.

Then, about 8:30 p.m., he went over to Darien Jade's. In a tank top and abbreviated jean shorts, her body seemed to fill the room. He'd slept with more than his fair share of women over the years, particularly in his high school and college days when he lived to get laid, but not many were the caliber of Darien. Yet it wasn't just the prospect of sex pulling him in. In fact, he couldn't have sex with her, technically, if Ashley Conner turned into a formal investigation, since she was someone who might eventually need to give testimony in court. But sex or no sex, he liked her smile, her nature, the way she tossed her hair.

Shit, he was in trouble.

After dark they walked over to the bar, the Soft Sell, to see if they could find anyone who had been around the area Saturday night and might have seen something.

When they walked in, Coventry could hardly believe his eyes. The place was packed. Darien grabbed him by the arm and muscled her way to the bar, telling him that if she was going to do this, she needed a shot, no, two shots, first.

"Do what?"

"Help you find your witnesses."

Three minutes later she climbed up on the bar and waved her hands in the air to get everyone's attention. As the eyes fixed on her, a chant went up, *Take it off! Take it off! Take it off!*

She pulled Coventry up on the bar next to her, peeled off her tank top, waited for the applause and catcalling to stop, and then shouted, "Now, listen to the man for a second. He needs to talk to everyone who was down here last Saturday night. This is important so please help us out."

Coventry was just about to start talking when the chant went up again: *Take it off! Take it off! Take it off!*

Chapter Ten

Day Two - July 12
Wednesday Morning

———————

TAYLOR SUTTON WOKE WEDNESDAY MORNING slightly hung over, in the bed of a man so incredibly good looking that she just had to climb on top for one more ride. Then he put her on the back of his Harley and dropped her off by the Little Bear, at the Porsche, giving her one long, last wet kiss.

Driving back to the city her thoughts turned to Nick Trotter. She called Brooke—in her capacity as the law firm's ad hoc investigator rather than as her sister—and asked if she could meet at Taylor's house in a half hour.

She could.

Brooke was actually waiting for her when she pulled into the driveway of her modest Lakewood home.

"Long night?" Brooke asked.

Taylor rolled her eyes. "About nine inches long."

Brooke shook her head.

"You are such a slut."

Taylor nodded. "We all have our vices," she said. "You should have seen this guy. I'm still shaking."

Inside the house, Taylor handed her sister the CD, and said:

"Here's the deal. I need to get going on an investigation ASAP but I'm slammed all day, so I need your help to get started. This is a confidential attorney-client matter, so you're acting as an independent contractor to the law firm on this. Keep track of your time. Listen to this CD. You're going to hear various conversations between Nick Trotter and some unknown guy who calls himself Northwest. My job is to find out who this Northwest guy is. He's freaking Nick out."

"Nick doesn't freak out," Brooke said.

"He does this time. These are all phone conversations, so we have that connection going for us. I'd suggest that you start there. Find the number or numbers of the phone that this guy used when he called Nick. Work with Nick's phone company. With any luck this guy called from a cell phone and we're done."

Brooke shrugged, as if to say, "Fine."

Taylor put a serious look on her face, to stress the importance of what she was about to say. "This is confidential stuff and, more importantly, serious. This Northwest guy's a killer and his passion is young women. So don't make yourself any more visible than you need to. You fit the profile too good."

"Then so do you," Brooke replied.

Taylor considered it. She was right, actually. Taylor—at the age of twenty-nine—was three years older than Brooke but they still looked like twins from a distance. Funny she hadn't even thought of that before. "One more thing," she said. "Nick is holding something back from me so keep your eyes open. He might say something to you that he wouldn't say to me."

THAT AFTERNOON, TAYLOR SUTTON was on the phone with in-house counsel for Sigman Corporation, negotiating an employment agreement on behalf of the woman they wanted to bring in as the new corporate CEO, when Brooke strolled in and danced.

Taylor couldn't help but grin.

The girl had some serious moves, as she should considering how much of her life she spent clubbing. When Taylor hung up, Brooke gave her the story. Nick's telephone company was happy to cooperate with her after Nick faxed over his approval for them to release his records to her. According to the phone records, all the calls to Nick from the creepy Mr. Northwest came from public phones. Most were made from Denver, but some came from New York, San Francisco and Santa Fe. Of the Denver calls, no two came from the same phone. The majority of them came from the downtown area but others originated in Boulder, Golden, Westminster, Littleton and other surrounding communities.

"I made a spreadsheet for you," Brooke said, handing her a stapled set of pages.

Taylor flipped through them. The calls were numbered from 1 to 42. Each call had columns showing the date, time, length, originating phone number, and location of the incoming phone.

"I am seriously impressed," she said.

After Brooke left, Taylor walked outside to the 16th Street Mall, sat down on the sidewalk, leaned against the building, slipped out of her shoes to cool her feet, and studied the spreadsheet. She pulled out a book of matches and lit them one after the other, throwing their spent remains in a pile on the sidewalk. Someone walked by and put a dollar bill in her shoe.

She looked up when he did. "Thanks," she said.

It turned out that one of the calls came from a public phone at a Texaco gas station in Westminster. Maybe that was because

Northwest was there getting gas at the time.

And maybe he paid for that gas with a credit card.

Chapter Eleven

Day Two - July 12
Wednesday Morning

———————————

NATHAN WICKERSHAM WOKE EARLY Wednesday morning, took a long heaven-sent piss and then headed down to the kitchen. He flipped on the monitor to find Ashley Conner asleep, curled in a fetal position on the bed.

She looked like a child.

If this was the first time he'd seen her, and someone told him she was eleven, he would have believed it.

He frowned at the sight.

She needed to be dead.

Gone.

There was too much work in front of him and he didn't need her still in the picture weighing him down.

He started the coffee machine, ate a nonfat yogurt with a plastic spoon, slipped into his jogging clothes and was three miles into a ten mile run before the sun came up. When he got back Ashley was still sound asleep in the exact same position. For a brief moment he thought she found a way to kill herself during the night, but then studied the monitor without blinking and saw the movement of her breathing ever so slightly.

He poured nonfat milk directly into the coffee pot and stirred it until the white cloud went away and the coffee turned a solid creamer color. Then he poured a cup and took a sip. Ah, delicious.

Today would be a big day.

An incredibly big day.

There was so much to do that he hardly knew where to begin.

He danced with the coffee cup in hand, twirling around like he was on stage, and then headed to the shower.

THIRTY MINUTES LATER HE WAS HARD AT WORK in the study when the phone rang.

"Is this Dr. Wickersham?"

"That depends. Who am I speaking to?"

"My name is Lindsey Abernathy. I got your name from Peter Sinclair."

Peter Sinclair.

Good.

Sinclair could be trusted. He had a lot more to lose than Wickersham did if the truth ever got out.

"How do you know Peter?" he questioned.

"He dates my sister."

"So you've met Peter, personally?"

"Yes, I . . ."

"Tell me about his dog." Sinclair had a dog, not just a dog, a best friend. Anyone who knew Sinclair knew his dog.

"You mean Ralph?"

"Yeah, Ralph."

"Ralph's a collie."

"That he is. Very good."

"I'm a Ph.D. candidate at Stanford, in physics. Getting that degree means a lot to me."

"It's a good degree to have."

"So . . . are you still in the business?"

Wickersham leaned back in his chair. "In fact I am. Did Peter tell you my rates?"

"He said $200 an hour, with a $50,000 non-refundable retainer upfront."

"It's actually a little higher, now, but if that's what Peter told you, I'll go with it. Are you interested?"

"Like I said, getting that degree means a lot. But I need guaranteed results."

Wickersham chuckled. "Don't worry about that. You need to appreciate the scope of the work upfront though. The average bill turns out to be in the one hundred to one-fifty range. I don't want you to get started on it if you can't go the distance, it wouldn't be fair to you."

"That shouldn't be a problem."

"Well, then, let me be the first to call you Dr. Abernathy."

They talked for another fifteen minutes and by the end Wickersham could tell that she had made the right choice calling him. She'd never be able to formulate, research, write and defend a dissertation in physics on her own. But with him as her ghostwriter and navigator, she should be able to get through the program just fine. Two years from now she'd be teaching college somewhere, or just dropping the degree at cocktail parties. Who knows and who cares, as long as the checks cleared.

With her as his latest client, that brought the current total number of projects to ten, meaning over a million dollars in the pipeline. Not bad for someone who worked out of a study at home; certainly a lot more than he ever made teaching at Berkeley.

HE WORKED HARD UNTIL NOON and then turned on the news to see if anyone was airing the Ashley Conner story yet. No one was and he knew why: because so far she was just a suspicious disappearance and not a dead body.

That would all change.

They'd get their body soon enough.

A week from now he'd be the number one story on everyone's lips. Two weeks from now he'd be the *only* story.

He opened a new blank document on Word, typed "Next visit: Weekend of July 14th," printed twenty-two copies and set about making envelopes.

Then he drove to the north edge of downtown, walked around until he found a mailbox that didn't have any security cameras pointed at it, and dumped them in.

They'd be delivered tomorrow, Thursday.

He'd strike either Friday or Saturday.

Before then, he'd dump Ashley Conner's body in a location where it would be found.

Just to be sure he had everyone's full attention.

The rock star was on stage.

Chapter Twelve

Day Three - July 13
Thursday Morning

——————————

BRYSON COVENTRY WOKE TO A PITCH-BLACK ROOM and realized that he was on Darien Jade's couch, it was the middle of the night, and he was no longer alone. Darien had left her bed and was there with him, her face close to his, her breath hot on his face, smelling of alcohol.

She said nothing.

Her breathing filled the room.

Her body was warm and her skin incredibly smooth. He touched her, letting his hands roam, finding that she had stripped herself of all clothing. Her lips came to his and, there in the darkness, he let her. Her hair cascaded down over his face and she pressed her body to his.

It was wrong.

But there was no stopping it.

Not even close.

THE NEXT TIME HE WOKE IT WAS 6:28 A.M. This time he was in Darien's bed and hints of orange daylight filtered into the room. She lay next to him asleep, breathing deeply.

He rolled onto his back and closed his eyes.

This is a place he could stay the rest of his life, if his life would let him. Right here, just like this. Never go anywhere or do anything else for as long as he lived.

Then he remembered Ashley Conner.

And the woman from Soft Sell who saw a van in the alley Saturday night.

Three minutes later he was in the shower, lathering up, thinking about the encounter with Darien last night and fighting to keep an erection down. When he came out she was in the kitchen pouring water into the coffee maker. She came over, put her arms around his neck and brought her mouth to his.

"How are we ever going to top that?" she asked.

He couldn't help but grin.

Good question.

Very good question.

"I don't know," he said. "But I'm willing to try."

She kissed him and walked back to the kitchen. "I've never slept so good in my entire life. Honest to God."

He frowned.

"What?"

"You're a potential witness," he said. "I'm not supposed to be messing around with you. That's Rule Number One in every book they've ever written."

She shrugged. "It's our business," she said. "No one else needs to know."

"I wish it were that simple."

She opened the fridge and pulled out the milk. "It is that simple." She looked into his eyes. "We have a secret."

"I guess we do."

"You've had secrets before, haven't you?"

"I guess so."

"Did you keep them?"

"Some of them."

"Well, me too. So what's the plan today?"

Coventry knew exactly what the plan was, at least the immediate plan. One of the women from the Soft Sell had seen a van in the alley on Saturday night, about 10:15. She was walking by when brake lights went on for a split second, no doubt from the driver's foot hitting the pedal inadvertently. She turned and saw enough to know that the vehicle was a van, but nothing more. She couldn't even tell if the color was light or dark, whether the rear doors had glass or were solid, or whether it was new or old. But it was definitely a van, not an SUV or a car.

That wasn't much to go on.

But it was more than they had twenty-four hours ago.

"The first thing we do this morning," he said, "is take a walk down Broadway and look for security cameras that might have picked up a van on Saturday night."

She smiled. "Perfect. I could use the exercise."

FIRST THEY STOPPED IN A LITTLE PLACE across Broadway called Mama's and grabbed breakfast. The waitress couldn't have been nicer and looked like she was barely making ends meet. The bill came to $8.49. Coventry waited until she came around, handed her a ten and a twenty and told her to keep the change. He knew better than to leave the money on the table.

"You made her day," Darien said as they stepped outside.

Coventry shrugged. "I was just showing off, trying to make you think I'm a nice guy." He looked at her. "Did it work?"

"Maybe. We'll find out later."

They walked north on Broadway. The temperature was supposed to bust a hundred again but right now, early in the morning, it was absolutely perfect. Darien wore shorts and a tank top, with lots of golden brown skin on display. Three or four cars honked at her within the first two blocks, even with Coventry walking next to her.

He spotted a bank a block farther up and picked up the pace.

"Shalifa Netherwood says you don't exist," Coventry said. He didn't know why he said it and as soon as the words came out he wondered if he'd made a mistake. He studied Darien to get her reaction.

"She's the one who came by the alley yesterday, right?"

"Right, the detective."

"So you had her check up on me?" she questioned.

Coventry shook his head.

"No."

"So she just took it upon herself?"

Coventry gestured with his hands, as if to say, *What can I say?*

"Why?"

He thought about it. "She has a bad habit of taking care of me sometimes."

"Why?"

"I don't know, she just does."

Darien grunted. "That's because she's hot for you." A concerned look fell over her face. "Have you ever slept with her?"

Coventry laughed. "Are you kidding, we work together," he emphasized.

"Meaning no?"

"Exactly, meaning no."

Darien paused, then said: "She's got an incredible ass."

Coventry couldn't agree more and said so.

"You could bounce a quarter off it," Darien added.

He laughed. "Now *that* I have done," he said.

She looked incredulous. "You have? When?"

"A bunch of us were in a dive bar once, getting falling-down drunk, celebrating the end of a case involving a guy by the name of David Hallenbeck."

"Never heard of him."

"Consider yourself lucky. Anyway, someone came up with a challenge to see who could bounce a quarter the highest off Shalifa's ass," Coventry said.

"And she went along with it?"

"Like I said, we were all pretty drunk."

She laughed, picturing it.

"You won, I suppose," she said.

Coventry shrugged.

He couldn't remember.

"We all won," he said.

They were almost at the bank now and Coventry had already spotted a number of security cameras mounted on the outside of the building. One of them sat above the entrance and pointed towards Broadway. It looked like it would pick up the traffic but he couldn't be sure.

"I don't care," Coventry said.

"Don't care about what?"

"Whether you exist or not," he said.

"Good."

"Besides," he added, "you'll tell me yourself when you're ready."

She retreated in thought, then said: "Don't count on it."

THE BANK WAS STILL CLOSED and no other good prospects were obvious from this vantage point. So they turned around and walked the opposite way on Broadway, passing the alley and continuing for another seven or eight blocks. Coventry spotted no security cameras. So they turned around and walked back to the bank.

It was open now.

It turned out that the security camera over the entrance did in fact pick up Broadway traffic. Coventry signed for two original tapes that included the time periods between 8 and 12 p.m. on Saturday night.

He walked Darien back to her apartment and then headed down to headquarters, anxious to see what the tapes showed, if anything.

Chapter Thirteen

Day Three - July 13
Thursday Morning

THE BIGGEST PROBLEM TAYLOR SUTTON had being a lawyer was sitting in a chair for longer than five minutes straight. Her body just wouldn't let her. So she constantly got up to refill her coffee or send a fax or walk over to the window and look out.

But even that wasn't enough.

Once an hour, at a minimum, she actually had to get all the way out of the office. This morning was no different. At a little after ten she slipped into her tennis shoes and headed for the door.

"I'll warn Denver you're coming," Claudia said.

Taylor made a face.

Outside the temperature had already climbed into the nineties and was in the process of baking the brick and mortar. The high today was supposed to be near a hundred, yet another scorcher with no relief in sight. She couldn't remember a summer this hot.

Fewer people than normal were in the street and those who were hugged the shady side. She passed a hotdog vendor sitting on a folding canvas chair, waiting for customers, seemingly dazed by the heat. He looked like he just walked across the desert. "Look up and you'll see buzzards," she said to herself.

A woman walking towards her caught Taylor's eye. The woman stared directly at her as she approached, almost as if studying her. Taylor half expected her to stop and say something but at the last second she averted her eyes and walked by.

Weird.

Three blocks later Taylor turned around to head back to the office. The woman was there again. She'd been walking behind Taylor. Now she was stopped and pointing her face into a store window.

Taylor pretended to not notice and crossed the street.

SHE WALKED DOWN THE MALL and then headed east on Glenarm, purposely not turning around, instead trying to find a diagonal window or something she could use to see behind her without giving herself away.

Nothing useful appeared.

So she stepped into an Einstein Bros and bought a coffee to go. She pointed her face to the street only when it would be normal to do so.

Sure enough.

The woman was outside.

On the other side of the street.

Down about twenty yards.

Pretending to study something in a store window. She looked to be about twenty-five, tanned and extremely fit. She wore khaki shorts, sunglasses, a baseball cap and black hiking boots.

Taylor stepped back outside and continued down Glenarm,

sipping the coffee, trying to think of why anyone would want to follow her. Maybe it was related to one of her cases. Possibly an opposing counsel trying to get some dirt on her. Well if that was the plan, they'd be out of luck. Sure, she slept around, but so what?

She finished the coffee, threw the cup in an overflowing waste receptacle, pulled out a book of matches and lit them as she walked, shaking each one until it went out and throwing it on the sidewalk.

Maybe she should just turn around and confront the woman.

No.

The woman would deny everything and then disappear down the street. Taylor would never get an answer that way. She turned right on 17th Street, wanting to get a good circular route going to be absolutely sure the whole thing wasn't just a big coincidence.

A man walked towards her, a businessman with a red power-tie, actually wearing his jacket in spite of the heat. He looked to be about thirty-five, muscular and important. She moved in front of him and stopped.

"Hi there," she said.

The man smiled. "Hi there back."

"This is really weird," Taylor said. "But I want to ask a favor of you."

"Oh you do, do you?"

"Look over my shoulder," Taylor said, "and tell me if there's a woman back there, a tanned woman with shorts and a baseball hat." She emphasized: "Don't be obvious."

The man looked that way, nonchalantly, and nodded. "Sure is."

"Is she stopped?"

"Yep."

"Okay, thanks."

"Wait."

"What?"

"I helped you, so you owe me now."

"Look . . ."

"I'm talking about supper," the man said. He already had a business card in his hand and was giving it to her. She looked at it: Sean Michaels, President and CEO of Fossil Oil and Gas Company.

"I don't date rich guys," she said.

He chuckled. "Okay, then. I'll give my money away."

She studied him. "What do you think of lawyers?" she asked.

"Why, are you one?"

"Maybe."

"I don't like them much," he said. "As a general rule."

"Me either," she said.

"So we have something in common."

She looked at the card, then back at him. "We'll see," she said. "Do me a favor. Don't look at that woman when you pass her. I don't want her to suspect we were talking about her."

TAYLOR WALKED ON. So, she was definitely being followed. Did it somehow relate to Nick Trotter? Or Nick's client—Northwest? How could Northwest possibly have connected her to Trotter? Was the woman Northwest's girlfriend or something?

No, probably not.

The woman looked normal. Plus she was fit and strong, not exactly the kind to be easily controlled or manipulated.

The matches were all gone now. She stuck the empty cardboard in her pocket and then came up with a plan. She headed over to the shops by the Hard Rock Café and lost the woman in the crowd.

Then she followed her.

She followed her to the Cash Register Building at 17th and Lincoln. There the woman entered the area for the elevator banks. Taylor had to stay back and wasn't able to see which bank she entered.

She did know one thing, though.

Nick Trotter's office was in this building, Suite 3450.

She waited a few minutes until she was fairly certain that the woman was gone. Then she took an elevator to the 34th Floor.

When it stopped, she got out, walked straight to Nick Trotter's office and pushed through the smoked glass doors into the reception area.

Chapter Fourteen

Day Three - July 13
Thursday Afternoon

WITH THE RADIO OFF, Nathan Wickersham drove around downtown Denver, without direction, not caring where he was or where he was going just so long as he was in the thick of traffic and there were lots of people around.

Ashley Conner was in the back of the van, chained down spread-eagle with a breathable gag in her mouth, wide-awake. Wickersham's cock tightened against his jeans just thinking about her back there.

Then at one point he drove down Cherokee Street, right past Coventry's office, and even waved at the building as he drove by. Then he headed over to California and took it towards the 16th Street Mall, getting caught at the light at the intersection. Dozens of people crossed in front of him as he sat there and smiled. Down the street, not more than a hundred feet away, two cops sat on horseback. Wickersham waved to them, as if they were old friends, but they never did see him.

Twenty minutes later he pulled into an open parking space on Bannock, not far from the Denver Public Library. He got out and looked around for surveillance cameras. Seeing none, he grabbed the black bag off the seat, put five quarters in the meter, walked around to the back of the van, opened the door with a key, climbed in and shut the door.

The heat immediately engulfed him.

He'd forgotten that the air conditioning didn't go back there.

It had to be a hundred and ten, minimum.

For a brief second he thought about going somewhere else, or maybe even taking the woman back home, but the look in her eyes told him she might never be this scared again.

She was gorgeous.

Drenched in sweat.

Straining at her bonds.

Pleading with him with those big brown eyes.

So alive.

"It's time," he said.

HE REACHED OVER AND LIGHTLY TWEAKED her nipples, touching her nowhere else, only on her nipples. Within a minute he had them rock hard in spite of herself.

"You comfortable, baby?" he questioned.

Her eyes pleaded with him.

So perfect.

Wickersham unzipped her shorts and slipped his hand in. Her pubic hair was short and silky. He tugged on it ever so slightly until she made a noise and strained even harder against her bonds.

Then he took off his shirt, so she could see his power, and studied her face.

She looked like a little girl.

He blindfolded her.

Then he leaned against the side of the van and watched her, occasionally reaching over and running a finger up and down her arm, ever so lightly, barely perceptible, just to remind her that he was still there.

He continued that for over thirty minutes.

Giving her plenty of time to contemplate her death.

Then he took her blindfold off.

"Here we go."

HE REACHED INTO THE BLACK BAG and pulled out a see-through garbage bag and some duct tape. He set the garbage bag on her stomach, then reached in his jean pockets and pulled out a pair of dice.

She already knew the ground rules from Tuesday night but he decided to repeat them again anyway. "I'm going to roll a pair of dice and you're gong to choose high or low. High means seven through twelve. Low means two through six. If you choose high and I roll a high number, then we go home. Same thing the other way—if you choose low and it turns out to be low, we go home. But if you choose wrong—if you choose high and it turns out low, or vice versa—then I put this bag over your head and duct tape it around your neck. You get to live for as long you can hold your breath, then nighty-night. If you don't choose either, you automatically lose. So high or low? What's your pleasure?"

Wickersham stopped talking and looked into her eyes.

Her expression almost made him come.

It was so goddamn perfect.

The fear, the exploding brain cells, the realization of total helplessness.

She pulled violently at her bonds as if she could rip them off by sheer willpower, but she could have been fifty times as strong and still not budged them.

"Okay, here we go," he said. "Blink once for low and twice for high."

She did neither.

Wickersham shook the dice in his hands, ready to roll. "Remember, not choosing is an automatic loss. High or low?"

She blinked twice.

"High?" he asked, just to be sure.

She nodded.

"Good choice," Wickersham said. "I didn't tell you this before, but it's better odds. There are twenty-one combinations that'll get you a seven to twelve, but only fifteen that'll get you a two through six. So statistically, you made the right choice." A pause, then, in a somber tone: "But you never know."

He got down on one knee, shook the dice in his hands and rolled them on the floor. She immediately tried to follow them with her eyes, straining her neck, but couldn't see from her position.

He smiled.

Then he looked into her eyes as he playfully rolled the duct tape around in his hands.

"Guess what?" he said.

Chapter Fifteen

Day Three - July 13
Thursday

BRYSON COVENTRY SHIFTED THROUGH the van photos extracted by the lab from the bank's videotapes. He separated them into three piles as he chewed on a turkey sandwich and drank coffee—decaf now, since 11:00 in fact.

Ashley Conner would have walked past the alley between 10:20 and 10:30. All vans time-stamped at 10:45 and after went into one pile as unlikely candidates. The second pile contained the vehicles before 9:45. The third pile—the important one— held the rest, about fifty all told. Some of them showed the driver's face, but they were blurred and almost unreadable. None of the photos showed license plate numbers.

He frowned and combed his hair back with his fingers. It immediately flopped back down over his forehead. Then his cell phone rang. He looked around but couldn't find it, finally following the sound to the inside pocket of his jacket.

Too late, no one was there.

Then it rang again.

He picked it up, lost his grip and watched it fall to the desk and then to the floor. Luckily it kept ringing, unbroken.

"Bryson, Jena Vernon here. Are you sitting down?"

He stood up, anxious, and said: "Yeah."

The minute he heard her voice he knew what she was going to say.

It turned out he was right.

As soon as he hung up he swung over to Shalifa Nether-wood's desk, grabbed her by the arm and said, "Come on." She must have sensed urgency in his voice because she got up immediately and fell into step without even asking why. They walked past the elevators to the stairs and started the three-story descent on foot. Shalifa said: "You really need to learn how to ride an elevator."

He grunted.

"No thanks."

"Why not?"

"Because I'm not a spider. When I turn into a spider I'll hang by a thread. But not before then." He added: "Jena Vernon's station got another envelope in the mail today."

"Same as before?"

"Yep, except the target date's this weekend."

She slowed her pace.

"This weekend starts tomorrow," she said.

She was right.

Tomorrow was Friday.

Technically, the weekend starts Friday night. He had been thinking he had until Saturday but now realized he was wrong.

"Yeah, I know that," he said.

WHEN THEY STEPPED OUTSIDE the heat pounced on them immediately. The grass—normally lush and green—was brown and parched, the victim of watering restrictions. They walked a short distance, to 14th Street, and waited under a tree. Three minutes later Jena Vernon pulled up in a silver Volvo. Coventry walked around to the driver's side and motioned for the traffic to go around. The car right behind Jena's had pulled in too close, and now had to back up to pull around. The driver, a young male, squealed out and gave everyone the finger.

Jena looked stressed.

"It's inside," she said, handing him a large manila envelope.

Coventry took it.

"Thanks. I owe you one," he said, turning to leave.

"Bryson, hold on a minute."

He came back. "What?"

She had a look on her face like she really didn't want to say what she was about to say. "The station's going to run the story. It's top billing at five o'clock. My guess is everyone else in town will be doing the same."

Coventry cocked his head, not sure if that was a good thing or a bad one. He did know, however, that he had no control over it in any event.

"We might want to hold a press conference later," he said. "I got to think it through. This guy's a publicity hound so everything anyone says is just going to fan his flames. But people need to know to be careful and call us if they see anything suspicious."

"Can you give me an exclusive?"

Coventry shook his head reluctantly. "This is too big, you know I can't. I'll give you a couple of comments on the side afterwards, though."

She reached out and squeezed his hand.

Three cars had jammed up behind her and one of them

started honking.

"I'll call you later," Coventry said as she pulled off.

"Send me a resume," she shouted. "The job's still open."

COVENTRY HANDED THE ENVELOPE TO SHALIFA. "Do me a favor and take this to the lab. Then round up every other envelope in town."

She took it. "What are you going to do?"

He already had his cell phone in hand. "I have to make a call. I'll be up in ten minutes." When she left, Coventry called Leanne Sanders, Ph.D.—the FBI profiler who helped on the Megan Bennett case earlier this year. She was a Supervisory Special Agent assigned to the National Center for the Analysis of Violent Crime (NCAVC) at Quantico, Virginia. Luckily he actually got her on the line. She listened patiently as he explained the situation.

"My preliminary thoughts are these," she said. "First, guys like this don't just wake up one day with a plan. He's been morphing into this for some time, meaning he has a past if you can find it. It would be something similar to what he's doing now but on a lesser scale, something in the nature of taunting the police or giving advance warning. Or just getting on the news. He might be the kind to set up a jeopardy situation and then jump in and be the rescuer to get his face in front of the cameras."

"We've already been searching on a national scale," Coventry said.

"Did you get anything?"

"We just started."

"Well, keep at it. We'll help if you want. He used the mail so we have jurisdiction to open a file if you want."

"I probably will," Coventry said.

"Second," she said, "I believe Ashley Conner is still alive."

The words shocked Coventry.

He always pictured her dead.

"Why do you say that?"

"Her death is part of the publicity, the proof that he not only warns but that he also carries out. When he kills her—and he will—he'll dump her body somewhere it can be found. It's the proof of how bad he is. If her body hasn't shown up, that's because she's not a body yet."

"Why would he still have her alive? He's had her since Saturday night, which is more than four days ago."

A pause. "I don't know. Maybe he's playing with her. Maybe he wants to leave her body at the site of the next abduction. Without more information it's hard to tell."

Coventry thought about it and suddenly felt out of his league.

"Can you come to Denver?"

"I'm up to my ass in so many alligators that I can't even see the water anymore. But let me work on it. I'll get back to you."

"You promise?"

"Yeah."

He almost hung up, then said: "Hey, can I say something sexist?"

"Please."

"I'm a little jealous of those alligators."

She laughed. "Thanks, you just made my day."

HE HEADED BACK UP THE STAIRWELL TO HOMICIDE, taking

the steps two at a time. First he filled in the chief. Then he pulled Shalifa Netherwood and Sergeant Kate Katona into a room and closed the door. "Leanne Sanders thinks Ashley Conner is alive," he said.

Kate Katona—a catcher of things since her tomboy days— licked her lips. For some reason her wash-and-blow hair seemed a little longer than usual. "Am I to assume that I'm now involved, since I'm sitting in this room?"

Coventry nodded and tried, as usual, to not get distracted by her world-class chest.

"We're setting up a task force and the three of us are going to head it up," he said. "Ashley Conner is going to be all over the news tonight, so we're going to call a press conference this afternoon. The chief wants it to look like the whole idea of going public is ours. So first, we plan what we want to say. Second, we start getting ready for this weekend."

"Get ready how?" Shalifa asked.

"I've got a few ideas," he said.

"Any of them any good?" Katona asked.

Coventry chuckled. "About the usual."

Katona looked at Shalifa and said, "We're in trouble."

Chapter Sixteen

Day Three - July 13
Thursday

TAYLOR SUTTON CLEARLY STARTLED Nick Trotter's receptionist when she pushed through the office doors at a hundred miles an hour. She looked around for the lady who had been following her but she was nowhere to be seen.

"Where's the woman?" she asked.

Before the receptionist could answer, Nick Trotter entered the room. He wore a crisp white shirt with an expensive silk tie, a subtle blue color. Confusion filled his face.

"What woman?" he questioned.

"The woman who just came in here. The one who's been tracking me."

Nick motioned for her to follow him. "Come on back to my office," he said. "Let's talk." On the way, Taylor stuck her head into every room they passed, including the coat closet, the Xerox room and the bathroom. The woman wasn't anywhere in the office suite.

She finally ended up in a chair in front of Nick's desk, twisting a pack of matches in her hand. Nick pushed an ashtray towards her and said, "Go for it."

She lit a match, blew it out, threw it in the ashtray and then told him the story. She could tell by the expression on his face that he wasn't connected to it in any way. At the end he said, "Let's go downstairs and wait for her."

THEY WATCHED FOR OVER AN HOUR down on the first floor by the elevator banks, waiting for the mystery woman to re-emerge from wherever she had gone. They chatted, read the paper, drank coffee, and took shifts while the other used the bathroom. At one point Taylor said, "You mentioned before that Northwest sent you a note with the cash retainer, something to the effect that he'd be calling you."

"Right."

"Do you still have that note?"

His face brightened. "I have to check but I think so."

"Make a copy for me but be careful not to touch the original," Taylor said. "Just in case we want to give it to the police at some point and have them run it for prints."

Nick smiled. "Now I remember why I'm paying you the big bucks."

"As for the money he sent, you put all that in a trust account?"

"Right," he said. "The bills themselves are long gone."

"Okay."

They waited another ten minutes and were just about to give up when the woman emerged.

"That's her!" Taylor said, bringing the newspaper up to hide her face. "The one with the baseball hat and the hiking boots."

"Got her," Nick said. "She's kind of cute."

Taylor frowned. "Do you know her?"

"Nope. Not even close."

The woman walked towards them, carrying an envelope that she didn't have before. They turned their backs, let her pass and then watched her as she headed for the Lincoln Street exit.

They followed, fifty steps behind, to the 16th Street Mall. When it became apparent that the woman was about to get on a shuttle bus, they decided that Nick would have to follow her alone. Taylor watched as the two of them got on the bus and disappeared down the street.

TAYLOR HADN'T EVEN NOTICED THE HEAT before but now it hit her hard. She walked back to the office, slipped out of her tennis shoes, peeled off her socks and sat down on the floor next to the air conditioning vent. As Claudia made fun of her, she filled her in.

"This has something to do with Nick Trotter's client," Claudia said. "This Northwest jerk."

Taylor agreed.

That was her gut feeling too.

"But what?" she said. "We didn't even get involved until two days ago and have hardly even done anything, other than listen to the CD and track down a few phone numbers. How could I possibly be on this guy's radar screen?"

Claudia shrugged. "I don't know but you are." She looked concerned. "Listen, I know you and Nick are close, but maybe he's setting you up somehow."

Taylor laughed, absurd.

"Not hardly," she said.

"Think about it," Claudia said. "Who knows that we're trying to track Northwest? You, me, your sister, and—dare I say—

Nick Trotter."

"He wouldn't do that," Taylor said.

Claudia headed back to her desk. "All I'm saying is do the math."

NICK TROTTER CALLED HER forty minutes later. "Bad news," he said. "I lost her."

"So you never got a license plate number or anything?"

"No," he said. "I think she spotted me, probably because the ponytail sticks out too much. She walked into Jackson's Hole down in LoDo and never came out. When I finally went in to check she wasn't there. I don't know if she slipped out the back or what."

Taylor thought about it.

For some reason she felt Nick was lying to her.

"Well, at least you saw her face," she said.

"Yeah," he agreed. "I really did lose her, Taylor. Trust me. I want to find out what's going on a whole lot more than you do."

"Yeah, I know," she said.

But heard no conviction in her voice.

Chapter Seventeen

Day Three - July 13
Thursday Evening

NATHAN WICKERSHAM FUNCTIONED BEST standing at the three-by-five foot board in his den with a blue marker in his right hand and an eraser in his left. He could fidget and pace while he worked and the concepts always seemed bigger and more exciting than anything he ever got using paper and pencil. That's where he was at 5 p.m., smoothing out a wrinkle in Albert Snyder's Ph.D. thesis, when it happened.

All three of the local TV newscasts opened with the Ashley Conner story. He grabbed a remote and turned the sound up on the middle unit.

It turned out better than he could have ever imagined.

Ashley Conner's face looked so beautiful.

Bryson Coventry looked so distressed.

Everyone out there in the listening audience was warned that the next visit was scheduled for this weekend. Women—especially young women—were cautioned to stay in public places and to travel in pairs.

"Stay turned to this station for updates."

He twirled around and danced as he watched.

Finally, it had begun.

"You're a goddamn rock star!"

THAT NIGHT, AFTER DARK, HE DROVE AROUND in the Camry looking for the next perfect spot to make his move. He ended up circling the Auraria campus, finding all the dark nooks and crannies where students walked after getting out of their precious little night classes. Taking a student was almost the perfect idea. They all thought they were bulletproof and few paid any attention to the real world. He doubted that one in ten would even be aware of the Ashley Conner situation, much less take it seriously. Plus, the campus didn't have any housing to speak of. Just about everyone commuted. And while lots of students drove, just as many if not more took public transportation and walked off campus to get to it.

It was almost as if someone had built the place just for him.

There'd be lots of foot traffic on Friday night. Even on Saturday, although there were probably no classes, the diehards would be hitting the main library or be down for some kind of activity or other. He even called and confirmed that the library was open until ten.

"Either night," he said, "this place will work."

He liked the idea of taking a student.

They'd be young.

And if he was patient, he'd be able to find a looker.

Just in case, however, he scouted out the side streets around some of the more popular nightclubs in Denver. Within an hour he found at least ten shadowy places where he'd be able to find a drunk single woman sooner or later.

He looked at his watch.

Ten o'clock.

Time to head to Coventry's house.

Coventry was the main guy hunting him.

If he wanted to play, then fine.

Wickersham could play too.

BRYSON COVENTRY, IT TURNED OUT, LIVED in a split-level house near the top of Green Mountain, third house from the end of the street, backing to open space. You had to wind up the side streets west of Alkire to get to it. The street dead-ended in a turnaround, a nice touch. From up there you could see a long band of city lights, stretching across the eastern horizon from Boulder to the Tech Center.

Wickersham swung by Coventry's house. The Tundra was parked in the driveway and lights were still on inside the house. He did a one-eighty in the turnaround, drove back down the street past Coventry's house and then parked the Camry in a dark spot midway between two streetlights. He put on a baseball hat and walked up the hill.

The temperature was just about perfect.

He made it all the way up to the turnaround and was starting to head back down the hill when Coventry's garage door opened. Wickersham ducked behind a pickup truck parked on the street and watched as Coventry carried a garbage can to the curb. A moment later a small dog ran over to Coventry from the neighbor's yard and humped his leg.

"Walter, your dog!"

The neighbor called out, "Finney, get over here, you little freak," and the dog ran towards the man's voice. "Sorry about that, Bryson."

"No problem," Coventry said.

Wickersham stayed where he was while Coventry walked back into the garage. Instead of closing the garage door, Coventry came back out a few minutes later wearing shorts and a T-shirt and jogged down the hill.

Wickersham looked around.

The neighbor wasn't outside anymore.

Or his horny little freak of a dog.

Coventry ran down the street and then disappeared to the right at the first side street.

Thirty seconds later Wickersham snuck through Coventry's garage and into his house.

Chapter Eighteen

Day Four - July 14
Friday Morning

BRYSON COVENTRY'S ALARM PULLED him out of sleep at 5:10 a.m., which was really strange because he had set it for 5:00. He shifted onto his back, getting used to the idea of waking up, while the weatherman told him the heat would shatter a hundred again, making it the tenth day in a row.

That wasn't good.

That meant that a lot of people would be out at night.

He shaved in the shower, popped in his contacts, threw on a pair of jeans and a blue cotton short-sleeve shirt, then mixed up a bowl of cereal with a sliced banana and nonfat milk, which he carried out to the Tundra and ate while he drove. By 6:15 he was at his office kick starting the coffee machine and standing there staring at the pot as it slowly filled up. Of course no one else was there yet, nor would they be for another two hours or so.

Coventry's gut told him that the so-called "visit" would come tonight, not Saturday. The guy would be excited to finally be on the news. He'd take the next victim this evening, if possible, then use tomorrow to kick back and watch the city squirm.

Shalifa Netherwood showed up about seven, more than an hour early, a real surprise. She wore gray pants and a nice white blouse that seemed extra crisp against her skin. She headed straight for the coffee, saying over her shoulder, "Thought you'd be here."

"Just got here," he said.

She sank down in the chair in front of his desk and propped her feet up. "This coffee sucks," she said.

Coventry shrugged, then saw that his cup was empty and walked over to fill it, shaking in powdered creamer and then pouring the coffee on top.

"I'm thinking our friend is going to strike tonight," he said. "I'm also thinking that Ashley Conner's body is going to show up somewhere before the five o'clock news."

She frowned.

"Don't even say that."

"He's not going to want two live ones around at the same time, is what I'm saying."

Suddenly his cell phone rang and the dispatcher's voice came through. "Coventry, we got a body. It's an African American woman, reportedly a streetwalker. She has a six inch knife buried in her eye."

Coventry looked at Shalifa.

They were the only ones there. No one else would be in for another hour, minimum.

"What's the location?" he questioned.

TWELVE MINUTES LATER THEY ARRIVED AT AN ALLEY off Colfax, just down from the Rainbird Bar, a long-standing hooker hangout. Three patrol cars guarded the scene, which had already been taped off. Trash and litter lay everywhere in stinking piles. Even at a casual glance, Coventry counted ten or twelve used needles on the ground around the body.

Shalifa recognized the victim.

"Well I'll be damned. That's Mary Williams," she said. "We went to East High together. She was in tenth grade when I was in eleventh, then she dropped out."

Coventry nodded.

"I slept over her house once," Shalifa added.

Now, according to Shalifa, the woman had a reputation for giving private S&M sessions. Supposedly she had a dungeon set up in the basement of her house over in the seven hundred block of Downing, although Shalifa had never personally seen it. There she let the Johns string her up and whip her for a hefty pile of cash upfront.

"So what do you think?" Coventry asked.

Shalifa shrugged.

"Maybe someone brings her back here to get a blowjob, he doesn't feel like paying, she goes to leave, he's not in the mood to be denied and sticks a knife in her eye."

Coventry considered it.

"Or a drug deal gone bad," he suggested.

Shalifa shook her head. "No, not drugs. She was never into that, believe it or not."

"Really?"

"She even got on my case once for smoking," she added.

Detective Richardson, a baby-faced up-and-comer in the Homicide Unit, showed up a little after nine and the three of them worked the scene until noon, at which point there was nothing left to do.

BY THE TIME THEY GOT BACK TO HEADQUARTERS it was coming up on one o'clock. Kate Katona cornered Coventry as soon as he walked in.

"The divisions are all set up for tonight," she said. "We're going to concentrate on places where young women can be found, which includes the major nightclubs, the LoDo area, and downtown—particularly around the Paramount, since someone's playing there tonight."

"Who?" Coventry asked.

"I don't know, I don't exactly travel in that circle anymore."

"Okay." He ran his fingers through his hair: "What about Broadway?"

She nodded. "That's on our radar screen, just in case this guy's gutsy enough to try the same trick twice, just to rub it in our faces."

Coventry nodded.

Good.

COVENTRY'S CELL PHONE RANG. It turned out to be Jena Vernon. "Bryson," she said. "If something happens tonight, can you call me? I want to be first on the scene and break the story."

He thought about it.

"Give me your cell number again," he said.

She did.

He wrote it on the back of one of his business cards and stuffed it in his wallet.

"I can't promise anything," he said, "but we'll see."

When she hung up, Coventry programmed the number into his phone.

THREE MINUTES LATER HIS CELL PHONE RANG AGAIN. This time it was Darien Jade. "Bryson," she said, "what are you up to tonight?"

"Driving around and looking for a van, until I fall asleep at the wheel."

"Can I ride with you?"

"That's against policy."

"Not if you're in your truck," she said.

He considered it.

Actually, she was right.

"Yeah, why not," he said. "But I'll have to drop you off somewhere if I get a call or something."

"Fine. Just slow down to at least twenty-five first."

Chapter Nineteen

Day Four - July 14
Friday Morning

TAYLOR SUTTON'S ALARM CLOCK went off before daybreak when the bedroom was still dark. She reached over without opening her eyes and turned it off. Normally this is where she'd pull the vibrator out but today she had too much on her mind and hit the shower instead.

She swung by the office to pound out paperwork and get coffee into her system, then got in the Porsche and headed north on I-25 to the Boulder Turnpike, finally exiting on 104th Avenue. Five minutes later she pulled into the Texaco where one of the phone calls to Nick Trotter had come from.

Inside, she milled around until two customers left and then walked over to the counter. The attendant was a scruffy looking older man with a beard and a thin face. He smelled like a forest fire. For some reason she pictured him drunk out of his mind every night on Jack and waking up to a hacking cough.

"Hi," she said. "I was hoping that you could maybe help me out with something."

"Sure," he said, showing yellow teeth. "What do you need?"

"Well," she said, "I'm a lawyer and I'm trying to locate a

man who made a phone call from the pay station outside on May 5th at 10:42 in the morning."

The man shook his head. "We rotate our surveillance tapes every five days."

Taylor nodded and tried to not look at his mouth, but found herself pulled back to it, as if it was a train wreck or something. "I suspected that," she said, "but I was thinking that maybe he made the phone call when he stopped to get gas, and maybe he paid with a credit card. I was hoping you could tell me if there were any credit card purchases around that time." She leaned on the counter. "I'm not looking for his credit card number or anything like that, just the name on the card."

The man looked confused.

"I wouldn't have a clue how to do that," he said. "I guess you'd have to get into our computer system somehow, but I don't have access to anything like that. Only corporate could do something like that."

"Okay," she said. "I understand."

"If you want to leave your card, I'll pass the request on and have them call you."

She hesitated, not particularly excited about someone that skuzzy having her phone number. She pictured him calling her at two in the morning with his dick in his hand.

But she handed him one anyway.

Then left.

FROM THE TEXACO SHE HEADED to the north edge of downtown, parallel parked the Porsche on Wazee, and walked a block until she came to an old three-story brick building with heavy construction taking place inside.

She called her sister on her cell phone and two minutes later Brooke walked out of the front entrance, looked around, and finally spotted her. Her face was dirty and smudged, and when she took off her hardhat her hair was matted in sweat. She was grinning ear to ear and never looked happier. "Here," she said, handing Taylor a yellow hardhat, "you got to wear this, otherwise six guys are going to chew my ass."

Taylor said, "Do me a favor. Kiss my hair goodbye for me."

Brooke did.

Then they walked inside.

THE CITY WAS STANDING ON THE CUTTING EDGE of getting the most extreme, chic, sensory-overload nightclub that imagination, creativity and truckloads of money could provide; an equal to the likes of Studio 54 back in its heyday.

Taylor could tell that Brooke was, at that moment, probably as happy as she had ever been. The six years of brain damage at the University of Colorado was finally starting to pay off. Without those two degrees—the bachelor's and the master's, both in business, both summa cum laude—Brooke probably wouldn't have been viewed as having the necessary pedigree to pull a project like this off. But she did have those two degrees. And she did have four years of hands-on experience as executive manager of Breathless, Denver's place to see and be seen. And she did have all the right connections. And she did have her finger firmly on the pulse of Denver. And she did have the beauty, poise and charisma to be in the business. In fact, modesty aside, she was perfect for something like this.

The whole idea for Image had been Brooke's brainchild from the start.

But she needed investors.

And now she had them, namely Richard Alexander and Tom Iverson, two experienced entrepreneurs who already owned a number of insanely successful and lucrative clubs in L.A., Chicago, Las Vegas and New York.

They put up the cash, bought this building, got the liquor license and were funding the construction.

Brooke's job was to develop the themes, quarterback the interior design, advertise and market, recruit all the right people, and then oversee all day-to-day operations once it got up and running. That meant she'd be responsible for human resources, security, reservations, bookkeeping, legal, purchasing, payroll, insurance, risk management, taxes, and all the rest. In exchange, she'd be a fifteen percent owner, receive a compelling base salary with a yearly escalation clause, and get a cut of the door.

Her squeeze—Aaron Cavanaugh—would have a crucial role to play, too.

At twenty-three, he was three years younger than Brooke, but that didn't bother her one bit. With those GQ looks, and that perfectly proportioned six-foot body, there wasn't a female in a hundred who wouldn't gladly sign up on the spot. He would be the front man for the new club, the pretty face that got the right people in the door and defined the standard of exclusivity, the meet-and-greet guy, the man with final say on who could move to the front of the line or reserve a table or booth on Friday night.

TAYLOR FOLLOWED HER SISTER AROUND and learned that the interior of the building was currently being gutted in preparation of reconstruction.

Taylor couldn't have been happier.

The project had pulled Brooke out of that dark mood that seemed to have a hold on her lately.

While they were standing in the center of where the main dance floor would be, Brooke's cell phone rang. "Might be business," she said as she looked at the number. "Nope, it's Aaron. Just give me a minute."

"Hey there, sexy," she said.

Then the smile dropped off her face.

Taylor watched as her sister listened intently to whatever it was that was being said. A furrow grew between her eyes, a familiar mark of stress. Then she looked at Taylor and said, "I'll be right back," and walked over to the wall as she talked, turning her face.

The conversation went on for about five minutes.

Brooke hardly talked at all but when she did it was in a serious tone.

Taylor wandered farther off, giving Brooke her privacy.

When Brooke finally hung up and walked over, she couldn't have looked more upset if she was being paid. "Trouble in paradise?" Taylor asked.

Brooke shook her head. "No, something else."

"Anything I can help you with?"

Brooke looked at her.

As if she wished that was possible.

Then said, "Unfortunately, no."

TAYLOR WENT TO HER OFFICE and hadn't been there for more than thirty minutes before the walls closed in. She ended up walking down Welton towards Broadway, leaving a string of burned matches in her wake, wondering what the hell was wrong with Brooke. She was sitting on the sidewalk in the shade, leaning against a building, when Nick Trotter called her.

"We need to talk," he said.

She sensed urgency in his voice.

"I got another call from Northwest this morning," Nick said. "He was talking about the Ashley Conner situation. You've heard about that, right?"

Yes, she had.

But what was it?

Oh, yeah.

"She's the art student who disappeared, right?"

"Right," Trotter said. "And whoever took her is supposed to strike again this weekend, according to the letters he's been sending the press."

"Right, that's the buzz."

"Well, Northwest was talking all about that case," Nick said. "Although he didn't come right out and say it, I think he's the one who took the Ashley Conner woman."

Taylor stood up and paced.

"You really think so?"

"Like I said, I'm not positive, but my gut tells me he's the one."

"Wow."

"Yeah, major wow."

A well-dressed man and woman in their late thirties walked on the other side of the street, close together, touching each other. For some reason Taylor sensed that they were cheating on their spouses.

"Did you tape the conversation?" Taylor questioned.

"I did."

"Good."

A pause on the other end of the phone. "I'm not sure it's so good."

"Why?"

"This is getting too heavy," Nick said. "I think I'm going to have to pull you off the case."

"Screw that," Taylor said. "Are you in your office?"

"Yes."

"Good. I'll be there in ten minutes."

Chapter Twenty

Day Four - July 14
Friday Afternoon

_____

NATHAN WICKERSHAM PACED BACK AND FORTH in front of the board, giving it dirty looks as if his expression alone could force answers to jump out of it. Face it—his concentration had gone to hell. The blue marks on the board were starting to look more like a child's scribbling than mathematical symbols. Most of his brain cells were focused on tonight.

When the rock star would take stage.

He needed to be careful, though.

If the perfect opportunity didn't present itself, he needed to wait until tomorrow, or even Sunday if necessary. Don't force the situation. That was important. There'd be plenty of police out there trolling around in the darkness. He'd be able to see some of them, but not all of them. Still, they'd be there. Don't forget that.

He capped the blue marker and set it on the desk, then wandered into the kitchen, pulled a nonfat yogurt out of the fridge and ate it with a plastic spoon as he walked around the kitchen island in circles. No fat and plenty of protein, the yogurt, good stuff.

Rock star food.

He walked into the master bathroom, took a piss, then pulled off his shirt and studied his abs in the full-length mirror. His torso was totally ripped.

"Ought to be on the cover of a magazine," he told himself, posing.

He had to admit, he wasn't at the absolute prime of his life but wasn't far off the mark, either. Just to prove himself right, he dropped down to the tile floor and did a hundred totally honest pushups.

That felt good.

In fact, it made him want more.

He walked into the master bedroom, dropped down to the carpet, and did two hundred stomach crunches. Then he went back into the bathroom and studied his abs again. The six-pack was incredibly defined. With a little more work he could probably get back to his eight-pack days.

Maybe he should go for it.

Just to prove that he could.

We'll see.

Outside, the afternoon sun pounded down relentlessly, trying to dry up every living thing on the face of the earth.

"We need rain," he said. "Bad."

He couldn't remember a more scorching summer.

But there was one good thing about hot days.

They made for perfect nights.

THE MONITOR SHOWED ASHLEY CONNER pacing back and forth in front of the bed. The fact that she won the game now twice in a row was a problem, but fair was fair. If he expected her to die by the rules when the time came then the least he could do was play by the rules until that time did come. One of the rules, as he told her upfront, is that they would play the game every forty-eight hours. That meant that her next play would be tomorrow afternoon. No doubt she'd lose at that point and he already knew what he was going to do with her body. One person had won twice before, like Ashley. But no one had ever won three times.

If he took his next victim tonight, then there'd be some overlap between her and Ashley. In a perfect world that wouldn't happen, but it didn't really appear to be too big of a problem. He'd be able to manage just fine. If fact, he could have his new captive actually watch Ashley Conner play the game tomorrow afternoon.

That would get her attention in no uncertain terms.

Actually, the more he thought about it, the more it intrigued him.

HE GRABBED THE KEY TO THE DUNGEON and walked downstairs to pay his little captive a visit. When he opened the door and walked in she was curled up under the covers pretending to be asleep.

"I know you're awake," he said. "Stand up and take your clothes off."

She didn't move, pretending not to hear.

"Now!" he shouted.

She jumped out of bed and had the most wonderful expression of fear in her eyes.

"It's not game time," he said. "That's not until tomorrow, so lighten up." He removed all the metal cuffs, except the one around her right ankle, which was chained to an eyebolt in the floor, and then said, "Take your clothes off."

She obeyed, removing everything except her socks.

"The socks too," he said.

She looked at him with pleading eyes.

"My feet get cold," she said.

He reconsidered.

He got no real pleasure out of having her uncomfortable.

"Fine," he said. "Leave them on." He studied her and then said, "Stay where you are, don't move."

He went upstairs and returned with a checkerboard and box of black and red checkers. "You know how to play checkers, right?"

She nodded, visibly apprehensive.

"Yes."

Her voice was barely audible.

He pulled all the blankets off the bed, set the board in the middle and sat on down on one side. "I'll tell you what," he said. "Every time you win, we'll extend the dice game for twelve hours." He smiled and motioned for her to sit on the bed. "Such a deal. Do you want red or black?"

WHILE THEY PLAYED, SHE HELD HER HANDS at odd angles whenever she moved a checker and then quickly pulled them back as soon as she could, protecting them from his vision.

He was curious but didn't want to let on that he knew.

So he took stolen glances whenever he could.

It turned out that her fingernails were scratched.

That's what she was hiding.

She had scratched some kind of messages or clues on them

for the police to find later, after he killed her.

Wickersham smiled.

What a clever little girl.

He was actually impressed.

They played ten games in all and he let her win six times. When they were done she actually thought that she had earned an extra three days before she would have to play the game again. In reality though, she had broken the rules.

That meant that they no longer bound Wickersham either.

He could take her whenever the mood struck him.

Fair is fair.

Chapter Twenty-One

Day Four - July 14
Friday Afternoon

ALTHOUGH MOST OF THE DENVER HOOKERS didn't come out until after dark, you could always find some around at just about any time because there were day Johns that needed to be serviced too. Coventry headed over there around five o'clock to see if he could find anyone who might know how or why Mary Williams ended up with a knife in her eye.

The Rainbird Bar sits on Colfax, just a few blocks down from Capitol Hill, smack dab in the heart of hooker-land. Coventry knew the place well. He was there seven years ago responding to blood on the linoleum, a drug sale gone bad. Then again three years ago—a woman cut down at the unjust age of twenty, stemming from an argument over five dollars. When he walked in, three scantily clad women had already checked him out from head to toe by the time he'd taken four steps inside the door.

All of them had made him for a detective.

Only detectives wore sport coats when it was this hot out.

Coventry walked up to the closest one and put his arm around her shoulders. She was a new face, a white girl about twenty-five, with needle marks on her left arm.

"How are you doing, darling?" he asked.

"Just dandy."

"Someone got killed last night, out in the alley," Coventry said. "You heard about that I assume?"

The woman nodded.

"Yeah, we know."

"I'd consider it a personal favor if you just serviced your regulars for a while, until we can catch this guy," Coventry said. He looked at the other two women as he said it, including them in the comment. One of them nodded. "If any of you know anything, I'd love to hear it," he added.

Silence.

"I really don't care what you do to get your grocery money," he said, "but I am going to care if you die in the process. That would sadden me quite a bit, in fact."

"Why would you care about us?"

Coventry looked surprised.

"Why wouldn't I?" He paused to let them know he was serious. "So, do any of you know why Mary Williams ended up with a knife in her eye last night?"

"You mean Paradise?"

"Right, Paradise."

"I never knew her real name."

All three of them avoided his eyes.

Then one of them spoke.

"She was into rough stuff," the woman said.

Coventry nodded. "I know."

The woman looked like she'd spoken her part and was done. "That's all we know."

"So you didn't see her with anyone in particular last night?"

One of them laughed. "We're the day girls, honey. You need to talk to the night shift."

Coventry thanked them and headed for the door. Just as he was about to step outside, one of them said, "She had a camera or something set up at her house. At least that's what she told me once."

Coventry was intrigued and walked back over.

"A camera, huh?"

The woman nodded. "That's what she told me once. I never personally saw it or anything."

"Interesting."

The woman looked hesitant and then added, "She really didn't have anyone there to protect her or anything, and she let the guys tie her up. So she used to take their pictures when they came in the house—I mean, they, the guys, didn't know it or anything, it was all on the sly. That way, if one of them got too rough or something, she'd have his picture. Then she'd give it to some friends of hers who'd even things up."

Coventry waited for her to continue, but she was done.

"Thanks," he said. Then he pulled three business cards out of his wallet and handed one to each of them. "That number's my cell phone," he said, pointing. "I carry it with me all the time. If any of you have any trouble, you call me day or night. Now, promise you'll carry this with you, for at least the next week or so."

They promised.

When he stepped back outside the heat hit him immediately. Still over a hundred, he thought. When in the hell is it going to rain?

COVENTRY TALKED TO A FEW MORE HOOKERS that he spotted milling around outside, got nothing of interest, then drove over to the victim's house. It turned out to be a small brick structure. The front yard was dead from the heat but the weeds were still thriving, giving the ground a spotted green appearance. He pulled into the cracked cement driveway, took the search warrant out of his briefcase, walked to the front door and pressed the doorbell.

No sound.

He pressed it again.

Nothing.

Then he rapped on the door with his knuckles.

No sound or movement came from inside.

One of the duplicate keys made from the victim's key chain found in her purse fit the front door. He opened it, said "Hello, anyone home? We got a search warrant," and got only silence back. He stepped inside. All the windows were closed and the place was an oven. The living room had a fireplace with a mantle, decorated with several pictures of a little girl. A pretty good sound system sat on the right side of the fireplace. Coventry turned it on and a rap song that he'd never heard before filled the room. It wasn't bad so he let it play but turned it lower.

The kitchen was tiny and separated from the rest of the house, with cheap painted pine cabinets and Formica countertops, but neat and clean. Inside the victim's bedroom there was a small closet. Inside that was an expensive combination safe bolted to the floor, hidden under a blanket and a box.

Coventry pictured the routine.

When the woman brought a John here he'd have to fork over cash in advance. She'd excuse herself and put the money in the safe before anything else happened.

Damn.

It was way too hot in here.

He opened every window, the front door and the back door, and then turned on every fan in the house.

The bondage area, located downstairs where it was much cooler, held three pieces of equipment—a long table that looked like a workbench, a cross, and a chair. All were fitted with strategically placed eyehooks where chains or ropes could be attached. There were also eyehooks in the ceiling at several locations, as well as the floor. A pair of cuffs hung from the ceiling on chains. Accessories hung on hooks on a wall—chains, ropes, cuffs, locks, ball-gags, hoods, blindfolds, spreader bars, whips, feathers, clothespins, and lots of painful looking stuff.

Coventry studied the corners and other dark areas, looking for a camera, but found none. Then he realized why. There was always a potential that someone would attack her upstairs and never even get to this part of the house. So the camera would be upstairs somewhere. In fact, if the woman was smart, she'd get the guy's picture before he ever entered the house.

He went back outside to the front entry and found it—a small digital camera—fitted inside the front porch light. At night, the light would be strong enough that a flash wouldn't be required. After a little exploring he found it was actuated from a foot pedal located under a smaller welcome mat over in the corner. So, while the woman was unlocking the door the man would be standing in front of the camera. She'd step on the pedal and he'd never be the wiser.

Very clever.

But where were the pictures?

No doubt they'd be downloaded into a computer but he didn't find one anywhere in the house. Maybe she had a laptop that she kept in the safe. In fact, the more he thought about it, the more he became convinced that was the case. He'd have the Crime Unit come up here later and get it.

Not that any of this really mattered that much.

After all, she got killed in the alley, not her house.

About all the pictures would be good for is if the guy was a regular and someone recognized him as being on Colfax on the night in question.

WHEN HE FINALLY LEFT IT WAS EIGHT O'CLOCK and he was drenched in sweat. Outside the sun was still bright but the shadows were a lot longer and heat wasn't quite as mean.

The evening was coming.

Then the night.

Somewhere out there in the darkness tonight, barring a miracle, a woman was going to be pulled into a van and driven off to Ashley Conner land.

He turned the Tundra's AC on full blast and headed over to Darien Jade's place. When he got there he found her in the shower, cooling off. She almost pulled him in with his clothes still on, but he managed to get out of them first.

For a long time they stood in the water, kissing and playing with each other with an increasing intensity. Then he laid her down in the tub and took her, forgetting about everything else in the world as the water sprayed down on his back.

Then they swung by McDonald's and ate in the Tundra as they headed downtown.

It was almost dark now.

Game time.

Chapter Twenty-Two

Day Four - July 14
Friday Afternoon

FRIDAY AFTERNOON STARTED OUT NORMAL but quickly escalated into a frenzied state of affairs as Taylor Sutton found herself trying to jam eight hours of paperwork, conferences and phone calls into a four-hour slot. She didn't even have time for one afternoon walk, much less three or four. Throughout it all, hour after hour, Nick Trotter's CD spilled out of two speakers, playing on endless loop from an old Yamaha CD player. Taylor hoped that if she heard it enough something would eventually jump out at her. But so far the only thing that jumped was Claudia: "Tell Nick Trotter he can stop worrying about his mystery client, because I'm going to kill him myself if I have to listen to this crap for five more minutes."

Taylor looked at her, just as a pile of papers fell off the end of her desk, and said: "I need to get drunk so bad my teeth hurt."

Claudia looked at her watch. "Hold off a couple more hours. I don't want anyone filing a bar grievance, charging you with lawyering-while-intoxicated."

Taylor laughed. "An LWI," she said.

"I can see it now," Claudia added. "You'd be the attorney to get a new group formed—CADL."

Taylor thought about it. "Meaning?"

"Clients Against Drunk Lawyers."

Taylor laughed, then lit a match—the first of the afternoon—and blew it out. "Thanks, I needed that."

"Does that mean you'll turn off Nick Trotter?"

Taylor shook her head, said "Sorry," then stooped down and picked papers off the floor, trying to sort them as she did.

AN HOUR OR SO LATER, BROOKE DROPPED BY, bringing some draft employment policies that Image wanted to use at the LoDo operation, but only after they got blessed first by a Colorado attorney, just in case this state had some quirks that the others didn't.

Aaron Cavanaugh was with her.

So cool.

Taylor got up from her desk, walked over and gave him a big hug, reaching around and feeling his ass, a familiar ritual. "God I love this guy," she told Brooke. Then to Aaron: "If you're ever in the mood for a *real* Sutton, let me know."

He chuckled and put his arm around Brooke's waist. "Already got one," he said. Then, referring to the CD, "What's with the talking?"

"Pay attention, because that's what a killer sounds like."

"A killer, huh?"

"That's right."

He chuckled. "A mean one or a nice one?"

"We're not sure yet."

It looked like Aaron was about to say something, but he didn't, and instead concentrated on the words and the voice. Taylor took the opportunity to tell Brooke about the latest call from the mysterious Northwest to Nick Trotter this morning. She added: "Nick thinks that the client is the same guy who took that art student—Ashley . . . somebody—the guy who's supposed to pay a so-called visit this weekend."

"You mean the guy all over the news?"

Taylor nodded. "One and the same." Then added: "Listen for yourself." She walked over to the CD player and put in the second CD, the one with this morning's conversation.

Everyone in the room concentrated on it, listening to every word. At the end, Brooke said: "He doesn't admit it."

Taylor agreed.

That was true.

"But he admires the guy way too much," Taylor said. "No doubt because he is the guy."

She watched Brooke as she thought about it and saw the doubt on her face. "Could be, could not be, too. I really don't see enough here to jump to that conclusion."

Taylor shrugged.

Technically, Brooke was right.

But that didn't change her opinion.

"I'm still with Nick," she said.

Brooke held her hands in surrender, then grabbed Aaron's arm and pulled him towards the door. "We got to go," she said. "Don't forget about those papers. The bigwigs want them reviewed by yesterday."

WHEN THEY LEFT, TAYLOR PUT THE FIRST CD back in the player and listened to it with half an ear as she wrote letters and tried to get stuff off her desk.

Then it was 5:00 and Claudia had her purse in hand, heading for the door. She stopped to say: "You know, this may just be my imagination, but I keep thinking that in one of those conversations, the mystery client tells Nick that he mentioned something in their last conversation. But I don't remember another conversation where it was mentioned. For whatever that's worth."

Taylor twisted a pencil in her fingers.

"I think I know what you mean," she said.

"Good, because I'm out of here. Happy drinking."

After Claudia left, Taylor lit matches one after the other, letting them burn down to her fingers before shaking them out and throwing them into an ashtray.

So if Claudia was right, what did that mean?

She paced back and forth, with her shoes off.

It meant a prior phone conversation was missing from the CD, but why?

Maybe because Nick hadn't taped it.

But maybe because he left it out on purpose.

"Goddamn it, Nick. What the hell's going on?"

Chapter Twenty-Three

Day Four - July 14
Friday Night

NATHAN WICKERSHAM HOPPED INTO THE VAN about 8:30 so that he'd be downtown by 9:30, right when it got dark. He turned the radio to an oldies station that just happened to be playing the exact same songs that he would have picked if he'd been in charge—"On the Poor Side of Town," "When a Man Loves a Woman," "You Can't Hurry Love," "Get Off My Cloud," "White Wedding." He actually hated to turn it off when he got downtown.

But he did.

It was time to concentrate.

Back home, Ashley Conner was busy thinking about what a bad girl she was. Wickersham went down to see her a half hour before he left, handed her a nail file and said, "File all that crap off your fingernails, and your toenails too. I'll be back in fifteen minutes to talk about your punishment."

The look on her face was priceless.

"But . . ."

Wickersham waved her off before she could say another word. "Don't make it worse than it already is."

When he came back down she was sitting on the bed, as nervous as a mouse in a snake cage. "I did it, just like you said." She held her fingers up to show him.

He inspected them.

She did good.

Whatever clues had been there were now long gone.

"Do you have any more anywhere on your body?" he question.

"No," she said. "Honest to God."

"Take your clothes off."

She did, immediately and without protest, obviously aware of just how tenuous her position was. He inspected her and found no scratches or cuts in her skin. Then he said, "Okay. I got to warn you, I'm not sure how mad I am yet. But you're going into the Punishment Room while I think about it."

She looked like she was about to say something to try to get out of it but didn't. "That's fair," she said.

He nodded.

"Okay, come over here."

Then he chained her up in the Punishment Room, in a standing position with her arms over her head and her hands separated by a spreader bar so that one hand couldn't get to the other. She was stretched tight, on her tiptoes. When her calves got too fatigued to hold her up, she'd have to hang.

"I want you to spend the time thinking about how bad you were," he said.

Then he closed the door, leaving her to the darkness and the sound of her own breathing.

If she went crazy, then too bad.

THE CITY WAS SO DAMNED INTOXICATING AT NIGHT, with the lights and the movement and the shadows. He drove around the outskirts of the Auraria campus first, to see if there was as much foot travel on the fringes as he originally envisioned.

There was.

Good.

He turned the radio back on and was glad he did because "Paradise By the Dashboard Lights" was playing. He turned it up and sang along.

There were no words in the English language that described the feeling of the hunt. You might as well try to explain the color blue to a blind man. When you experienced it, you understood it. And if you never experienced it, you never would. It was that simple.

And—if he dared say—the feeling just keep getting better each time. He wasn't sure why that was, but maybe it had something to do with the fact that he wasn't as nervous anymore, not with a string of successes under the belt. Without the nervous edge he seemed to be able to better focus on the euphoria of the event.

Better than drugs.

"Even better than rock 'n roll, Meat Loaf."

Better than sex?

Mmm, now that was an interesting question.

"Yes," he finally decided.

The black bag sat on the seat next to him, and he reached over without looking at it, just because he liked the feel of it. He checked it three times this afternoon. Everything was there.

HE WAS IN NO HURRY. In fact, he was toying with the idea of just driving around for a couple of hours before picking his prey, maybe even stopping somewhere for a salad first.

Just for grins, he drove over to Ashley Conner's neighborhood, to see if there were extra patrol cars circling around. There were, lots of them. So many in fact that he didn't even turn his head to look down her street. He kept going, straight down Broadway for more than two miles, before cutting over to I-25 and looping back to downtown.

So, the cops were definitely taking the whole thing seriously, as they should.

Coventry had organized them well.

Too bad it wouldn't do them any good.

Just to be on the safe side, he put on the black rim glasses, the mustache and a baseball cap.

Ten minutes later he was driving north on Speer, singing along to one of the world's most perfect songs—"Friday I'm In Love"—when the light turned red at 14th Avenue. Ordinarily, he would have stepped on the gas and gone through, but tonight he needed to be on his best behavior.

The cross-traffic took off.

A bunch of ordinary mortals.

Getting in his way.

For some reason the last car caught his attention. It was a pickup truck, actually, not a car. There were two figures inside. The passenger was a woman and, even in the dark and at a distance, he could tell she was stunning. She had a dark tanned face, raven black hair and looked vaguely familiar. For some reason, she stared right at him as the truck went through the intersection.

She even turned her head to look back.

Then suddenly the brake lights went on, the truck slowed

and then came to a screeching halt. The woman and the driver had both turned around at this point and were looking at him, talking to each other in an animated way.

Then he realized who the woman was.

The light turned green and he immediately stepped on the gas.

"Shit!"

Chapter Twenty-Four

Day Four - July 14
Friday Night

THEY PASSED A 7-ELEVEN and Coventry swung back and pulled in, a spur of the moment thing. "Coffee," he said. In the back seat, he had three or four used thermoses. He grabbed the closest one, unscrewed the cap and took a whiff. It had a definite pungent odor but didn't seem like anything that would kill him.

"Good enough," he said.

Darien waited in the truck while he ran inside, poured five French Vanilla creamers into the thermos, topped it off with fresh caffeine, grabbed two empty Styrofoam cups and paid.

When he got back in the truck Darien was looking at him strangely. He unscrewed the thermos and poured coffee into one of the cups. "You want some?" he asked.

She nodded, "Yeah, but I'll just share yours."

Fine.

She was still looking at him funny.

"What?" he asked, concentrating on not overfilling the cup.

"I'm just trying to think of what we are," she said. "Are we just Bed-Buddies, or something more?"

Coventry chuckled. "Way more," he said, "at least from my point of view."

She seemed relieved. "Good, me too."

Coventry got serious. "The truth is, I've been waiting for someone like you for a while."

She cocked her head. "You don't know anything about me."

That was accurate, to a point. She continuously deflected every question that related to her past. He still didn't know where she grew up, if she had brothers or sisters, if her parents were alive, how old she was when she lost her virginity, or what she did for a living.

But he did know how he felt when he was around her. And he knew how her body moved in the dark.

"I know enough," he said.

She paused. "I'm scared."

He looked at her.

"Why?"

"I'm scared you're going to find something out about me that's going to make you change your mind."

"What might that be?"

She looked away.

"Nothing, really."

"You're not really a guy, are you?" he asked.

She laughed. "No."

"You've never been a guy?"

"No."

"Well, okay then."

Coventry cranked over the engine and looked behind the truck to be sure he wasn't going to run anyone over. It was a good thing, too. A teenage girl was right behind him, apparently cutting through the parking lot while she talked into a cell phone, oblivious to the fact that his backup lights were on and his engine was running. He waited until she passed and then backed up.

"Time to catch a killer," he said.

TWO HOURS LATER THEY WERE DRIVING east on 14th Avenue, listening to one of the best songs ever made—"Friday I'm In Love"—when Darien Jade said, "I know that guy from somewhere."

Coventry looked in the direction she was staring and didn't see anything, other than a string of cars waiting at the red light on Speer Boulevard.

"Who?"

"The guy driving the van."

Something in his gut made his foot go to the brakes. "Where do you know him from?"

"I don't know."

Coventry brought the rest of his weight down on the pedal, with so much force in fact that the antilock brakes kicked in.

He turned in his seat.

The first vehicle at the red light was a van. The driver seemed to be looking their way but shielding his face with his hand—on purpose or just a coincidence? Either way, Coventry couldn't make out his features.

"That guy right there? In the van?"

"Yes."

"You know him?"

"No," she said. "I don't *know* him, but I've *seen* him." She looked confused. "Why? What's the big deal? I'm just making small talk . . ."

Coventry wanted to back up to Speer, but the traffic had already taken off and a string of cars was turning onto 14th, right towards him.

"Shit!"

"Bryson, what are you doing? All I said was I've seen the guy."

"Yeah," he said, "probably from your neighborhood, when he was checking the place out. He has a van."

"That's awful thin."

"Thin is better than zero."

He cut back to Speer as fast as he could and then weaved north through traffic. The van was nowhere. It had vanished. To make matters worse, both he and Darien had been looking at the driver so hard that neither of them noticed anything in particular about the van, other than it was a van.

"I can't even say if it was white or black," Darien said.

Coventry nodded.

"Me too," he said. "It was him though, I can tell by the way he took off when the light turned green. Maybe we scared him enough that he'll call it quits for the night."

"You think?"

Coventry thought about it and then shook his head. "I wouldn't, if I was him. You got to show a little guts."

THEY GOT A **BOLO** OUT ON A VAN with a white male driver wearing black glasses, then continued the drive around the city, hoping against hope to just bump into him again.

"I wonder what the odds are," Darien said at one point, "of actually finding someone like this."

Coventry shrugged.

"I don't know, but we did it once," he said.

She cocked her head. "So what are the odds of actually finding someone like this twice?"

Coventry couldn't help but laugh.

"Somewhere less than fifty-fifty, I'm guessing."

He looked at his watch. It was eleven o'clock, meaning the city traffic would still be pretty thick for another couple of hours and the van would be hard to spot. Things would thin out after two or two-thirty, though, and they'd be able to concentrate a lot better on what was out there driving around.

Coventry emphasized the fringe areas around Larimer Square and LoDo, hunting down every van on the road, getting into position so they could see the driver's face, then dropping back so that Darien could write down the vehicle's license plate number.

Before long it was three in the morning.

And still nothing.

Chapter Twenty-Five

Day Five - July 15
Saturday Morning

———————

WHEN TAYLOR SUTTON OPENED HER EYES she immediately knew she had slept well into the morning. The room was still fairly dark, thanks to thick curtains, but the light that did manage to finger its way in was strong.

She propped herself on her elbows and looked around.

She was alone in a bedroom that she'd never seen before; and not just any bedroom, but something out of a magazine. The place oozed money. The bed itself was big enough to play soccer on. The ceiling was vaulted and a massive flat-panel TV hung on the opposite wall, strategically positioned about two feet above an expensive maple dresser. The master bathroom, although not fully visible, had an oversized Jacuzzi and a large glass shower, all befitted in muted tile that looked to be a hundred years old.

She sank back down on the pillow, still slightly hung over, trying to judge how much her head hurt.

Not as much as it should, she decided.

The room, in fact the whole world, was quiet. Not a sound came from anywhere. She remembered the sex last night, the drunken, crazy sex. She recalled using her mouth and tongue for a long time, giving a deep teasing blowjob. The memory was so real and fresh that she reached between her legs and, over the next twenty minutes, brought herself to a slow explosive orgasm.

Then she got up and showered.

She found her purse on a dresser but couldn't find her clothes anywhere. So she grabbed a long-sleeved shirt out of the master closet and put it on as she walked down a winding staircase to the lower level.

DOWNSTAIRS IN THE DESIGNER KITCHEN a pot of coffee waited for her with a clean cup sitting next to it. She found cream in the Sub Zero, poured a little in the cup, then topped it off with coffee. It was a blend she had never tasted before, something exotic and expensive.

Damn good, she had to admit.

On the granite countertop in the island she found her Porsche keys sitting on top of a handwritten note: "I had a driver bring your car over this morning. Hope you don't mind. Leave your number before you go, otherwise you'll break my heart."

She walked across a well-furnished room the size of Kansas and looked outside. The Porsche sat in the middle of a cobblestone circular driveway that surrounded a contemporary water feature. The neighborhood houses looked like castles. Unlike the rest of the world, the lawns here were lush green. She must be in Cherry Hills somewhere.

She refilled the coffee cup and wandered around the house.

It belonged to Sean Michaels, the businessman she met on the street on Tuesday, who looked over her shoulder for her when she was being followed. She bumped into him after work yesterday at the Paramount Café and let him buy her a drink—too many drinks, actually. She remembered him taking her to some club in a Ferrari, where they danced to pounding music in the middle a thousand crazy people.

Suddenly she remembered where her clothes were.

In the Ferrari.

She had them off by the time they got to his place. .

She went to the garage to see if the Ferrari was there by any chance. It was, sitting next to three motorcycles that looked like chromed Harleys on steroids, with the wildest, most intricate paint jobs she'd ever seen. Inside the Ferrari, on the floor, she found her clothes and put them on, then hung his shirt back up in the master closet.

Before leaving she stopped in the kitchen long enough to turn off the coffee machine and throw one of her business cards on the counter.

She was almost out the front door when she came back into the kitchen and wrote her home phone number on the front of the card.

Ten seconds later she was in the Porsche.

It had to be every bit of a hundred and twenty degrees in there.

IT TOOK SOME TIME TO FIND HER WAY out of the neighborhood but she finally managed. She needed to get to the office and listen to one of Nick Trotter's conversations again. And knew exactly which one it was. But first she swung by her house and picked up her gym bag, then headed over to 24 Hour Fitness to do cardio until all the alcohol sweated itself out of her system.

Halfway through the workout a breaking-news report popped up on the TV monitor. When it ended she immediately got off the elliptical, walked briskly to the locker room, grabbed her bag and headed for the front door, still in a deep sweat.

It was clear where she needed to be.

Sixth Avenue at Federal.

And she needed to be there now.

This very minute.

Chapter Twenty-Six

Day Five - July 15
Saturday Morning

THE HUNT CAN BE A HELL OF A LOT more exciting than the kill. In this particular case, the kill had been a non-event. Wickersham had almost given up last night, in fact *had* given up, when something unexpected happened just before three in the morning—a broken car on the side of the road, a woman standing next to it, a woman by herself.

Alone.

Unprotected.

Ripe for the taking.

He pulled over and found she was insanely drunk, with a flat tire. She had no spare.

"If the cops find you here like this, they'll slap you in the drunk tank so fast it'll make you head spin," Wickersham told her. "I've been there. They'll give you a DWI too. The best thing you can do is just lock it up and let me drive you home."

She hopped in.

"Thank God you came by."

Then she hit on him.

Big time.

The alcohol had turned her into a total slut.

She kept rubbing his cock and he let her. Then she unzipped his pants and gave him a blowjob as he drove. He pulled off the road, in a dark secluded spot, and let her continue for fifteen minutes. He couldn't leave his DNA in her mouth, but almost did, not pulling his cock out until a split second before he came. Then he tied her down spread-eagle in the back of the van and played the dice game with her.

She lost.

He dumped her body and headed for home, taking nothing with him except her driver's license, the smell of her perfume and a very satisfied dick.

WHEN HE GOT BACK TO HIS PLACE it was almost five in the morning. Ashley Conner was still in the Punishment Room, passed out and hanging limp by her wrists. He got her down, rubbed the circulation back into her body, and laid her in the bed. Then went upstairs and fell asleep immediately.

He woke up a short time later, still tired but too excited to sleep any longer. The camera showed that Ashley Conner was awake now, dressed and pacing in front of her bed. She looked terrified. He wasn't sure, but he guessed that she'd do just about anything in the world to avoid going back into the Punishment Room again.

Last night's kill hadn't made the morning paper.

Probably because no one found the body.

But they would.

And that would be today.

He chuckled just thinking about it and wished he could be there to see Coventry's face.

"You're a goddamn rock star," he told himself.

Then he had a neat idea. He gathered together what he needed, walked out to the Camry and pointed the front end of the vehicle towards Coventry's house.

Chapter Twenty-Seven

Day Five - July 15
Saturday Morning

COVENTRY WAS TAKING DARIEN HOME, heading east on the 6th Avenue freeway in the middle lane with a cup of coffee in his left hand, when an 18-wheeler started riding his ass. He sped up to get some breathing room. It didn't work. Then it moved into the right lane, pulled next to him and blew the horn.

Coventry looked over and found the driver pointing to Darien, who wore black shorts and a white tank top. He waved at the guy as if to say, "Yeah, I know, she's hot, " and expected that to be the end of it. But the honking continued and the truck didn't speed up even though the lane was clear ahead.

"I think he likes you," Coventry said.

She looked at him, then back at the driver, a heavyset man with a full beard who now had his arm all the way out the window, pointing.

Honk.

Honk.

"He reminds me of that guy in *Thelma and Louise*," she said. "Disgusting."

"Never saw that movie," Coventry said.

"You didn't?"

"No, it's a chick-flick, right?"

"Well, sort of."

"I don't do chick-flicks."

Honk.

Coventry slowed to let the trucker get ahead but the dumb ass decelerated with him and kept honking. "What's with this guy?" Darien must have seen something he didn't because she unfastened her seatbelt and climbed halfway in the back seat. "I thinks he's pointing to the bed," she said.

Then she screamed.

"What?"

"An arm! There's an arm in the back!"

"Shit!"

COVENTRY HIT THE BRAKES—dumping the coffee—and pulled over to the side of the freeway as fast as he could, sliding to a stop. He jumped out, wiping his pants, and looked in the back.

Goddamn it.

An arm stuck out from under the tarp and wood. He pulled the coverings back and found a woman.

Dead.

Naked.

She looked to be about thirty, with short black hair, slightly overweight, with more tattoos than she needed. He kicked the tire and then punched the side of the truck so hard that it dented.

"You son-of-a-bitch!"

He paced all the way around the vehicle, then again, then

again. Darien watched him but said nothing. "Okay," he finally said, "calm down. Calm down and catch the little shit."

Ten seconds later he called the Crime Lab. Then Jena Vernon.

"Hello?"

She was breathing heavily and he pictured her on a treadmill.

"You wanted me to call you so I am."

"Where are you?"

"6th Avenue, east bound, at Federal."

"I'll be there in ten minutes."

SEVERAL PATROL CARS PULLED IN behind the truck. Coventry had them set up a perimeter that no one was to cross without his express permission. A few minutes later the Crime Lab pulled up and Coventry was relieved to see Paul Kubiak at the wheel.

"Don't lose a goddamn fiber," Coventry told him before he could even open the door. Kubiak looked at him, as if to say you're blocking the way, and then got out when Coventry stepped back. He immediately walked around the pickup, dragging that big old gut of his, stared at the woman for a few moments, then told Coventry: "It looks like you made another mess. What I need you to do is close that lane of traffic and get a bottleneck going so we don't have the truckers blowing through here at a hundred miles an hour."

"You got it." He felt a layer of stress fall away. "By the way, good morning."

Kubiak looked at him and chuckled. "You know, they make diapers for adults."

Coventry looked at his pants.

He had to admit, it did look like he wet himself.

"I want this guy," he said.

THE DEAD WOMAN HAD BRUSING on her wrists and ankles, as if she'd been cuffed and then pulled like a maniac to escape. There were no other visible marks on the body. Her face still had fear etched on it.

Traffic had bottlenecked now and the uniforms were doing their best to keep the Lookey-Lews moving. Jena Vernon shouted at him from behind the perimeter but he didn't have time for her right now.

He'd just have to apologize later.

Shalifa Netherwood showed up about the same time that Coventry noticed a news helicopter overhead. "Are you okay?" she asked.

He could care less if he was okay nor not. This wasn't about him.

"Yeah, fine," he said.

He needed coffee in the worst way.

A visit to a restroom wouldn't hurt either.

She pulled out a notepad. "Let me get your statement before you go all senile on me," she said. He gave it to her, standing there next to the truck, while they watched a Crime Unit Detective by the name of Lieberman photograph the body. Coventry and Darien Jade drove around last night looking for the van. They gave up about three in the morning, went to his place and fell asleep almost immediately. They got up about nine, briefly stopped at the Einstein Bros on Union to get two coffees to go, and were driving down the freeway when some trucker next to them got all excited and started blowing the horn.

"Did you get out of the truck at Einstein's?"

Coventry nodded. "Yeah, for about five minutes, tops."

"Okay."

"The body didn't get dumped there," he added. "There were too many cars around. It had to have been at my house, sometime between three in the morning and daybreak."

She nodded.

He looked at her, then back to the victim.

"We need to get this poor woman identified," he said. "I want to know where she was last night and where she got taken. That's a crime scene and the longer we take to find it the less it's going to help us." He looked at the helicopter, briefly distracted, then back at her. "The other crime scene is at my house, where he put the body in the back. In fact, would you mind going over there and securing it?"

No, she wouldn't.

"Love you," he said as she walked away.

He looked around for Darien Jade but couldn't find her. She must have slipped away during the commotion, probably to find shade.

It was already in the nineties and you could feel the temperature rising. Even the coffee on his pants had already dried.

HE WASN'T QUITE SURE AT THIS POINT what to do next. He couldn't wander outside the perimeter; otherwise he'd be barraged by reporters. So he slipped into the front seat of the pickup where he at least had some shade, left the door open, and called the FBI profiler, Leanne Sanders. She was about thirty seconds away from stepping into a meeting when she answered, so he gave her the reader's digest version of what just happened.

"Okay," she said, "I'm going to mull this over tonight, but here's my preliminary thoughts, which may change later. This guy probably got a bigger charge out of putting the body in the back of your truck than he did actually killing the woman. I wouldn't doubt it a bit if he actually followed you around this morning to see the look on your face when you discovered the body. In fact, it wouldn't surprise me if he's watching you right now."

"You mean he's here somewhere?"

"That's exactly what I mean. What fun would it be to cause such a big fuss and then not be there to watch?"

Two minutes later Coventry motioned for Jena Vernon to come over.

"I'm going to give you some one-on-one time in a bit," he said. "In the meantime, I want you to film as much of the crowd as you can, but don't be obvious. Get in different positions and make it look like the cameraman is focused on you, but get the crowd."

He watched her process the information.

"Do you think the man who did this is actually here some-where?" she asked.

Coventry shrugged.

"We don't know. It's possible." Then, looking up: "Is that your chopper up there?"

"Yes."

"Is there any way for you to get the word to them to get some film of the crowd too, as well as the cars parked around here?"

She nodded and pulled out a cell phone.

"Done," she said.

She turned and almost got away before he grabbed her by the arm. "By the way, here's a scoop. We'll be setting up another crime scene at my house soon."

She looked startled.

"How soon?"

Coventry looked at his watch. "Ten minutes, I'm guessing. Detective Netherwood is on her way right now."

She looked like she just won the lottery. "Coventry, this is huge," she said. "This'll be national news. I'm talking CNN and all the rest of them."

He hadn't thought about it.

But she was right.

The case was about to explode.

And that would only inspire the guy more.

Chapter Twenty-Eight

Day Five - July 15
Saturday Morning

TAYLOR SUTTON BROKE MORE THAN A FEW speed limits as she raced down the 6th Avenue freeway to the crime scene location reported on the gym's TV monitor. Traffic was already backed up to Wadsworth, so she got off there and took the side streets to Federal, then parked the Porsche in the lot of a seedy hotel and walked over to all the commotion.

The epicenter of the storm was a white pickup truck.

From her vantage point, slightly higher in elevation, she could make out the naked body of a woman in the truck's bed. A large crowd stood around and at least a dozen cops were strategically positioned to keep everyone out. Others, like her, were walking down to the scene.

Sweat dripped down her forehead and into her eyes. She pulled her shirt up and wiped her face as best she could, flashing a flat, tanned stomach to anyone who might be looking.

That helped but not much.

She really didn't know what she expected to find here.

All she knew is that the dead woman was probably the work of the man all over the news who bragged about his "visit" this weekend. And, if Nick Trotter's theory was correct, this is his mystery client, the man she was trying to find.

She squinted.

Back at her car, safe and sound, she had sunglasses and a visor. For a heartbeat she considered getting them but didn't really feel like making another 200-yard trek in the heat.

So she wandered around to the other side of the crowd instead. There, at least, her face pointed away from the sun.

It was too damned hot.

The whole world was drying up.

She couldn't believe the size of the crowd. There had to be two hundred people, minimum, plus the cops and news crews, and vehicles all over the place. Three helicopters floated above it all, washing the air with a deep, vibrating rumble.

BEFORE LONG IT BECAME CLEAR who was in charge—a man about six-two, strong looking, with long brown hair that kept flopping down over his forehead in spite of the fact that he repeatedly raked it back with his fingers. His tanned face belonged on a magazine cover. He was a little too tall for her taste, but other than that, eminently doable. He wore jeans and a blue cotton short-sleeved shirt, punctuated with a black holster and weapon. She'd seen him on TV a number of times but he looked bigger and better in person.

Right now he was intense.

Almost mean looking.

She was glad she wasn't on the receiving end of whatever it was he was thinking.

She worked her way through the crowd to get closer to him. There was something about him pulling her in. For some reason she pictured the two of them together in a cool quiet place somewhere, intoxicated, on the verge of screwing like rabbits.

He was talking to a female who also wore a weapon, no doubt another detective. She had short wash-and-blow hair and an easy smile. Judging by her manner, she held Coventry in high respect. She also seemed to have a lot of chest under her clothes. Some of the guys in the crowd were actually focused on her with some intensity.

Taylor worked her way in even closer.

So near that she was now able to actually pick up the conversation.

"HERE'S THE PISSER, KATE," Coventry said. "I think I actually had this guy in my crosshairs last night. If I'd been smart enough to react a little faster, this poor woman might be alive right now."

The woman—Kate—looked puzzled.

"What do you mean?"

"Okay," Coventry said. "Darien and I were going through a green light at the intersection of Speer and 14th."

Kate interrupted him. "Darien doesn't exist."

Coventry chuckled.

"Not according to Netherwood," Kate added.

"That's the rumor," Coventry said. "But trust me, she does." He then told her about a man with black glasses, driving a van, who disappeared down Speer before they could catch him. "He's our guy," Coventry said. "I had the little shit in my hands and let him wiggle out."

Kate looked skeptical. "Nothing personal, Coventry, but that's a pretty big stretch. So what if the guy took off fast? Everyone in the world floors it as soon as the light turns green."

"It's not just that," Coventry said. "I think Darien recognized the guy because he'd been hanging around Ashley Conner's place. Remember, Darien lives across the hall from her. My guess is that this guy was checking out the neighborhood, certainly before he took Ashley, but maybe afterwards too. I haven't told you this yet, but I've been in contact with Leanne Sanders."

"The profiler?"

"Yes," Coventry said. "In her opinion, our man's a moth who loves to be around the flame."

Kate looked as if that made sense.

"Can Darien give us a composite?"

Coventry shook his head. "Unfortunately, no. It's just one of those vague things, when you see someone and know you've seen them before, but really don't have enough of an image in your mind to describe their features."

"But," Katona said, "she might be able to pick him out of a lineup, if we got to that point."

Coventry shrugged.

"You never know."

Suddenly Coventry, who had his back to Taylor, turned and looked directly at her.

"HI THERE," HE SAID.

Taylor stared at him, unsure what to do. There was something about his eyes that wouldn't let her look away. Then she figured it out—one was blue and one was green.

"Hi there back," she said.

She had a sudden urge to light a match and instinctively

reached down to her pocket, before she realized that she still wore her workout shorts which didn't have any pockets. That's why she carried the Porsche keys in her hand.

"Did you hear all that?" Coventry asked.

Her first instinct was to lie.

But his eyes wouldn't let her.

"Maybe a little," she said.

Coventry nodded. "Hot out again," he said and raked his hair back with his fingers. "That stuff about the van and the black glasses is confidential. Do you think you could help me keep it that way and forget about it?"

She nodded.

"Forget about what?"

"Thanks," he said. "I appreciate it."

SHE HUNG AROUND FOR ANOTHER FIFTEEN minutes before finally deciding there wasn't much more she was going to get out of it.

From there, she headed home and stood under a cool shower until her core temperature came down to normal. Then she called Nick Trotter, apparently catching him on a golf course somewhere. "Nick, quick question," she said. "The guy who ran you off the road. He was driving a pickup, right?"

"Right."

"It wasn't a van."

"No, it was a truck."

"Okay," she said. "One more question. I know you said you couldn't see his face, because it was dark. But could you tell if he was wearing black glasses or not?"

A pause on the other end of the phone, then: "I don't think

so."

"You sure?"

"Pretty sure," Nick said. "I didn't see his face, but I did see the outline of it. If he'd been wearing glasses, I think I would have noticed."

"But you're not sure?"

"Not a hundred percent," Nick said. "Why?"

"No reason. Just trying to narrow things down."

Chapter Twenty-Nine

Day Five - July 15
Saturday

NATHAN WICKERSHAM JOGGED UP the old gravel firefighting road on the west face of Green Mountain, maintaining a steady pace under a blistering sun. He wore a small, lightweight backpack that held a pair of Bushnell auto-focus binoculars and a water bottle. The mountain was pretty much his and his alone thanks to the heat. All the sane people in the world had found shade or air conditioning somewhere.

He liked the heat.

In fact, he liked just about anything extreme—temperature, wind, waves, workouts, whatever. Life was crisper and more intense at the edge.

Green Mountain traditionally lived up to its name and was actually green. But this summer the sun had sucked the color out of it and painted it a dead brown instead.

It had no trees.

Not a one.

Not even a scraggly Pinon, which can grow just about anywhere in Colorado. Wickersham couldn't figure out why, because across the valley, on the other side of C-470, the hills were no higher but were thick with Ponderosa Pines.

Trees there.

None here.

Weird.

The jog to the crest of the mountain was about two miles. Then he ran along the wide, flat ridge, able to see many miles in all directions. The view to the east displayed Denver and the endless flatlands beyond. The view to the west dropped into a valley and then lifted up into the Rocky Mountain foothills.

Seriously stunning.

He slowed down to a walk about a half mile before he came to a transmission tower. There he sat in the shade and drank most his water in one long swallow.

Damned good.

At first he thought he would rest there for five minutes or so, but was too excited, and almost immediately got up and continued east on the ridge at a brisk walk. In three-fourths of a mile he should be able to see Coventry's house.

The rock star was watching.

HE WASN'T WORRIED ABOUT THE FORENSIC TYPES finding anything useful there. Putting the body into the back of Coventry's truck had been quick and simple. About four in the morning, while it was still pitch-black out, Wickersham parked the van at the end of Coventry's street, in the turnaround, killed the engine and sat there with the windows open for a full five minutes, listening for any sounds of life.

There were none.

Once he knew it was safe, he coasted down the hill in neutral with the engine off and stopped directly in front of Coventry's driveway. He opened the back of the van, pulled the woman out, carried her body over to the truck and quietly set it in the bed. He pushed it against the cab as far as he could and covered it with a tarp and some wood lying in the bed, so Coventry wouldn't see it when he got in. That way he would drive around with it for a while. Then he got back in the van and coasted all the way down to the stop sign. There he fired up the engine and disappeared into the night.

Not a single dog barked.

Not a single light on the street came on.

Not a single eye saw the invisible man.

COVENTRY'S STREET FINALLY CAME INTO VIEW, snaking up a valley. Sure enough, a Crime Unit van and two patrol cars were parked in front of Coventry's house.

Perfect.

The game was on.

It would be interesting to see if the Crime Unit spent any time inside Coventry's house. If so, that meant that Coventry figured out that there was a reason his alarm clock was off by ten minutes the other morning, the reason being that someone had entered his house and changed it.

Two news vans were on the street too, with cameras rolling while female reporters talked into microphones, no doubt telling the world that this is where someone put the body into Coventry's truck last night.

Wickersham kept walking along the mountain ridge, more than three hundred yards away, feeling like he was watching his own baby being born. All this was because of him.

The rock star.

The magnificent one.

Even if someone saw him here, he was just one more guy out for a walk in the hills. Suddenly a helicopter rumbled in from the east. A news chopper, getting even more footage for this evening's top story.

Damn it.

He was hoping to find a spot where he could lay down and pull out the binoculars. Scratch that idea, as long as the dumb-ass helicopter was up there. So he just kept walking while the aircraft got into position over Coventry's house and hovered there.

Although the ridge of the mountain was flat, and had a fairly worn hiking path, it was also so rocky that Wickersham had to keep a constant eye on where he put his feet.

Up ahead, about fifty yards away, a middle-aged female power-walked in his direction. She wore a big hat and sunglasses. She was smiling and looking at him. Even from this distance he could tell she was a serious hiker by her tan, her stride and her outfit, no doubt a housewife trying to keep the pounds off. He'd have to mutter something when she passed, but needed to hide his face.

How?

Bingo.

He swung the backpack around and pulled out the water bottle. He would put it to his mouth and drink just as she passed. She wasn't more than ten yards away when it happened.

He saw it right before she got to it.

A rattlesnake.

Six feet long.

Thick as a baseball bat.

Lying there invisible in the dirt, not moving a muscle, soaking up the sun.

Her foot came down on it near the tail end, almost on the rattle. The snake reared and struck immediately, before her foot even came off. It sunk its fangs into her calf and held on for a heartbeat while it injected venom.

The woman went down hard, smashing her body on the rocky ground. When she looked up, he had never seen such fear before. The snake was still there; its fangs not more than a foot from her face.

"Help me!" she screamed.

Chapter Thirty

Day Five - July 15
Saturday Afternoon

THE DAY GOT SO BIG SO FAST that Coventry couldn't hear himself think. He told Netherwood he'd be right back, then walked past the elevator, down the stairs to the parking garage, and took an unmarked car over to Darien's, parking in front of the bondage paraphernalia shop on Broadway.

She actually answered the door this time.

"You scared the shit out of me," he said. She grabbed him by the shirt and pulled him in. Even though the windows were open and three fans were blowing, the place was so hot that she must have just got home. "Where'd you go?" he asked. It was a good question too. She disappeared almost immediately after they pulled over this morning with the body in the back.

"You were busy. I walked home," she said.

Coventry wasn't satisfied. "You should have said something."

"I didn't want to bother you."

He wasn't sure if that was the reason, or because she didn't want to be around the news cameras. But he wasn't in the mood to press it.

"You're sweating," she said. "I have a cure for that."

She took him into the bathroom, turned on the shower and felt it with her hand as it warmed up. When it was just about right—refreshing but not too cool—she turned off the lights and allowed the room to slip into darkness, except for the faint illumination coming from around the door. By the time Coventry had his clothes off she was already under the spray.

They held each other.

It felt so damn good being there with her.

Knowing she was safe.

At least for the moment.

"I'm on this guy's radar screen," Coventry said. "That means he knows about you. He could go after you at any time, just to show me what a clever little prick he is."

"I already know that, Bryson," she said. "And I'm not cooling it, if that's what you're getting at."

"It's the last thing I want, but we can't afford to . . ."

She cut him off. "I run my life, not some creep. So screw him." She squeezed his hand. "If something happens to me, it's on my shoulders, not yours."

Unfortunately that wasn't true.

She'd have a much better chance of staying out of this guy's brain if she distanced herself.

"In my ideal world, you go somewhere for a while," he said. "I'll pay. California or wherever you want. That's the only way you're going to be a hundred percent safe."

"Yeah, well, I don't want to be a hundred percent safe," she said. "I don't even want to be seventy-five percent safe." Coventry started to argue but she cut him off. "This discussion's over. Protect me if you want but don't expect me to go anywhere."

Coventry swallowed.

"Okay?" she added.

"Are you sure?"

"Positive."

He bit his lower lip.

Then raised an eyebrow. "Are you always this stubborn?"

"Pretty much, so get used to it."

His cell phone rang, barely audible, coming from the pocket of his pants. He suspected it might be Shalifa, reminding him of the press conference scheduled for 2:00. He pressed the light button on his watch to see what time it was.

Shit!—1:47.

He slapped Darien on the ass and stepped out.

"Got to go," he said. "I'll pick you up at eight if you're still alive."

She grabbed his arm. "Hey, you didn't ask me if I'm free. You're just assuming."

He got back in, pulled her stomach to his and gave her a deep kiss.

"Well are you?"

"Am I what?"

"Free."

"No. I'm cheap, but I'm not free."

He chuckled. "Close enough. See you at eight."

COVENTRY ARRIVED AT THE PRESS CONFERENCE ten minutes late, running to the podium as if he was catching the last subway train. His hair was soaked and he had no time to put on a tie. He intended all day to jot down a few notes on cue cards beforehand, but hadn't done that either.

Afterwards Shalifa said, "If you were trying to give the impression that we're so busy trying to catch this guy that we don't even have time to prepare for a press conference, it worked."

He laughed. "Well, that pretty much is the truth."

"Although I'm not quite sure if I understand the wet hair thing," she added.

"It's my new look."

"Here's a clue. It's not working."

They walked up to homicide. Coventry found a half cup of cold goop sitting on his desk, dumped it in the snake plant, refilled and joined Shalifa and Kate Katona, who had already pulled up chairs.

"The most important thing," he said, "is to find out who the woman is. I don't want to use a picture of her actual dead face, so let's get a sketch artist to give us something as accurate as possible, without the scary look, and get it all over the news. Who wants that assignment?"

Katona nodded. "I can handle that."

"Okay, good."

"If this guy's true to form, we'll get her driver's license in the mail pretty soon anyway," she added

"Maybe, but we don't have that kind of time. Once we find out who she is, we can hopefully figure out where she got abducted. I want to process that scene while there's still a chance of getting something useful out of it."

Then they outlined the other pressing things that needed to be done.

Hours later, after everyone else had left for the day, his cell phone rang. He crumpled an empty McDonald's bag, tossed it in the trash, burped, and answered, "It's me."

A man's voice came through, one he didn't recognize, garbled as if the guy was talking while chewing a pencil, deliberately disguised. "I'll tell you her name, if you want."

Coventry's mind raced.

"No thanks," he finally said. Then he hung up and kicked the trashcan.

Chapter Thirty-One

Day Five - July 15
Saturday Night

ASHLEY CONNER, IT TURNED OUT, lived in a seedy apartment building south of downtown. The elevator was broke so Taylor Sutton took the stairs to the fourth floor, immediately spotting a door with yellow police tape.

She had no idea what she was doing here or hoped to accomplish. All she knew is that if the man terrorizing Denver was in fact Nick Trotter's mystery client, then this was where his first victim lived.

She tried the doorknob and found it locked.

She jiggled it just to be sure.

Sure enough, locked solid.

Okay, now what?

She walked down to ground level, sat on the front stairs of the building, and watched a half-dozen moths dart as close as they could to a streetlight. She pulled out a book of matches and lit one. Then she blew it out and threw it on the cement walkway where it landed about five feet away. She lit another one and threw it, trying to get it as close to the first one as she could. It landed about eight inches away, not bad. Before she knew it there were thirty or more matches on the ground, more than a few of them still burning.

The door opened behind her and she instinctively moved over to let them pass. There were two people, a man and a woman. Both looked too young and full of life to be in a place like this. They walked to a mid-sized SUV parked on the street. When the man turned to get in she recognized him.

Bryson Coventry.

What the hell was he doing here?

Certainly not investigating.

Not the way he and the woman were hanging on each other.

They rolled through the stop sign at the end of the street and crossed Broadway, which was one-way south. She suspected that they were cutting over to Lincoln to head north. Taylor didn't know why but she ran to the Porsche and sped in that direction. She didn't really expect to catch them but ended up next to them at a red light at 8th Avenue. Coventry actually glanced in her direction for a second before she could cover her face with her hand.

When the light turned green she let him take off, then dropped back and followed in his lane with another car between them. She flicked the radio buttons, suddenly starved for good music, skipping over a number of duds before finally powering off altogether.

Then she powered it back on, determined to find something worth listening to. When she landed on the B-52's "Roam," she nodded and left it there.

That was better.

Coventry passed the State Capitol Building and turned right on Colfax.

She followed.

NICK'S STORY ABOUT BEING RUN OFF THE ROAD had been nagging at her all day. Nick was over six feet, built, and had a bare-knuckles attitude about everything. If someone had played car bumper like he said, and that's all there was to it, he would have been the first person on the face of the earth to run the guy down and pull his ass out of the car.

Plus there was no damage to his vehicle.

Which seemed unlikely, given how long the chase seemed to last.

Chances are there was more to the story than he was telling.

But then again, maybe he was just being on his best behavior. After all, his life wasn't exactly what you'd call normal anymore. Not since his lovely wife Sarah disappeared without a trace two months ago, halfway through a brutally ugly divorce.

Nick had no alibi.

But the police had no body or credible evidence.

Things would eventually shake out. In the meantime, everyone in town had an opinion.

Suddenly Coventry's SUV pulled into a parking space in front of a liquor store. She continued past, parked the Porsche a block down and then headed back on foot.

Maybe the woman with him was a hooker and he was dropping her off.

That would be interesting.

Then her cell phone rang. "It's me, Sean. A few buddies of mine have their hands on a company jet. We're heading down to the Hard Rock in Vegas to tear it up. I thought you might want to come."

She turned and headed back to the Porsche, already picturing a wild night of partying, gambling and sex. Then she surprised herself, stopped in her tracks, and said, "I'd love to but the timing's wrong."

"Oh, come on. You'll be back in time for work Monday morning."

"Why? When are you coming back?"

"Tomorrow night."

She almost gave in again, but said, "Call me then."

SHE LEANED AGAINST A BUILDING about fifty yards down from Coventry and the woman, who were talking to hookers. The woman had long black hair and started to look more and more like a model. A dark van slowed as it passed. Taylor couldn't make out the face of the driver but it was clear from the silhouette of his head that he was checking her out.

He probably thought she was a hooker.

She turned her body away from him.

He sped up and disappeared down the street.

She lit a match and then threw it on the sidewalk.

Then another.

And another.

She watched them burn out.

Then threw more.

Coventry and the dark haired woman—the model—were still talking to hookers. It appeared that Coventry was showing them something.

She pulled out her cell phone. There were three new voice messages at her office number. The third one got her attention.

"Yes, um, Ms. Sutton? This is Bradley Winters, from Texaco. It's my understanding that you're trying to locate someone who may have been at our Westminster station at May 5th at 10:42 in the morning. We usually don't give out information, but since you're an attorney, I'm going to assume this is legit. In any event, there were two credit card transactions near that time. The first was at 10:35, a gas purchase by someone named John S. Martin. The second was at 10:49, another gas purchase, by someone using the card of a company called Seven Circles. Hope this helps. Call me if you have any questions, my number is . . ."

She immediately called Nick Trotter to see if he recognized either of those names.

He didn't answer.

Chapter Thirty-Two

Day Five - July 15
Saturday Night

THIS WAS PROBABLY A STUPID IDEA but Nathan Wickersham really didn't care. The TV coverage had him dancing—so perfect. He walked downstairs, fastened a three-foot chain to Ashley Conner's ankles so she couldn't run, and then brought her upstairs.

She chewed on her lips, apprehensive.

Obviously wondering if he was going to kill her.

"You're okay for now," he told her. "We're just getting some fresh air."

They headed out the back door to take a walk in the north forty. Ashley wore a steel collar around her neck, fastened to a lightweight alloy chain attached at the other end to Wickersham's belt. She carried the chain in her hand to keep the weight off her neck as best she could.

It was almost dark.

Wickersham's property went forever and was totally hidden from view.

Secluded.

Perfectly private.

Ashley Conner seemed grateful to be outside.

She remained quiet, however, not saying anything. Then, out of the blue, she spoke. "Do you have a gun?"

"Why?"

"I don't want to die by suffocation," she said. "I'd rather be shot in the head."

Wickersham nodded.

Understanding.

"We'll see," he said. "You're all over the news. Everyone in the world's looking for you."

She was shocked.

"Really?"

"Yep," he said. Then he laughed: "Everyone except me."

An orange moon rose over the tree line to the east. Way off in the distance a pack of coyotes yelped and Wickersham pictured them running down a jackrabbit. "This was all farm at one point," he said.

"Oh," she replied. "Can you do one thing for me?"

He was curious.

"What's that?"

"When I'm dead, I don't want anyone to find me without clothes on."

He chuckled.

"Trust me, you won't care at that point."

But she was insistent. "I really don't want everyone looking at me. That's all I ask. Just that one small favor."

Wickersham thought about it.

"We'll see," he said.

"Thank you. That's all I ask. That and the gun."

THEY WERE AT LEAST A HALF MILE INTO THE FIELD. Now the night was almost black and the house was visible only because of the lights inside.

Ashley was weak and needed to sit down. So they headed over to the edge of the field where Wickersham found a log. They sat in silence and watched the moon. If they stared right at it and concentrated, they could actually see it rise. The orange had already faded to yellow and would soon be white. It got smaller and smaller as it lifted off the horizon. Wickersham broke twigs in two as they watched. The snapping of the wood sounded extraordinarily loud against the deathlike quiet of the night. There wasn't a car or other sound to be heard from any direction.

"Don't even think about shouting," he said. "If you do, then you won't get any of those little favors you want."

"I won't."

"A woman got bit by a rattlesnake today," he said. "Right in front of me."

"Really?"

She seemed interested.

"Yep," he said. "She stepped right on it not more than ten seconds before I would have. It bit her in the calf and she fell to the ground. Then it bit her in the face. She twitched for about thirty seconds and then stopped moving. It was one of the strangest things I'd ever seen in my life."

Ashley said nothing.

Ten minutes passed.

The temperature was just about perfect.

It was weird being out here in the middle of nowhere at night. Good weird, though.

Then something happened.

They heard voices.

Deep voices.

More than one.

Someone was out there.

Not far away.

"Help me!" Ashley Conner screamed. "He's going to kill me! Over here! Help me please!"

Wickersham jerked on the chain as hard as he could and tried to snap her neck. She fell to the ground, momentarily stunned, but continued to scream.

"Please! Help me, he's . . ."

Wham.

He delivered a fist as hard as he could to the side of her head. She groaned and then fell silent.

Out in the field not more than a hundred feet away lights appeared.

Flashlights.

Two of them.

Pointing in his direction, sweeping back and forth.

He frantically worked to get the chain off his belt, couldn't, and then took the belt off altogether.

Good.

At least he was free.

The flashlights were closer now.

Coming fast.

"Hey, lady, where are you?"

Silence.

Then, "John! Over there! I see him!"

Both flashlights pointed directly into Wickersham's eyes.

Chapter Thirty-Three

Day Five - July 15
Saturday Night

AT NIGHT, AFTER DARK, SOME SECTIONS of Colfax Avenue get darker shadows than they should. The shops close, the dangerous people multiply, the hunt for drugs and sex begins in earnest, and transvestites pop out of nowhere. There were even still a couple of old adult video arcades where guys jerked off with the doors open. Coventry drove down one of the seedier parts of the street in a silver 8-cylinder 4Runner, a rental paid for by the department until the Crime Lab could decide what to do about Coventry's truck.

He parked on the street in front of a liquor store. He and Darien got out and hoofed it over to the alley where Mary Williams—Paradise—managed to get a knife in her eye. Darien wore jeans and a T-shirt, and looked apprehensive.

"You sure know how to show a girl a good time," she said.

Coventry chuckled. "Yeah, lots of women are stuck in some stupid restaurant right now, being forced to eat lobster and drink wine. You can thank me later for saving you from all that."

"Oh I will, trust me."

A car drove by and slowed down. Someone yelled out the window, "Hey dude, how much for the girl?"

Coventry flashed his badge.

The car sped off.

"Asshole," he said.

In his left hand he carried an envelope with about a hundred pictures inside. They came off Mary Williams' laptop, which came out of her safe, which came out of her bedroom closet. The men in the pictures had all been over to her house, probably for some rough stuff. The plan tonight was to interview the night-shift hookers to see if anyone remembered any of these guys being around the night Paradise got killed.

He hoped to get a few hits.

Unfortunately he got more than that.

Within the hour he had a stack of about thirty guys that the women recognized on some level or another, although no one was sure if any of them were around during the night in question. Coventry was just about done when he spotted one more woman down the street, someone he hadn't talked to yet.

"One more," he told Darien.

AS THEY WALKED IN THAT DIRECTION, Coventry shook his head. "The guy we're looking for—not the guy who killed Paradise, the one who dumped the body in my truck—called me on my cell phone, just before I left to pick you up tonight."

Darien looked shocked.

"He did?"

Coventry nodded.

"What'd he say?"

"He asked me if I wanted to know her name, meaning the name of the woman in the back of the truck," Coventry said.

"And?"

"And I said no thanks and hung up," Coventry said. "I've been kicking myself ever since. It was the absolute worst thing I could have done."

Darien looked at him, processing the information.

"I just got pissed off," Coventry added. "I mean, the guy has the balls to think that we need his help to catch him. It was like a slap in the face. I guess hanging up was my way of saying that we were smart enough to get him on our own."

Darien nodded.

"I don't blame you," she said. "The asshole."

"What I should have done," Coventry said, "if I'd been a professional, is let him tell me the name of the victim and then keep him talking for as long as possible. Every word would have been another clue."

"Can you call him back?" Darien asked.

"Tried," Coventry said. "But he called from a pay phone."

Darien locked her arm through his.

"I think you were right the way you handled it," she said. "Who does the asshole think he is? You *will* get him and it'll be without his help. Hanging up was a way to show him he's dealing with a superior, not a wimp, and that you're pissed. I personally think that sending that message is more important than getting a scrap or two of information."

Coventry considered the argument.

Then smiled.

"You're not being nice to me, just to get in my pants, are you?" he asked

She squeezed his arm.

"Maybe, you never know."

THEY REACHED THE NEXT WOMAN. She was tall, tan, and wore a short glittery dress that showed off shapely, muscular legs that were just about perfect. A pink scarf wrapped around her neck and cascaded over ample cleavage.

Coventry looked at Darien who studied the woman. By the look on her face, she was starting to figure out that the woman was a man.

"Evening," Coventry said.

"Well aren't you the cute one," the woman said.

"Well likewise. What's your name, darling?"

"T-Von."

Coventry nodded, said "Nice," and then explained the situation.

"Here's what I know," the woman said. "I was walking past the alley Thursday night, sometime around two in the morning. I guess that would be Friday, technically. Paradise was in the alley with someone. She was telling him that he needed to pay first, twenty dollars. The man said, 'No problem.' He must have given her the money, because she said something like, 'Let's see what we have down here.' By that time I was past the alley and didn't hear anything else."

"How'd you know it was her?"

The woman laughed, a deep laugh. "Everyone knows Paradise," he said.

Coventry scratched his head.

"Did you see the man?"

T-Von shook her head. "That alley's dark as a bitch."

Coventry nodded.

That was true.

"Did you recognize his voice?"

"No, sorry."

Coventry receded in thought.

"Would you recognize it, if you heard it again?"

The woman cocked her head, weighing the question.

"Maybe."

"Do you know who found Paradise first?"

"No, why?"

"Because when we got to her she didn't have any money. So someone must have taken it first. I could give a crap about that, but I'd like to get my hands on that twenty for fingerprints. I'd swap another bill for it, so no loss."

T-Von nodded.

"Paradise was a good person," he said. "I'll ask around. You got a card?"

He did indeed.

Chapter Thirty-Four

Day Six - July 16
Sunday

IN HER DRIVEWAY, TAYLOR SUTTON got the oil plug for the Porsche loosened with a crescent wrench and then unscrewed it the rest of the way with her fingers. When she pulled the plug away, as always, oil spilled out so fast that she couldn't get her hand away fast enough. She made an evil face and wiped her hands with a rag as the spent petroleum drained like a waterfall into a black container. Her cell phone rang just as "Boys of Summer" came on the radio. She almost didn't answer, but did. It turned out to be Nick Trotter, getting back to her regarding the message she left last night in connection with the Texaco credit cards.

"Never heard of anyone called John Martin or the Seven Circles Company," he told her.

"How about Andrew or Mary Campbell? They're the directors of Seven Circles, according to the Secretary of State records."

"Nope, nothing."

"Okay," she said. "They're probably nobodies. I can't find any of them in the phone book, either."

"Not even Seven Circles?"

"Nope."

"Probably a dummy corporation of some type," Nick said. "Let me guess, they use CT for their registered agent."

"Yep."

"It's a shell of some kind," Nick said. "Probably set up to manipulate taxes."

Taylor agreed.

"There aren't any tax deductions for killing lawyers that I'm aware of," Nick added.

Taylor laughed.

"Good thing," she said.

Oh well, a dead end.

She finished changing the oil on the Porsche, then did the laundry, grocery shopped at King Soopers, and cleaned the house. Then she Googled Bryson Coventry, discovered something interesting, and headed for Cherry Creek.

THE CHERRY CREEK SHOPPING DISTRICT is a several block cluster of high-end trendy stores, restaurants and coffee shops. There's hardly any parking except on the streets, and those always went fast. So Taylor felt lucky when she found a spot on St. Paul, directly across the street from the Carr-Border Gallery.

It even had shade.

Unfortunately, when she walked over to the gallery it was closed. One of Coventry's paintings was in the front window, however. It was an eight-by-ten landscape depicting a field that rolled into a cluster of pine trees, with soft lavender foothills in the background, all under a muted cerulean sky. Although the composition was fairly simple, the colors and the brush strokes brought the piece to life. She was astounded at how good it was.

She squinted to read the price tag.

$650.00.

She resolved to come back next week and buy it, then walked over to Starbucks, bought a decaf and sipped it on her way back to the Porsche. Tons of people paraded around in expensive clothes and lots of them had dogs on leashes, everything from Pugs to ridiculously fluffy Afghans.

Their little babies.

She got back to the Porsche and, once inside, decided to just sit there for a while, one of her favorite pastimes. There was something about the smell of the leather and the round no-nonsense gauges that gave off a slight aura of danger. It was fun just being there even when the vehicle wasn't moving.

She powered down the windows and sipped coffee, more than content. She almost turned on the radio but instead put Nick Trotter's CD in and fast forwarded to about where she needed to be. She finally found the conversation she was looking for, the one that referred to an earlier conversation that wasn't on the CD. Cross-referencing to the spreadsheet that Brooke prepared, the conversation that she did have took place on May 5th. The one before that was April 15th. That meant that the missing conversation took place somewhere between those two dates.

She jotted down a few notes on the spreadsheet so she'd remember it later.

The coffee was gone now.

And going right through her.

She looked around, wondering where she could relieve herself. Then she powered up the windows, locked the door, and walked to the Tattered Page Bookstore. They had a restroom downstairs. Plus, she needed a couple of new books anyway.

The sun beat down hard as if trying to brand her with a tank-top tan.

THE TATTERED PAGE BOOKSTORE was her favorite place in the world to kill time on a Sunday. She wandered around, picking up whatever book caught her eye. Over in the photography section she found a coffee-table book called *Denver After Dark*. The photos inside, all night or twilight shots, were absolutely incredible, a lot more like art than photography.

Seriously impressive.

A picture of the photographer was on the back cover.

Taylor studied her face.

The woman looked familiar but she couldn't place her.

Maybe she'd seen her at a club or something.

She set the book down, bought a novel called *Night Laws*, and headed back to the Porsche.

She had one more stop to make before heading home.

One very important stop.

Chapter Thirty-Five

Day Six - July 16
Sunday Morning

———————

ASHLEY CONNER WAS ON THE BED in the dungeon, breathing but still not waking even when Wickersham shook her, evidently in a coma. The blow to her head last night, out in the field, must have done serious damage.

Wickersham paced back and forth, half watching her, half trying to figure out if there was any way the events of last night could come back to bite him in the ass.

If there was anything else he needed to do, now was the time.

His plan last night had been simple and had worked. When the two flashlights came in his direction he ran into the night, away from Ashley Conner, across the field. As he predicted, one of the two men was faster than the other. Wickersham let the sucker stay on his heels until they were well separated from the second man. Then he turned, knocked him to the ground and snapped his neck. The other man, when he finally caught up, was bigger and harder to kill, but eventually went the same way.

Then he ran back to Ashley Conner.

Thank God she was still there.

Exactly where he left her.

Still unconscious.

He carried her back to the dungeon, put her on the bed and locked her in.

Then he had to deal with the two bodies out in the field.

He grabbed a flashlight and walked back to see who they were. They turned out to be teenagers, about seventeen, probably on summer vacation before their last year of high school.

Shit.

That really complicated things.

They probably lived in the area.

The search would be vicious.

Mommies would be crying for their babies.

Well, too bad.

They were the ones trespassing.

They were the ones chasing him.

So screw them.

HE WORRIED MOST ABOUT DOGS. He didn't know where the kids came from or where they were going, but one thing he did know is that he didn't want dogs following their scent onto his property and having it stop there.

So he came up with a plan.

He ran back home, got the jeep and drove back out to where the bodies were. He took off their pants and shirts and left them there on the ground, marking the location with a wooden stake. Then he threw their bodies in the back of the jeep and took them to the barn.

He walked back to the stake, picked up their clothes and dragged them along the ground, heading off his property, to

County Road 6, and then up the road for a full mile. Then he stuffed the clothes into a black plastic garbage bag, sealed it and walked back to the house.

He put their clothes back on, threw their bodies in the back of the van, and drove about thirty miles east, way out onto the plains, where he dumped them in a wooded area about two hundred yards from the road.

When he got home he burned his clothes and his shoes, then scattered the ashes and remains on the south edge of his property, more than a quarter mile from the house.

That was last night.

HE FELT ASHLEY CONNER'S PULSE. She was definitely alive but not responding to anything, even when he pinched her hard. The coma was definitely real.

The only thing that bothered him about the events of last night was the fact the jeep tracks—if the cops could trace them—started at the barn, went to a point where the boys had been, and then came straight back to the barn. He decided to remedy that defect by taking the jeep back out in the field and driving all over the place.

Which he did.

If asked, he would just say he likes to 4-wheel around the property, which was actually true.

When he got back to the house he wasn't quite ready for what he saw. A cop car was pulling into the driveway.

There were two cops inside.

They came fast. *Goddamn it!*

Chapter Thirty-Six

Day Six - July 16
Sunday Morning

WHEN COVENTRY WALKED into the kitchen he was surprised to find pancakes and coffee waiting for him. Darien wore one of his long-sleeved white shirts and lifted it up just long enough to flash a black thong.

"Careful," he warned, "I'm a morning guy."

"Yeah, right," she said. "An all-day guy is more like it."

"All day includes the morning."

He was halfway into his second plate of pancakes and his fourth cup of coffee, and starting to think seriously about giving Darien some first-class rug burns, when Shalifa Netherwood called. "We got her name," she said. "It's Jennifer Holland." Coventry stood so fast that he dumped coffee all over the table.

"How'd we get it?"

"One of her girlfriends saw her picture on the news before going to work this morning. Apparently she called the hotline and left about ten messages."

Coventry talked for another few minutes, poured what was left of the coffee pot into a thermos, and told Darien, "I have to run."

"I'm coming with you."

"Can't," he said. "Police business."

"I'll wait in the car."

He considered it.

"Unless you want to leave me all alone with a target on my back," she added.

Fifteen minutes later they were at a BNSF switchyard in Golden. The victim's friend turned out to be a 32-year-old biker-looking woman by the name of Sandra Black, an engineer running a red switcher. Coventry rode with her in the cab so she wouldn't fall behind schedule while Darien waited in the 4Runner.

She held back tears.

"You sure you should be driving this thing being so upset and all?" Coventry asked.

She nodded and dried her eyes with a Kleenex.

"I'm okay," she said.

Coventry waited.

"We went out drinking Friday night, me and Jennifer and another lady named Samantha Winger, and closed a bar called the Camel's Breath," she said. "Do you know the place?"

No, he didn't.

"It's one of those dives north of downtown, near the South Platte, off 38th Street," she said. Coventry found himself half listening and half in awe of all the gauges and the way she handled the engine. She stopped the conversation while she talked to one of the crew on the radio, coupled a car and then moved forward, pulling a string of four. "We were all shit-faced," she said. "None of us should have driven home but we all did." She looked at him: "That's our secret, I hope."

"Absolutely."

"Anyway, that's it. We all left about 2:30 in separate cars. I didn't talk to her or see her after that, until the news this morning."

Coventry had a few questions, then a few more, and then some follow-up. After forty-five minutes, he had as much information as he needed for the time being. He gave her one of his cards and wrote a number on the back. "This is a counseling service for families and friends of victims. It's free and they're good people. There's nothing wrong with talking to someone."

She was working an area of track about a half mile away from the 4Runner, but Coventry said, "You can just let me out here so you don't get behind."

"Thanks." She slowed the engine and Coventry felt the cars push against it, grinding to a stop.

Before he got out he said, "This story is already huge and getting bigger every minute. I'm not going to release your name to anyone, but the news will know Jennifer's name by the end of the day. Sooner or later they'll find out about you so be prepared."

She shrugged.

"I really don't mind talking to the news. Especially if there's any chance it can help catch this guy."

"That's your choice," he said, then had one more thought. "If you don't mind talking to the news, I have a TV friend who would love to get an exclusive. Her name's Jena Vernon."

"I know her, she's the blond. Tell her to go ahead and call me if she wants."

"Just don't say anything to turn yourself into a target."

WALKING BACK TO THE CAR, he dialed Shalifa Netherwood,

who should have arrived at the victim's house by now. She answered on the second ring.

"Talk to me," he said.

"I'm here," she said, "walking around the perimeter. No one's home, so we'll need a search warrant."

Ouch.

That would be tougher than normal, on a Sunday morning.

"Call Clay at home," he said. "I think he knows a judge or two who won't totally kill him if he bothers them on a Sunday."

"He's going to love hearing my voice. You said she drove home in her own car, after the bar closed, right?"

"Right."

"There's no car here."

"There isn't?"

"No, wait, there are a few down the street. What does she drive?"

"A black Honda, an older model, maybe ten years old or thereabouts."

"Nope," Shalifa said. "Nothing like that anywhere around here."

"Okay," he said. "She may have got taken somewhere between the Camel's Breath and her house. I'm thinking that we're not going to find anything useful at the house, so I'll tell you what. Call Richardson at home and have him coordinate the search warrant. Then meet me at the Camel's Breath ASAP."

THE CAMEL'S BREATH WAS A SEEDY PLACE sandwiched between a railroad yard and the South Platte River, in that no-man's land north of Brighton Boulevard and south of I-70. It sat there alone, an oasis of alcohol in the mist of a harsh urban environment. Pulling up, Coventry was surprised that he'd never been called there on official business before. It looked like the kind of place where life was cheap.

The gravel parking lot was empty.

Coventry brought the 4Runner to a stop near the front door, kicking up a cloud of dust that drifted to the east. He got out and walked with Darien around the building, a paint-peeling wooden structure. It turned out to be a lot bigger than it appeared from the front. It could probably hold three or four hundred drunks if you squashed them in with a shoehorn and ignored the fire codes.

"Well, her car's definitely not here," he told Darien.

Two minutes later Shalifa Netherwood pulled up in her personal car, wearing white shorts and a sleeveless shirt. Without her weapon, her body took on a lot more curves than Coventry was used to.

Shalifa and Darien hugged.

Coventry swallowed.

"Don't tell me you two are friends now."

They simultaneously looked at him and grinned.

"We've had a few talks," Darien said.

"Great. Excuse me a minute."

He wandered around to the shady side of the building, leaned against it and worked the phone until he had the information he wanted. When he came back, he said, "We're looking for a 1993 Honda CVR, black, plate number 727-CLZ. I'm thinking that our best bet is to just start here and take the most logical route to her house."

They pulled out and hadn't gone more than a half mile when they found the car on the side of the road, sitting there with a flat tire.

"You bastard," Coventry said. "Pretending to be a nice guy."

Chapter Thirty-Seven

Day Six - July 16
Sunday

NICK TROTTER'S MANSION sat in a gated community in Greenwood Village. Taylor Sutton stopped the Porsche at the gate, already doubting the wisdom of what she was about to do. She almost turned around but then thought, *Screw it*, and pressed the buzzer for Nick's place.

No one answered.

She pressed it again.

No one answered.

She put the Porsche in reserve and was just starting to back up when Nick's voice crackled from a speaker: "Hello?"

She hit the brakes. "It's me, Taylor. Can we talk?"

"Of course. You got some news for me?"

"Something like that."

The gate swung open.

Driving up the street, she had no idea what the people who lived in the place did for a living, but whatever it was, they did it right and they did it big. It was almost hard to believe that this kind of money existed in Denver.

Nick's contemporary showpiece was the fifth house on the

right, strategically placed on two acres of well-manicured grounds.

Nick met her at the front entry, which was in and of itself an architectural statement.

He looked good.

Happy.

Tanned.

"Not a bad place," she said.

"Almost all of it comes from Sarah's side of the equation," he said. "Which is why everyone thinks I killed her."

"Not everyone," Taylor said.

He put his arm around her shoulders and squeezed. Then got brighter: "Come on, I have an idea."

THEY ENDED UP IN THE BACKYARD HOT TUB, adjacent to the pool, just down from the waterfall. Nick had somehow set the temperature so that it was absolutely perfect, not too hot or too cold. From here you couldn't see a single other house. They wore visors and sunglasses and had large glasses of diet Pepsi.

Taylor decided to get right to the point.

"You need to tell me what you're holding back," she said. "Otherwise I'm getting out of the case."

He looked shocked.

"What do you mean?"

She frowned.

"You withheld one of your taped conversations," she said. "One that took place sometime between April 15th and May 5th. Sarah disappeared May 1st. So the timing bothers me. What's going on?"

He looked as if he was going to deny it, but then shook his

head as if beaten and asked: "How'd you figure that out?"

"I didn't, Claudia did."

"Smart gal, that Claudia."

Taylor nodded. "Also, that story about the hit-and-run, I keep bouncing it around in my brain and still can't get it to fit right. I guess that's a weird way of saying that I'm not quite believing it."

He chuckled.

"You're smarter than I thought."

"So it's not true?"

He shook his head. "No."

She couldn't believe it.

She stood up to leave and said, "I'm out of here." But he grabbed her by the arm and pulled her back, so hard in fact that she lost her balance and her head went under water.

"At least hear me out," he said.

She shook water out of her ear and almost stood up again, but instead said: "This better be damn good."

"Actually, it's damn bad."

OKAY, HERE'S THE DEAL," he said. "Most of what I told you is true. By the way, what I'm about to tell you is highly confidential. You're my attorney. What I'm about to say stays with you and you alone. I don't even want Claudia knowing about it, or anyone else. Agreed?"

She nodded. "If you want."

"I'm serious," he added. "It's not that I don't trust you, I do, which is why I chose you in the first place. But we're about to go to a new level. So I need your word, both as my attorney and a friend, that you'll never share what I'm about to say with anyone, unless I personally okay it."

She nodded.

And sensed that he was about to tell her that he killed his wife Sarah.

Chapter Thirty-Eight

Day Six - July 16
Sunday

WICKERSHAM LOOKED OUT the kitchen window, just to see if it still seemed hot outside, and was shocked to spot a group of five or six police officers off in the distance, on his property, trailing behind two dogs.

Shit!

He wasn't in the mood for any more cops. The two that pulled into his driveway this morning—asking if he'd seen or heard anything about two missing teenagers—had been enough.

He grabbed the binoculars from the distressed maple cabinet above the Sub Zero and pulled the scene in closer. The group was following the same path that the two kids used.

What to do?

Think!

Think you asshole!

He powered up the dungeon monitor and confirmed that Ashley Conner was still in a coma in the exact same position he'd left her. Then he turned it off.

Good.

At least if the police ended up in the house, to talk to him or something, there wouldn't be any screaming or hollering coming from downstairs.

Now what?

Don't get caught.

If they come for you, don't be here!

He grabbed his wallet, put on a good pair of jogging shoes and bounded out the front door, locking it behind him. Keeping the house between himself and the cops, he worked his way into the trees on the opposite side of the property, then edged his way closer to the getaway car. When he was halfway there he hid behind a log and focused the binoculars on the search party.

THEY SEEMED TO BE HUNG UP where the two kids first came at him, before they chased him the other way, into the field. The dogs seemed confused, almost as if they kept getting pulled back into ground they had already covered. After about five minutes, however, they picked up the track where the two kids ran after him, and headed that way. A few minutes later they were at the location where the two assholes ended up getting their stupid little necks snapped.

The group stopped there.

Two or three of the cops bent down, looking at something.

Wickersham held his breath to see if they put anything in an evidence bag.

They didn't.

But they did talk to each other with intensity.

Shit!

What the hell were they saying?

Just keep moving, assholes.

There's nothing there.

Just move your big fat asses.

But they didn't.

They hung there, walking around the area, looking at the ground.

Then Wickersham remembered something.

He took the stake with him last night, the one he used to mark the location of the clothes; it wasn't there anymore. But he never bothered to fill in the hole.

Had they spotted the hole?

He doubted it.

And even if they had, so what? There'd be no way to figure out what it meant.

Maybe they were looking at blood.

From his broken lip.

Or from the second kid's bloody nose.

Now that would be a problem.

The dogs tugged on their leashes, anxious to keep moving. The cops talked some more and finally let the animals lead them away. Then something wonderful happened. The dogs followed the exact line where Wickersham dragged the kids' clothes. In fact, they followed the trail perfectly, without stopping, all the way to County Road 6, and then walked east on the gravel shoulder. They were still heading up the road, exactly as they should, when Wickersham lost sight of them.

He slapped his hand on his knee.

"Oh yeah, baby."

He headed back to the house, wanting to be there, to find out what they knew in case they came to talk to him. He milled around in the yard, wanting to intercept them there if they came, rather than have them in the house. He dragged the hose over and washed the Camry, staying outside for as long as he could stand the heat.

A full hour at least.

No one came and he finally went back inside and poured a glass of wine.

He was in the kitchen, dancing, when someone knocked on the door.

Chapter Thirty-Nine

Day Six - July 16
Sunday

THE INVESTIGATION OF JENNIFER HOLLAND'S black Honda took hardly any time and turned out to be a major letdown. It had a flat tire and there had been no attempt to change it, most likely because there was no spare in the trunk. From what Coventry could figure, the woman got a flat and either flagged the van down or got spotted. Either way, there was no sign of a struggle. In fact, he doubted that the driver of the van even got out of his vehicle, meaning there'd be no forensic evidence at all at the scene.

"A great big zero," he told Darien, when he finally went back to the 4Runner. "At least the press didn't catch wind, so we were able to work in peace."

"What now?" she questioned.

"Now I'm going to put you to work," he said.

"Oh, that sounds good."

He chuckled. "Not that way. Real work."

They met Jena Vernon at the TV studio. She took them into a fancy room with lots of wood and a number of monitors. She cued up a tape and the biggest monitor on the wall lit up. It was the scene from 6th and Federal, the footage of the crowd that showed up to see what was going on. Coventry wanted Darien to look at it and see if anyone there looked like the driver of the van that got away from them Friday night.

Jena set it on slow motion.

Coventry watched Darien's face as she viewed the tape, hoping against hope to walk out of the room in the next ten minutes with an actual photograph of a suspect.

She was serious, concentrating.

"Nothing yet," she said.

"That's fine," he said. "Just do your best."

Then, at one point, she said: "Stop!"

Jena froze the picture.

Coventry searched the screen for someone with black glasses but didn't see anyone.

"What?"

"That woman," she said, "that woman in the crowd that you're talking to."

Coventry recognized the woman. She was the one who overheard part of his conversation with Katona, referencing the van and the black glasses.

The cute one.

Even though she was all sweaty.

A little too short for his taste, but still nice.

"I've seen her somewhere," Darien said.

"Where?"

She had a distant look, reaching deep. "Oh my God, yes. She was on Colfax last night, just down the street from us."

Coventry wrinkled his forehead.

"You mean when we were there showing the pictures?"

She nodded. "Yes. I remember she kept lighting matches

and throwing them on the ground, which got my attention. Then the more I looked at her the weirder it seemed, because she wasn't dressed like a hooker and didn't walk over to any cars or anything. I just thought it was strange that she was there. You don't remember seeing her?"

Coventry shook his head.

"No, not at all."

"Well, you were busy talking," Darien added.

Maybe it was just a coincidence, or maybe it meant something. Right now Coventry wasn't in the mood to think about it much. "Let's watch the rest of the tape," he said.

HIS CELL PHONE RANG AS THEY WATCHED. It turned out to be the FBI profiler, Leanne Sanders, returning his call. "I'm going to take this in the next room," Coventry said. It turned out there was no next room, so he wandered down the hall until he found a quiet spot.

"Thanks for calling me back," he said. "I have some more information I want to run by you regarding our little friend out here in Denver."

"You have quite the storm brewing," she said. "I can't even turn on CNN anymore without getting the latest and greatest."

Coventry frowned.

"I'm way out of my league," he said. "Come to Denver and save my ass, please."

She chuckled. "You're doing fine. So what is it that you need to tell me?"

He swallowed. "You're going to kill me, because I screwed up big time." With that, he told her about the phone call he received from the mystery man who asked him if he wanted to know the victim's name. "It was our guy," Coventry added. "There's no question in my mind."

A pause on the other end.

"Jesus," Leanne said, "I thought you were kidding when you said you screwed up."

"Apparently not."

"First of all," she said, "get a cell phone that records. Second of all, keep him talking next time. That's always Rule Number One. The more he says the more we learn. This is no time for egos."

He frowned.

She was absolutely right.

"Thanks," he said. "My ass needed a good kicking."

"Well, then, consider it kicked."

He brought her up to speed on everything else going on, including the fact that they were screening the crowd even as they spoke. At the end of the conversation she had just a few parting words of advice. "You're too much on this guy's radar screen. He'll make a play for you, or for that woman you're hanging around, before this is all over. That'll be his ultimate victory."

Coventry agreed.

"I already know that," he said.

"I know you do," she said. "I just want you to hear it from someone else so you'll take it seriously."

Chapter Forty

Day Six - July 16
Sunday

TAYLOR SUTTON WAS WRONG about thinking that Nick Trotter was about to tell her that he killed Sarah. In fact, sitting there in the hot tub, those were the first words out of his mouth. "You're thinking I'm about to confess to killing Sarah," he said. "Well I didn't." He looked away momentarily. "At least not directly."

Not directly?

What the hell does that mean?

"Okay, here's the situation," Nick said. "Everything I told you about the mysterious Northwest sending me a retainer out of the blue and then calling me and bragging, as reflected in the CD I gave you, is absolutely true. So is the fact that I really don't know who he is."

Taylor listened, wondering where he was headed.

"Okay," she said.

Nick took a long swallow of diet Pepsi and shifted his body into a more comfortable position.

"Then Sarah and I start going through this god-awful divorce," he said. "All those assholes who run the newspapers couldn't find a real story to save their lives, so they start filling their empty pages with stories about me and Sarah. You read all that crap."

She had indeed.

All the marriage money came from Sarah.

There was a pre-nup.

Nick Trotter, the infamous criminal lawyer himself, was about to learn how to live like a mere mortal.

Which served him right.

The womanizer.

The drunk.

The egomaniac.

How's it feel, Nicky-boy?

"Meanwhile," Nick continued, "my mystery client is reading all this. One day he calls me up. I'm in a pissed mood and have a few drinks in my gut. He starts talking about quote-unquote *the bitch*, and how she'd be better off dead. Of course, I couldn't agree more. Then he says something like—and I don't remember the exact words, but it's something like this—*I'll tell you what, since I'm such a nice guy, I'll take her out for you.* I laughed, and said something like, *Perfect. Thanks a lot.*"

Taylor processed the information.

"You were joking, of course," she said.

He looked hesitant, but said: "Of course. I was just ranting and raving. I didn't think he was serious and never gave it another thought."

HE LOOKED AROUND THE GROUNDS, almost vacantly, then back at her. "That conversation took place about a week before she disappeared. It's one of two conversations that I didn't put on your CD. Then, after she disappeared, which was on May 1st, he called me again. He says it was done and that he buried her body out in the north forty."

"So he actually killed her?"

"According to him, yes," Nick said. "Needless to say, it shocked the shit out of me."

"I can imagine."

He nodded. "So there I am, all of a sudden, a co-conspirator to first-degree murder."

That didn't seem right.

"What do you mean, a co-conspirator? You were just kidding," Taylor said.

He shook his head.

"True," he said. "The problem is, I've pissed off too many D.A.'s over the years and they'll just twist it around. The way they'll see it, I already knew the guy was a murderer, or at least should have reasonably suspected it. When he offered to kill Sarah, my words encouraged him, whether or not I was joking. That, in their minds, would give them enough of a toehold to charge me as a co-conspirator, whether they could actually prove it or not. And in this state every conspirator to a felony offense is as guilty as every other conspirator. They'd go for the death penalty. That's a given."

He looked down.

Beaten.

"Shit," Taylor said.

"Major shit."

"Do you still have those two conversations?" Taylor asked.

He looked at her as if she was crazy. "No way," he said. "They're long gone, erased, history."

Silence.

"I need a goddamn drink," he said, muscling his way up. "You want one?"

She did.

"Jack okay?"

"Fine."

WHEN NICK LEFT, SHE PULLED HERSELF OUT of the tub to use the facilities. Her body felt heavy, no longer supported by the water, but the sun felt great on her wet skin. When Nick came back he handed her a water glass half filled with jagged ice and Jack. It looked like the ice got chipped from a block with an ice pick, and briefly reminded her of *Basic Instinct*.

She made a mental note to rent that again.

Or better yet, buy it.

"Thanks for not bolting," he said. "I was afraid you'd dump me, once you found out what was really going on."

That wasn't an issue.

She'd known him forever.

He wasn't the one who came up with the idea of killing Sarah.

He wasn't the one who did it.

His words had been in jest, irrespective of how the law might treat them.

"Anyway," he said, "I kept trying to figure out what this guy was up to. After all, no one kills somebody for someone else and doesn't expect something in return. I've come up with two theories."

"Which are?"

"The first theory is this. He knows he's eventually going to get caught, for one of his past crimes or a future one. He's going to ask me to defend him. And I'm going to be motivated as hell, because he's going to make me an offer I can't refuse. If I don't give him the defense of the century, he's going to tell the cops that I asked him to kill Sarah. He'll say it was all my idea. Then he'll tell them where the body is. Sure, he'll be confessing to another murder, but at that point it won't make any difference."

"Wow."

Nick nodded.

"Basically, when I eventually defend him, I'll be defending myself. I'll be on trial as much as him, only no one will know it except him and me."

"Talk about getting an attorney in your corner," Taylor said.

"Exactly, get the attorney in the muck with you," Nick agreed. "The second theory is this. He tells the police that I asked him to kill Sarah and he shows them where the body is. He then agrees to testify against me in exchange for life in prison instead of the death penalty." Nick shook his head in apparent admiration. "I'm his trump card, in effect. He's a clever guy, you've got to hand him that."

Nick took a long swallow of alcohol.

Taylor did too and felt it drop warm and fiery into her stomach.

"That's where you came in," he said. "I wanted you to find out who he is so I can find out where Sarah's body is. I lied to you about the hit-and-run because I needed you to think he was trying to kill me, so you'd be motivated to find him. I didn't want to tell you all this other stuff, for obvious reasons. Forgive me?"

She did.

But she also had a question.

"What are you going to do if we find out who this guy is and where he buried Sarah?"

He cocked his head. "I'm going to dig her up and dump her where she'll never be found. Then, if this guy does in fact eventually go to the police, his story will be total baloney because there won't be a body."

"And you're off the hook," Taylor said.

"Exactly." He sipped the Jack and looked her in the eyes. "So my life is in your hands. That's why I came to you instead of a private investigator to begin with—I don't know any investigators well enough that I'd trust my life to them."

Chapter Forty-One

Day Seven - July 17
Monday Morning

THE DAWN BECAME LIGHTER with each passing minute and then started to take on a warm golden color. At this rate the morning sun would be visible above the horizon line in the next ten minutes or so. Nathan Wickersham picked up the pace, now running five-minute miles according to his best guess. Black-and-white magpies were in the sky, already searching for food. From somewhere off in the far distance came the familiar sound of a tractor firing up. He didn't particularly like to run in the morning, but with the temperature scheduled to break a hundred again today, there wasn't much choice. Either get up early or get fat.

He'd take early.

He reflected on yesterday, the day from hell.

The knock on the door had been the cops, telling him that they'd traced the missing boys to a path that went through his property and wanted to rope off a few areas and bring experts in to have a look.

Did he mind?

Or would they need to get a warrant?

"Of course I don't mind," he said. "Anything at all to help."

They came back later, eight people all told, and spent over an hour in the field. Wickersham intentionally walked out to visit them, just to be absolutely sure that his scent was at the scene, and from the scene to the house, in an explainable way. The dumb asses never suspected a thing. He walked all over the area with them and listened in on their discussions. About all they could tell was that the boys made an abrupt change in direction at two different locations. At one of the locations, it looked like the grasses were matted down more than normal, almost as if they had milled around there for some reason.

But they found no forensic evidence.

No clothing.

No footprint impressions—the ground was way too hard and dry for anything like that.

No blood.

No nothing.

No stake hole.

In the end, the zigzag line of scent was interesting but unexplainable.

SEVEN MILES INTO THE MORNING RUN he still felt good and decided to go for twelve instead of ten. Plus that would give him more time to think. The burning question he needed to resolve, and resolve fast, is what to do with Ashley Conner.

He didn't like having her in the house with so many cops hanging around. If they somehow came to the conclusion that he was implicated in the disappearance of the two boys, they might surprise him and show up with a search warrant—unlikely, but possible. The safest thing to do would be to kill her and dump her, and the sooner the better.

Then he needed to clean the dungeon like a madman to be sure her fingerprints and DNA were gone. He needed to check every square inch of it also, to find out if she scratched or wrote her name or other incriminating comments somewhere. He wouldn't put it past her to pull up the carpet somewhere and scratch something on the concrete underneath, especially after the fingernail incident.

He also needed to wipe her down so he didn't leave any DNA or fingerprints on her body. The best thing to do would be to stick her in the bathtub after she was dead and scrub her with antiseptic soap or bleach, wearing gloves of course. Then wrap her in a clean bed sheet, carry her to the van and dump her somewhere after dark.

But not in Coventry's truck this time.

Coventry would be smart enough to have surveillance cameras installed by now.

Maybe he'd dump her where the other woman had the flat.

Her car would be towed by now.

It was a remote location.

Plus, it would make a neat tie-in.

He could almost read the headlines already: Victim One's body is found where Victim Two was taken!

He smiled.

Yeah, that was neat.

He could live with that.

That's what a rock star would do.

HE STOPPED RUNNING A QUARTER MILE from the house, to give his heart and metabolism an opportunity to slow down.

Then he showered, rounded up the duct tape and plastic bag and headed downstairs to the dungeon.

Ashley Conner was in the exact same position he had left her, lying face up on her back. She hadn't moved a muscle.

He pinched her.

She didn't react.

She wore gray drawstring sweatpants and a plain white T-shirt. Her chest hardly pushed the shirt up at all. She had no real tits to speak of. The flat chest made her look like a little girl.

He ran his fingers through her hair.

It was soft, a lot softer than his.

"Well," he said. "Time's up. It happens to all of us sooner or later."

He picked up the bag and positioned it over her head.

He could actually feel the grim reaper in the room.

Then he picked up the duct tape.

"Nighty-night," he said.

Chapter Forty-Two

Day Seven - July 17
Monday Morning

BRYSON COVENTRY'S MORNING TURNED INTO a rapid-fire series of events. A security company installed a motion detection system and a surveillance system at his house. Darien came down to headquarters to view the videotape of the vans obtained from the bank on Broadway, but none of the drivers' faces seemed familiar. Coventry gave her a cell phone while she was there and programmed all his numbers on speed dial. He had a series of coordination meetings with Shalifa Netherwood and Kate Katona.

Then the autopsy report for Jennifer Holland landed on his desk.

A true disappointment.

She hadn't been raped or sexually assaulted. No DNA had been found anywhere on her body—no skin was found under her fingernails, no third-party saliva showed up on her nipples, mouth or face. Nor had any fingerprints been found on her body. There were no strange fibers or third-party hairs in her hair or anywhere else. The cause of death was suffocation. A trace of duct tape glue was discovered on her neck. The best guess is that someone had put a plastic bag of some sort over her head and then duct taped it around her neck. She was tied down at the time, which explained the bruises on her ankles and wrists. Other than those marks there was no physical trauma evident on the body.

The little shit.

Unfortunately, he'd been smart enough to remove the bag and tape before dumping the woman's body in the back of Coventry's truck, probably because he knew they were such good conductors of prints.

He was a careful little prick.

You had to give him that much.

Coventry wanted Darien to be somewhere safe, and Jena Vernon offered to invite her along for the day. At first Coventry balked at the idea. Jena knew too many things from Coventry's growing-up years, not all of which were flattering. No doubt Darien would end up with an earful before the day was over. But after reconsideration he really didn't care. He had bigger things to worry about right now and liked the idea of Darien being with someone he could trust. The last thing he wanted was for her to be alone, anywhere, which not only meant her apartment but his house as well.

He was at his desk, downing yet another cup of coffee, when the phone rang.

IT TURNED OUT TO BE T-VON, THE TRANSSEXUAL from Colfax, the human with the Adam's apple of a man and the legs of a goddess. He had some bad news to tell in that semi-feminine voice of his, no doubt because that's the way Coventry's life worked lately.

"No one knows where Paradise's money went," he said, which meant that any chance of recovering the twenty-dollar bill and printing it were gone. Coventry wasn't surprised. Money disappears faster than innocence on Colfax. "Also, I remembered something after you left," T-Von added.

"What's that?"

"Well, basically, I remembered seeing Paradise after I saw her in the alley," T-Von said. "So whoever was in there with her wasn't the one who stuck a knife in her head anyway."

Coventry frowned.

Oh well.

It figures.

Back to square one.

"Hey, thanks anyway," he said. "I really mean it," which was true.

A pause, then T-Von said: "I did hear something else though, but don't know if it means anything or not."

Coventry raised an eyebrow.

Curious.

"What's that?"

"Apparently, Paradise got out of the bondage scene a month or two ago, except for the regulars that she could really trust."

Coventry thought about it and didn't find the information particularly helpful. "Okay," he said.

"All right, then."

Coventry's eyes fell on the snake plant. For some reason it seemed even bigger than he remembered and had to be every inch of six feet now. He wasn't sure if he could take it in a fair fight anymore.

"So she got out of the business, huh?" he said.

"Yep, apparently."

Coventry was about to hang up, but asked, "Why?"

"Some guy just about killed her, apparently."

"Really?"

"Big time."

"How? What happened?"

T-Von then told him a long story with such vivid imagery and so many details that Coventry felt like he was right there.

WITH THE RADIO OFF, THE MAN cruised up and down the darkest and seediest part of Colfax Avenue in the nondescript vehicle, on the hunt for one very special woman.

On his third pass he spotted her, strutting her ass on the other side of the street. She had hot-pink shorts that barely covered her precious little crotch, a pierced belly button and firm tits with one nipple hanging halfway out. Up top she wore a cheap blond wig; and down below, cheap red heels. Midway between the two was a world-class ass.

He felt his cock tighten against his jeans.

He drove past her for two blocks, scouting the territory, spotting no cops. Then he circled back and slowed down as he approached her. By the time he came to a stop she was already by the side of the car, leaning over, giving him a cleavage show.

A taste.

He powered down the passenger window. Her face and tits immediately leaned into the car, filling it up.

"Are you a cop?" she questioned. Her teeth were brilliant white, or maybe the contrast against her dark skin just made it seem that way.

The man chuckled at the absurdity of the question. "Me? Not hardly."

"What are you doing out here all alone, sugar?   You looking for a party?"

"That depends," the man said.   "Are you Paradise?"

She nodded, then pulled a tit out and played with the nipple. "Tickets to Paradise are a thousand bucks, sweetie.   Regular is a lot cheaper."

The man fiddled with his wallet and then handed her ten hundred-dollar bills.

"Hop in."

She slid in next to him   "What's your name, honey?"

"I got lots of names," the man said.

"Oh, mystery man." She played with his cock, making the five-minute drive to her bungalow seem like thirty seconds. Inside, she poured them each a jigger of vodka, which they drank in unison, bottoms up.

Then they went downstairs to the dungeon.

It was fairly simple, a rack by one wall, an X-frame against another.   In the middle of the room there were eyebolts in the ceiling with chains hanging down.   Perfect.   The man tied her feet together and then strung her up with her arms stretched tight overhead.

Completely naked, of course.

She had already explained the ground rules. The session would last one hour.   If he started to hurt her too much she'd tell him, and he'd have to lighten up.   If he didn't, she had people who would hunt him down like the dog he was.   If he made her bleed or welt up, that was an extra thousand, no questions asked, no excuses accepted.

After he had his fun, she'd blow him for an extra fifty if he wanted, or screw him for a hundred. Or he could just lie down on the floor and jack off for free; she really didn't care.

He stood behind her, reached around and massaged her nipples, touching her nowhere else, only on her nipples. Within a minute he had them rock hard.

"You comfortable, baby?" he questioned.

"Oh, yeah."

The man reached down to her crotch.

Her pubic hair was pitch-black and coarse, like a Brillo Pad.

He tugged on it ever so slightly and she made a sound somewhere between pleasure and pain. Then he picked up the whip, a flexible two-foot cane with a leather tip.

He circled around her, took off his shirt and studied her ass.

It was the strongest part of her body, rippled with muscles, taut.

He blindfolded her.

Then walked over to the wall, slid down until he was sitting on the floor, and watched her, playing with the whip in his hand.

For a while she didn't say a thing.

Then she got tired of waiting.

"Come on baby," she said. "Don't be afraid. Make me hurt."

He chuckled. "I'm really not into that," he said.

"What do you mean?"

"I'm more into watching."

"Whatever, man, it's your money."

He sat there, studying her. In a few minutes she started to say something, and he cut her off: "No talking," he said.

He used most the hour to study her. Occasionally walking over and running a finger up and down her stomach, ever so lightly, barely perceptible, just to remind her that he was there.

Then he took her blindfold off.

He went over to his backpack and pulled out a black garbage

bag and roll of duct tape. He draped the bag over her shoulder, then reached in his jean pockets and pulled out a pair of dice.

"Hour's up, sugar," she said. "You did good. Now let me down."

The man smiled.

"Actually we have five more minutes," he said. "I'm going to roll a pair of dice and you're gong to choose high or low. High means seven through twelve. Low means two through six. If you choose high and I roll a high number, then I let you go. If you choose low and it turns out to be low, I let you go. But if you choose high and it turns out low, or vice versa, then I put this bag over your head and duct tape it around your neck. If you don't choose either, or if you scream, you automatically lose. So decide woman, what's it going to be?"

The man studied her as she pulled viciously at the chains.

"Session's up, chump! Get me down! Right now!"

The man smiled. "Remember, not choosing is an automatic loss. You have five more seconds."

"Oh God . . . *high* . . ."

He got down on one knee, shook the dice in his hands and rolled them on the floor.

He grinned.

Then looked into her eyes.

She stared at the dice, trying to read them.

"Can you see what they say?" he asked.

"No, get me down!"

"Eight," he told her. "I guess you chose right."

She pulled at the chains. "Get me out of here you asshole!"

He walked to her, shaking his head with amusement. "Relax, sweetie," he said. "I was just messing with you." He started to release her. "Remember," he said, "I paid a thousand bucks. I'm entitled to a little something."

"Yeah, well, that wasn't funny—asshole."

She dripped with sweat.

"Lighten up," he said. "We both got what we wanted."

AFTER T-VON TOLD HIM THE STORY, Coventry walked over to Shalifa's desk. "We got a new wrinkle," he said. "A big new wrinkle. Get the team together ASAP so we can all go over it together."

He walked over to the coffee pot, found it was empty except for an eighth-inch of brown goop in the bottom that was starting to bake onto the glass, and made a fresh pot.

Now he knew why Paradise ended up with a knife in her eye.

Bodies were going to start showing up in Denver.

Dead by suffocation.

Sooner or later Paradise would make the connection and tell the police about her little incident.

She'd seen the man's face.

She'd be a witness.

So she had to be eliminated.

Chapter Forty-Three

Day Seven - July 17
Monday Morning

AS USUAL, THE LAW PRACTICE got in the way of Taylor Sutton's life. She wanted more than anything to spend the entire day on Nick's case, and not just because he gave her an additional $25,000 retainer. But she had other files flapping in the wind so bad that they'd turn into malpractice suits if she wasn't careful. So she got in the office before dawn and hammered out one thing after another.

When Claudia came in, Taylor wanted to tell her about the meeting with Nick yesterday. But she'd given Nick her word, so she didn't. Plus, she already knew what Claudia would say: "So, according to Nick, it was all the idea of this mysterious client to kill Sarah. How do you know Nick's not lying about that? How do you know it wasn't all his big fat idea to start with? I'm telling you, honey, he's lying to you again and you're falling for it again. Thank God you got me around to wake you up every now and then."

Taylor wouldn't have an answer to that, not a good one anyway.

All she would be able to say is, "It wasn't Nick's idea. I could tell by his eyes."

At which point Claudia would say something like, "Nick had the idea from the start and in fact probably paid the guy to do it. Now he's afraid that the money's going to be found in this guy's safe, with his fingerprints all over it."

Anyway, that's an argument she didn't need and wouldn't have.

BY 10:00 SHE COULDN'T STAND HER DESK anymore and headed over to Broadway where the air smelled like bus diesel, French fries and bar carpet. She left a string of burned matches in her wake, more than usual.

More than one person gave her a dirty look.

Such a litterbug.

She had one good piece of information today that she didn't have before her meeting with Nick, namely that Sarah's body was buried in the "north forty."

No doubt meaning a farm.

Although she really needed to get back to the office, instead she scrambled around until she was able to find a place to buy a map of Denver that included the surrounding communities.

She carried it back to the office like a treasure.

Then she put a red mark at the location of every phone that Northwest had used to call Nick.

She drew a line around the farm areas that had the greatest proximity to those phones. They turned out to be north of Denver outside the I-25 corridor, halfway to Loveland to be precise, where the population thinned and basically stayed that way all the way to Fort Collins.

She smiled and realized that she still had her shoes on.

She kicked them off, walked over to the coffee machine and poured a fresh cup.

Then walked back over to the map, looked at it, and said, "You live there somewhere."

AN HOUR LATER BROOKE SHOWED UP to get the employment policies that Taylor had managed to review so far. She looked at the map.

"What's that?"

"Nick's mystery client lives somewhere in this area," Taylor said.

Brooke looked worried. "You need to get your ass back to lawyering and out of the sleuth business."

Chapter Forty-Four

Day Seven - July 17
Monday Morning

———————

WICKERSHAM PULLED OFF A STRIP OF DUCT TAPE and reached down to wrap it around Ashley Conner's neck when he noticed her T-shit had ridden up and her belly button was showing.

For some reason the sight caused him to pause and lean back. He reached down and gently poked a finger in it. Her stomach muscles were taut and firm and pushed back.

Great stomach.

Not as good as his but still pretty damn nice.

He put his full hand on it.

A warm feeling washed over him, a naughty feeling, the kind he got when he used to pull the legs off spiders, back when he was a little kid.

He moved his hand around. Her skin was incredibly soft and smooth, almost like a baby's. His fingers reached under her shirt and went up to her tits. He found a nipple and ran a finger around it in little circles.

Her coma face didn't change.

There was no reaction at all.

She wasn't telling him to stop.

HE GOT AN ERECTION, a full three inches worth. He reached down and rubbed himself, a reminder of how puny he was.

For some reason his dick had never grown up. Everyone has at least one physical flaw and his particular unfortunate draw of bad luck was ending up with something more like a stub than a real cock. In a relaxed state it was two and a half inches; when excited it was slightly bigger. There was no problem with the width. It was certainly as wide as it should be. Nor was there any problem with performance. He could get hard and come with the best of them. The only problem was the length.

And what a problem that was.

Normal sex was just about impossible.

He discovered that early on, at the age of seventeen.

The minute the woman started moving with any significance at all he'd pop out. There just wasn't enough length to keep it in, even with a tight woman. If the woman was loose then totally forget it. Just go watch TV and don't even try.

By age nineteen he had pretty well gotten the message pounded into his thick horny skull that sex with women just wasn't going to happen, not now, not ever.

That's when he stopped trying.

HE MOVED ASHLEY CONNER'S ARMS over her head and pulled her T-shirt up and off. She looked so damn beautiful that he could hardly believe it.

This was something new.

An unconscious woman.

Why had he never thought of this before?

He took off his pants and straddled her stomach, rubbing his dick on her soft tight abdomen. God that felt good. Now he thrust his dick back and forth in a steady motion and felt his ass muscles grow increasingly tighter.

He could actually come like this!

He closed his eyes and kept up the pace.

Her body was perfect.

So warm and soft.

He brought his head down to hers and kissed her on the lips. He thrust even faster now and the sound of his own breathing filled the room.

He stuck his tongue in her mouth as deep as he could.

Then screamed and exploded on her stomach.

Chapter Forty-Five

Day Seven - July 17
Monday Morning

THE PLAN WAS TO AMP-UP THE SEARCH for the person
who stuck the knife in Paradise's eye, the theory being that he
was the same person terrorizing Denver.

Coventry took the photos of the men from Paradise's house,
together with a cup of coffee, and went into one of the empty
meeting rooms. He closed the door. Of the thirty or so photos
of the men who had been recognized by the Colfax hookers on
some level or another, he placed a piece of masking tape on the
bottom right corner, just so he wouldn't forget who they were.
Then he arranged all eighty or so of the pictures in chronologi-
cal order.

According to the transvestite, T-Von, the incident that
freaked Paradise out happened a month or two back. Working
in that timeframe, Coventry found someone who might be the
man that sparked the big change in Paradise's life.

The man wore a small backpack; maybe with the duct tape
and plastic bag inside.

He also wore a baseball hat.

And not just any baseball hat.

One that shielded his entire face.

Coventry slapped the desk in frustration.

Shit!

Why doesn't anything ever work right?

Maybe he was wrong. Perhaps it was one of the other guys. He double-checked his analysis, but only became more convinced that the guy in the baseball cap was the one he was looking for. That's because after him the visitors to the wonderful house of Paradise were much less frequent.

He was the catalyst.

The one who scared the shit out of her.

Unfortunately, his picture absolutely sucked.

Not only did the baseball hat not have any writing or distinguishing marks, being a uniform dark blue in color, but Paradise wasn't in the photo either, unlike most of the other ones. Thus there was no good way to figure out the man's height, no good reference point to compare it to.

Coventry was sick with the thought that they almost stumbled upon a perfectly good picture of the guy but he happened to escape by nothing other than blind luck.

"You better thank someone, you little asshole."

SUDDENLY THE DOOR OPENED and Shalifa Netherwood walked in. "You're not a very good hider," she said.

Coventry handed her the picture.

"This is our guy."

"He is?"

"Yep."

"You got a better picture than this?"

"Of course not."

"Ouch."

"This guy is such a lucky son-of-a-bitch that I can't even believe it," Coventry said. "If he just had his head cocked a little different, we'd have his ass in custody by nightfall."

"And maybe have Ashley Conner back," Shalifa added.

He nodded.

Right.

Shit.

"It's encouraging that her body hasn't shown up," Shalifa said. "If he's playing the dice game with her, like he did with Paradise, then she must be winning."

"Yeah, well I've been to Vegas and can tell you firsthand that that won't last long," Coventry said. Then, picking up his coffee cup: "I'll be right back."

She fell in step.

"Me too."

He stopped and looked at her.

"We're both going to the men's room?"

COVENTRY PICKED UP DARIEN FOR LUNCH and they ended up in a booth at Wong's on Court Street, with plates of rice, vegetables and chicken. Clanging plates and Chinese banter filled the air. He ate there as often as he could because Wong was a good guy and nobody ever rushed him.

One of the younger waitresses came by the booth, a pretty little flower of a thing. She looked at him and Darien, and said, "You want threesome?" She had almond eyes and straight black hair. Coventry looked at Darien, then back at the woman, shrugged, and said, "Yes, I think threesome would be nice."

The look on Darien's face almost made him bust out in

laughter but he managed to hold it in. He held his teacup up and the woman filled it.

He said to Darien, "You want tea some, too?"

She shook her head and chuckled. "Got me."

Coventry grinned.

"Yes I did."

"Look at you, all proud of yourself."

"Yes I am."

When the waitress left, Coventry leaned forward and asked the question he'd been dreading. "Okay, so what'd Jena tell you about me this morning. Because in fairness, I should get some rebuttal time."

Darien put on a face, as if there was so much stuff that she didn't know where to start. "Let's see, what have I learned so far?" she said. "You played guitar in a band in high school, you had a 1966 Mustang, you kept two copies of Playboy under your mattress . . ."

Coventry chuckled. "She knew that?"

"*Everyone* knew that, apparently."

Ouch.

"You had them dog-eared to your favorite pages."

Double ouch.

"What else? Oh, you had long hair past your shoulders, you were the president of your senior class, and other boring stuff." She paused and put on a serious face: "She's still hot for you, you know."

He shrugged.

"What about you?" he asked.

"Maybe."

"Then maybe that's all that matters."

When they were almost finished eating, she had a stray

thought: "Oh, I almost forgot," she said. "You remember the guy with the glasses, driving the van on Speer, the one I recognized?"

"No, who's he?"

She smacked his arm.

"Not funny," she said. "Anyway, I remembered where I saw him."

Coventry raised an eyebrow.

Oh yeah.

"Go on."

"Do you remember the day you came to the apartment building, not the first time in the morning when we met, but later that afternoon? When the news crew showed up at Ashley's door."

He did.

"Well, that guy was part of the news crew."

Coventry couldn't believe it.

"You're kidding," he said.

No, she wasn't.

"I passed them all in the stairwell," she added. "I sort of remember him because he gave me a creepy look. I didn't turn around after he passed, but I got the feeling he did. I could feel his eyes on my ass."

Coventry processed it.

So the whole thing had been a great big false alarm.

Oh well.

"Sorry," she said.

"It's okay. That's how my life works."

HE PLANNED TO SPEND A QUIET EVENING with Darien at

his house, maybe have a beer or two and chill out after a long day, pop in a DVD, say *A Perfect Murder*. But he ended up pacing back and forth until she finally jumped in front of him and said, "All right, what's going on in that brain of yours?"

What indeed?

He wasn't quite sure.

"I need to make some progress on this case," he said. "I'm floundering and people are dying. We tied the guy to the murder of Paradise but it hasn't done any good. We're no further now than if we'd never made the connection at all."

"You checked her house, right?"

He nodded.

Right.

But only once.

He looked at her and reached for the car keys. "Do you feel like going to a dungeon?" he asked.

"Oh, kinky. I like that."

A HALF HOUR LATER they were at Paradise's house, downstairs in the dungeon. Coventry had no idea what he expected to find but felt better being in motion than sitting on his ass.

They both put on gloves before they walked in.

The place was exactly as he left it.

Wrist cuffs hung from chains in the middle of the room. Darien walked over and studied them while he wandered around, looking for who knows what.

Maybe another camera.

When he looked back, Darien had reached up and grabbed the chains, as if chained herself. "Put me in the cuffs," she said.

Coventry shook his head.

"Are you nuts?"

"I want you to," she said. "I've never been tied up. Besides, don't you have to get inside this guy's mind if you're going to catch him?"

He walked over to her.

Not really convinced that this was a good idea.

"Are you sure?"

She nodded.

Against his better judgment he reached up to fasten a wrist, but before he could do it, she said: "Blindfold me first. He had her blindfolded, remember?"

He did indeed.

He looked around for a blindfold.

There it was.

Hanging on the wall.

A leather one with padding on the inside and a strap at the back, like a belt. Then it dawned on him. The guy would have handled this. His prints might still be on it. With any luck no one had used it since, or even if they had, there was still a chance they didn't smear his.

He cocked his head and said, "This may not be such a bad idea after all."

"Are you going to blindfold me, or what?" Darien asked. She was in the process of slipping out of her clothes. Coventry must have had a startled look on his face because she said, "She was naked, remember?"

He used her tank top as a blindfold, secured her in the cuffs and then tied her feet together. This is exactly how Paradise had been, at least according to the stories she told everyone afterwards.

Then he sat down against the wall and watched her.

When she started to say something he said, "No talking."

She shut up.

He imagined that he would play the dice game with her at the end of the hour. What he was seeing, then, was the last sixty minutes of her life, if she lost.

It was his to savor and enjoy.

He was the grim reaper and she didn't even know it.

"Remember," Darien said, "he touched her sometimes."

Coventry pushed against the wall to rise to his feet, walked over, pulled off the glove and ran the index finger of one hand in slow wavy motions up and down her body. She trembled under his touch.

Chapter Forty-Six

Day Seven - July 17
Monday Evening

TAYLOR SUTTON WORKED AT THE OFFICE until 6:30 in the evening because she didn't feel like messing with the roads until the rush hour thinned. Then she stopped at a Subway, bought a turkey sandwich with everything except mayo, plus a diet Coke and bag of Cheetos, and ate in the Porsche as she drove north on I-25 to farmland.

She kept going until the roads were no longer called street or avenue but had a CR designation instead, meaning County Road. She got off the interstate when civilization seemed sufficiently diluted, and stopped at the first gas station she came to.

It was one of those two-pump dinosaurs that probably hadn't changed an iota in twenty-five years. She pictured an inch of dust in the back storeroom. An old fart sat behind the counter fighting with a crossword puzzle.

He smelled like a cigar and wore a flannel shirt.

"I'm a lawyer from Denver," she said. "I'm looking for someone who lives around here somewhere, but I don't know his name. He drives a van and has black glasses. I thought maybe you'd know him."

The man studied her.

He seemed to think about it.

Then shook his head.

"Can't say that rings a bell," he said.

She nodded.

"Okay, thanks," she said, handing him a business card. "If he does show up, give me a call, will you?"

He looked at the card and then stuffed in his front shirt pocket.

"Sure thing," he said.

IN THE NEXT THREE HOURS she made twenty more visits just like that one. No one had any recollection of seeing anyone similar to the man she was looking for.

She left her business card at every location.

If she couldn't find him, she'd let him find her.

Chapter Forty-Seven

Day Seven - July 17
Monday Evening

AFTER SUPPER, NATHAN WICKERSHAM went grocery shopping at King Soopers, a thirty-mile roundtrip, exactly like he did every Monday evening. He didn't particularly like the idea of leaving Ashley Conner alone with so much heat around, but wasn't partial to breaking his habits either, just in case anyone was paying attention.

Plus he needed food.

And liquor.

Sure, the kitchen island had lots of wine bottles in the built-in chiller, but those were the expensive units to impress guests. He needed some cork that he could actually pop without having to worry about taking out a second mortgage.

When he got back home it was almost nightfall. He hadn't turned on any lights inside the house before he left and the windows were dark when he returned, as they should be. The temperature was bearable and, in fact, just about perfect. Somewhere in the upper eighties. Of course, that would change fast once the deeper night settled in. He parked the Camry as close to the front door as he could, popped open the trunk, muscled up two bags of groceries and walked towards the entry.

What he saw he could hardly believe.

The front door was wide open.

And he wasn't the one who left it like that.

In fact, he had checked it twice before he left, just to be absolutely sure it was locked.

What the hell?

He set the bags down and then stood there frozen, listening, ready to bolt in whatever direction seemed best. Seconds passed and nothing happened.

No headlights raced down the road.

No caravan of cops squealed into the driveway.

No sounds came from inside the house.

No nothing.

HE KEPT A GUN IN THE DEN, in the bottom drawer of the desk. He took two steps inside the house, slow careful steps, as if sneaking up on someone, and stopped. Still he heard nothing. He walked all the way to the den, one careful step at a time, and pulled out the bottom drawer as quietly as he could.

He reached down into the black space.

The gun was there.

Right where it should be.

So sweet.

He brought it out without making a sound, took off the safety and then headed for the kitchen.

He still heard no sounds from anywhere.

The kitchen was empty.

He almost turned on the lights but didn't.

Instead he tiptoed back to the front door and looked around

outside. Nothing had changed. He started to feel better now. If the cops were coming for him they would be here by now.

Wouldn't they?

He searched the rest of the house, one room at a time. A window in the spare bedroom was broken. A rock sat on the floor in a pile of glass.

But no one was in the house.

He went to the dungeon. The door was locked, as it should be. Inside, Ashley Conner lay on the bed, still in a coma.

HE WALKED AROUND THE PERIMETER of the house but found nothing out of the ordinary. Back inside, he turned on the lights and searched the house again.

Everything was absolutely normal except for a couple of things. Someone had riffled through his bills. Some of his old phone bills were sitting on the desk. It looked like some of them were gone. Also, some of the pictures around the house were missing, frames and all, pictures of him and friends.

He slipped into warmer clothes, all black, turned off all the lights in the house and stepped outside, locking the front door behind him. With the gun and binoculars in hand, he took a position in the trees, about fifty yards from the house, and watched.

If anyone came for him tonight he'd disappear into the woods.

Then make his way to the getaway car.

Never to be seen or heard from again.

Chapter Forty-Eight

Day Eight - July 18
Tuesday Morning

SOONER OR LATER THE ASSHOLE'S luck was going to run out. Coventry was excited, pounding down coffee well before dawn, more than hopeful that today was the day. He was already waiting for Paul Kubiak when the man's big old gut pushed through the door on the sixth floor. "All this stuff," Coventry said—pointing to evidence bags holding blindfolds, whips and cuffs—"comes from Paradise's dungeon. I'm pretty sure our guy handled at least some of it, particularly the blindfold. I need everything printed ASAP. Then we're going over to her house to print a wall. I'll show you where."

Kubiak looked at him, pulled a glazed donut out of a white bag, and took a bite. "Do you work here?" he asked. Coventry grinned and was almost gone when Kubiak shouted at him, "Thank you Paul."

Coventry half turned and hollered over his shoulder, "Thank you Paul."

TEN MINUTES LATER THE FBI PROFILER, Leanne Sanders,

called him with startling news. He was just hanging up, still flabbergasted, when Shalifa Netherwood walked in. He grabbed her by the arm and headed for the door: "Come on," he said. "We're going to New Mexico."

The words surprised her. "New Mexico the state?"

"Santa Fe to be precise."

At the elevator she reached to press the down button but he yanked her arm and led her to the stairway.

"Oops," he said. "Be right back." Forty-five seconds later he fell back into step, this time holding a thermos of coffee and two Styrofoam cups.

They headed south on I-25, initially caught in the rush hour mess but finally breaking free after Belleview. Coventry brought the 4Runner up to 78 and set the cruise control. Before long they had Dry Creek Road in their wake and entered an open stretch of freeway that carved its way through a stunning and relatively undeveloped topography. To the west lay the Rocky Mountain foothills. To the east, somewhere out there, lay Kansas. Santa Fe would be a six or seven hour trip, meaning at least an equal number of rest stops, thanks to the thermos. That was okay, because Coventry knew where they all were.

"The chief called me at home last night," he offered. "He wants me to tee up the Nick Trotter case again. He says nothing's happened in over a month—which is true—and he's getting flak from a number of directions."

Shalifa frowned.

"I don't see how he can bother you with that at a time like this," she said. "You'd think he'd be more interested in getting Denver off the CNN evening news."

Coventry agreed.

But understood the chief's viewpoint.

"He's not looking for much," he said. "Just something he can take back and say, *See, we're working on it.*"

She reclined her seat and closed her eyes.

"Where are we at on that, anyway?"

Good question.

"I can't tell yet if Nick did it or not," he said. "Sometimes I think yes, sometimes I think no."

"Why is that even our case? I thought they lived in some ritzy estate in Greenwood Village."

"They do," Coventry said. "But the wife disappeared downtown, remember?"

Now she recalled. "Right, okay."

"Nick has motive," he added, "millions and millions of motives in fact, and no alibi. But since we never found the abduction scene, we have squat for evidence. Her car was clean. There were no eyewitnesses. Basically, we have no choice but to sit back and wait for the body to show up."

"So what are you going to do?"

He shrugged.

"I guess I'll just call him in again for some more questioning."

"That's called harassment."

"It's also called keeping my job."

Shalifa shifted thoughts.

"So how are you and the mysterious Darien Jade getting along?"

He briefly recalled last night, working her into a sexual frenzy in Paradise's dungeon.

"Not bad."

"Not bad, huh?"

"No, not bad."

"Meaning what? Good?"

He nodded. "Better than good, probably."

"Better than good. So we're talking, what? Excellent? Something like that?"

"Right."

She grinned and punched him in the arm. "Coventry, you're in love, you dog."

He denied it. "No way."

Shalifa shook her head, as if contemplating a distant thought. "That poor girl," she said.

He chuckled. "Yeah, you got to feel for her."

THEY CAUGHT A LATE LUNCH AT MICHAEL'S KITCHEN in Taos—slightly out of the way but worth it—and ended up rolling into the Santa Fe Police Department in the middle of the afternoon. Coventry immediately headed for the restroom and his cell phone rang on the way.

"Coventry," he said.

"Mr. Coventry, this is Archie Baxter."

Coventry drew a blank.

"We met on the bus, I just lost my job and you gave me a number to call."

The confusion dropped off his face. "Right, how are you?"

"I'm good. I just wanted to thank you."

"So you got hooked up?"

"I sure did. I've been meaning to call you and say thanks."

"Not a problem."

When he got out, Shalifa was nowhere to be seen. Then he spotted her down the hall waving at him and headed in that direction. Time to catch a killer.

Chapter Forty-Nine

Day Eight - July 18
Tuesday Morning

TAYLOR SUTTON FOUND HERSELF LOCKED in a conference room with two of her client's in-house lawyers and the head of the Human Resources Department, Martha Gatlin, a terrible looking woman with too much sugar in her smile.

They were noise in her ears.

From the information she had been able to process, it appeared that one Joel Smith, a young African American man with a family to support, filed a discrimination case in the United States District Court yesterday, alleging that his discharge nine months ago was racially motivated. Apparently two of the claims in the Complaint, the ones based on negligence and defamation, might be covered under the company's insurance policy, so the prudent thing to do would be to promptly file a claim with the insurance carrier. Then, if . . .

Noise, noise, noise.

After the meeting that never ended, she pointed the Porsche north on I-25 and spent the rest of the day crisscrossing back and forth through farmland, being told that no one knew anything about a driver of a van with black glasses, and watching her business card get stuffed into the pocket of one gas station attendant after another.

THAT EVENING SHE SWUNG BY NICK'S HOUSE, spread the map of Denver out on the granite countertop in his kitchen, and sipped a glass of wine while she showed him the location of the phone calls and the farmland areas she'd been working for the last couple of days. He had the flat-panel TV in the adjacent family room turned to a Rockies game, with the sound low but not off.

When she first started talking he concentrated more on the game but then increasing focused on her story. He wore his hair loose instead of in the ponytail and kept pushing it out of his face.

He paced as she talked.

Clearly stressed.

Not saying a word but in heavy thought.

Then he cut her off. "You've turned yourself into a target," he said. "Goddamn it."

"Not really," she said. "If someone from a gas station sees him and calls me, he won't know anything about it. But if someone knows him, and gives him my card and says I've been snooping around asking about him, I'll only be a person of interest. I'm hoping enough of an interest for him to call me."

Nick drained the rest of his wine and looked like he was about to throw the glass against the wall. Instead he softly and deliberately set it on the counter.

"You underestimate this guy," he said. "And I can't let you do that. That's why I'm going to have to pull you off the case."

The words shocked her.

"What?"

"It's for your own good," he said. "I can't have your blood on my hands. We agreed upfront that you'd keep a low profile. You went way past that line, so it's over."

She shook her head.

"No, I can't stop now. I'm too close."

"I'm serious, you're off the case."

She started to protest but he held his hand up in a "Stop!" motion. He was not only serious but wasn't going to change his mind. "Now we need to get you some protection," he said. "I'd let you stay here but it won't look so dandy if another woman moves in two months after my wife disappears."

She stood up and scowled at him.

"You know what? Screw you, Nick."

SHE BURNED RUBBER LEAVING HIS DRIVEWAY and then screeched past the too-perfect houses. Before she got to the gate she called him with her cell phone. When he answered she said, "If you think I'm off this case you're living in fantasyland."

Then she hung up.

Chapter Fifty

Day Eight - July 18
Tuesday Morning

NATHAN WICKERSHAM STAYED IN THE TREES all night, shivering his ass off and slipping in and out of a fitful sleep. By morning no one had come back to the house and he was getting more and more convinced that the break-in was the work of kids. So he went back in, verified that the place was still as he left it, kicked off his shoes, and let his body fall into the middle of the bed.

He woke around noon, still groggy but feeling a hundred percent better. He showered, ate cereal topped with strawberries, and was in the study answering e-mails and working on his third cup of coffee when the phone rang.

He picked it up in a good mood.

The rock star was returning.

"Yo," he said.

"Yo," a man's voice said. "That's cute."

He didn't recognize the caller.

"Who is this?"

"It's the boogieman in your closet, asshole," the man said. "Listen carefully because you're going to live or die depending on what you say in the next two minutes. First of all, I know you're the person terrorizing Denver, so let's just get that out in the open right off the bat."

"Who . . ."

"Shut up and listen!" the man said. "Personally, I don't give a rat's ass if you kill every stinking bitch in the city. But here's what you're going to do to get me off your ass. There's a woman called Janelle Parker. Get a pen and write her name down."

Wickersham did, with a shaking hand.

Scared shitless.

"She's in the Denver white pages, the only Janelle Parker there, and lives near Wash Park. She's twenty-eight, a photographer, cute too. You're going to like her. You be damn sure that she's your victim when you pay your next little visit this weekend. Take her out on Friday, Saturday or Sunday. I don't give a shit which, but one of them. Now, here's the part of the deal you can't refuse. After you do that, you're never going to hear from me again. You have my word on that. But if you don't, then I'm going to place a little call to Bryson Coventry. He'll get a nice picture of you too, one of the ones I took from your house yesterday. So my advice to you is don't screw up."

The line went dead.

Wickersham threw the pen. It flew across the room and smashed into the flat-panel TV.

"Goddamn it!"

He pulled out the phone book and frantically turned to the P's. There she was.

Janelle Parker.

The only Janelle Parker there.

Just like the guy said.

"Okay, think!" he told himself. Do it? Or just get the hell out of Dodge, right this second, while the getting is good?

HE GRABBED HIS WALLET AND RAN to the Camry, knowing it was better to be anywhere in the universe right now other than here. He couldn't have been more than a mile down the road when a cop came from the other direction. He instinctively looked at his speed and was shocked to find it was eighty.

A look in his rearview mirror confirmed that the cop was turning around with the light bar flashing.

Goddamn it!

Chapter Fifty-One

Day Eight - July 18
Tuesday Afternoon

CANYON ROAD IN SANTA FE IS A NARROW LANE that twists and picks its way among adobe structures, rich green trees and bright flowers. In most places it narrows so much that the traffic runs only one direction. Coventry found a parking spot for the 4Runner on a side street and he and Shalifa walked back to where the action was.

He knew the place well.

At one time it was *the* place for artists to live, the colony. The artists sold their work directly out of their studios. The road developed an increasing reputation as a place to buy quality art at starving-artists' prices. The buyers came, the display areas increased in size and the houses eventually turned into full-fledged galleries. Now it was one of the best places in the western United States to buy high quality art.

About halfway up the road they came to the gallery they were looking for. It had two large windows, one on each side of the front door. Each held a couple of paintings. In the right window there were two large abstracts, contemporary pieces, with thick paint, bright colors, framed in bright white wood, totally in-your-face.

They did nothing for Coventry, unless cringing counted.

But in the left window there were two southwest landscapes, laid loosely with an impressionistic brush, with colors true to life and considerable attention paid to the interplay of dark and light.

"I could live with that," Coventry said, nodding.

"It's gorgeous," Shalifa agreed.

The work inside was equally impressive. Shalifa moved around the gallery from one piece to the next, as if they were M&Ms and she couldn't eat them fast enough. There were sculptures too: a horse-drawn wagon falling over a cliff, an Indian warrior deflecting an enraged eagle, a nude woman carrying a water jug on her right shoulder.

Coventry was drawn to one painting in particular, an exciting southwest landscape filled with brush and gullies and foothills and mountains, all under threat of a impending afternoon storm.

"I like it," Shalifa said.

Coventry nodded and twisted the price tag so he could read it: $3,500. Reasonable enough, given the quality.

AN ELEGANTLY DRESSED WOMAN in her twenties sat behind a contemporary desk working a computer, ready to answer questions if they had any, but otherwise content to leave them alone. She had short, stylish blond hair and wore lots of turquoise jewelry.

Coventry walked over to her and said, "You're Jacquelyn Davis-Wade." The woman looked at him and seemed drawn to his eyes. "One's blue and one's green," Coventry offered. "Some kind of genetic mutation, I imagine."

"I've never seen that before," she said. "From an artistic point of view, it's sort of cool. So who are you and how do you know my name?"

"We're detectives from Denver," he said. "Bryson Coventry and Shalifa Netherwood. You were attacked last year. We believe that the man who assaulted you is doing the same thing up in Denver. We're hoping we could talk to you and maybe get some information to help us."

She fidgeted.

"How'd you find out about me?"

"An FBI profiler by the name of Dr. Leanne Sanders is helping us out and found out about you through some database research," he said. "The man in Denver is playing a dice game with his victims, then suffocating them with a plastic bag if they lose. From what we understand, that's pretty much what happened to you."

She nodded.

"The bastard."

Coventry sat down on the edge of her desk. "We've already met with Detective Harrison. We've reviewed the file and he showed us your statements," he said. "But for me, there's no substitute for hearing the story firsthand. I know it's painful, dredging up all these old memories, but we need to catch this guy."

"Is this the guy on CNN? The one who sends the letters?"

"It is."

"I've been following that," she said. "There's nothing in the news about dice and plastic bags."

Coventry agreed.

It was recently discovered information.

They were trying to keep it quiet.

She nodded, convinced.

"Okay," she said. "What do you want to know?"

Coventry, as usual, wanted to know everything, every single last little detail. So he let her tell the story in her own words first, then brought her back to the beginning and this time asked a hundred and one questions.

It happened in the gallery, shortly after closing. The man hid in the back room and grabbed her from behind, knocking off her glasses. He wore a ski mask. He tied her to a chair and then draped a garbage bag over her shoulder. He said they were going to play a little game, she was going to choose a number and he was going to roll the dice. If she didn't choose right then he'd wrap the bag around her head.

"He actually rolled the dice," she said. "That's when the cleaning people opened the front door—they have the keys—and he bolted out the back."

"So you never saw his face?" Coventry asked, just to be absolutely sure.

"No, but I'll never forget his voice."

Interesting.

Very interesting.

That little fact hadn't been in her prior statement.

He smiled and then hugged her on the shoulders.

"Jacquelyn Davis-Wade, you done good."

"Get me a voice to listen to," she said. "I'll tell you if it's him or not."

BY THE TIME THEY WRAPPED UP, it was way too late to head back to Denver. Shalifa called a number of hotels and soon discovered that Santa Fe in July is pretty much a reserved town, unless you wanted to stay at a dive. The best she could find in any place decent was one room, a last minute cancellation.

"Two beds or one?" Coventry asked.

"Two."

He shrugged.

"If we do it, we can't tell anyone," he said. "HR would have a heart attack."

She cocked her head. "Okay, but don't even think about bouncing a quarter off my ass."

He chuckled.

"Darien told you that I told her about that?"

She rolled her eyes. "Women talk, caveman. Get a grip."

Chapter Fifty-Two

Day Nine - July 19
Wednesday Morning

———————

TAYLOR SUTTON WAS ASLEEP when someone rolled her over and straddled her. She opened her eyes. The room was still dark but with enough light to make out Tarzan, with his long blond hair and rugged jungle looks. At first she couldn't quite place him. Then she remembered last night, bar hopping, all wound up and pissed at Nick Trotter for trying to take her off the case. She remembered walking up to Tarzan, a complete stranger, and whispering in his ear.

She recalled the incredible passionate sex.

"Morning, glory," he said.

"Morning, yourself," she said, stretching her arms above her head.

"You wanted me to wake you at six-thirty," he said.

That was true.

She remembered now. It was a workday and she had piles of neglected papers on her desk.

"I made some coffee," he added.

"Well aren't you the nice one?" She pulled his head down and kissed him. This time, unlike last night, he took his time with her, building her up deliberately and skillfully until she couldn't stand it anymore.

THE FIRST THING SHE DID when she got to the office was rip Nick Trotter's retainer check into tiny little pieces and stick them in an envelope. Then, to make a statement, she called a courier service to have the envelope hand-delivered to Nick's office. She'd already earned a good portion of the retainer but screw it.

She didn't want his money.

As far as dropping the case, though, that wasn't going to happen. She started the job and she'd finish it, with or without him. If he didn't have the balls to save his own ass then he at least ought to be grateful that she did.

She was pounding out a trial brief for Judge Anderson, to bring him up to speed on the latest developments in sexual harassment, all of which favored her client, when the phone rang.

"Taylor Sutton," she said.

"Ms. Sutton, this is Bob from the gas station," a man said.

She recognized him by the scratch in his voice and pulled up an image of a middle-aged man who smelled like smoke and looked as if he knew his way around cow dung.

"Bob, I remember you," she said.

"Really?"

"Yes," she said. "You have those beautiful blue eyes. So what's up?"

Bob told her. A man came in for gas this morning, driving a van. He didn't wear glasses, but Bob told him anyway that a lawyer from Denver was trying to find someone in the area who drove a van and wore black glasses. The man said he sometimes wore sunglasses and maybe the lawyer was looking for him. So Bob gave him her card and the man said he'd give her a call.

"If you gave him my card, how'd you know my phone number?" Taylor asked.

"I remembered your name and that you're a lawyer. You're in the phone book," he said.

"Yes I am," she said. "Thanks. I'm probably going to be in the area this afternoon. If I am, I'll stop by and say hi."

AN HOUR LATER SHE WAS HEADING FOR THE DOOR when it opened and Nick Trotter walked in holding the envelope.

"Got your package," he said. "I pity the guy who eventually marries you."

She wasn't sure whether to laugh or smack him. So instead, she told him about the phone call from Bob. "I'm heading out there, right now."

"What for?"

"To drive around the area and look for a van."

"That seems like a long shot, even if you were still on the case."

She cocked her head. "Well if you have any short shots I'll be glad to take them."

Nick looked at her, as if pondering a decision.

"You're really not going to drop this, are you?"

She shook her head. "Apparently not."

He chuckled. "You've always been too damn cocky for your own good."

"Look," she said, "since I'm not going to drop the case in any event, why don't you get on your own team and help me out. I've got a gut feeling that this guy's shadowed you at one time or another and that you might recognize his face if you saw it again. So come with me, right now. If we find a van and the driver seems like someone you've seen, then bingo, we got him. It's that simple."

He studied her.

"God you're a stubborn thing," he said.

She grabbed his tie and pulled him towards the door. "You have no idea."

Chapter Fifty-Three

Day Nine - July 19
Wednesday

THE COPS SHOWED UP MID-MORNING and checked in with Wickersham to let him know they were going to be conducting additional investigation out in the field. He took the opportunity to hand them the speeding ticket he got yesterday—eighty in a forty-five. They apologized and agreed to take care of it in appreciation for all the cooperation he was giving. Then they spent an hour in the field. He sensed that they were just trying to stay in motion because they'd run out of anything solid to do. Either that or they were trying to rattle him. Either way, he watched them with the binoculars just to be sure that they didn't get too excited about anything.

They didn't.

When they left he worked the Internet to see what he could find out about Janelle Parker, who may or may not be his next victim. He wasn't sure yet whether he would actually yield to the blackmail scheme or just call everything quits and get out of the country, maybe even as early as tonight. But it couldn't hurt to scope the woman out.

Maybe he'd learn something to tip the scales one way or the

other.

She turned out to be a photographer and, in fact, recently came out with her first book, titled *Denver After Dark*. She had a nice author website that showed several photos from the book as well as the upcoming one, titled *Secrets of the Desert*. According to the Tour Information page of her website, she was scheduled for a book signing at the Tattered Page Bookstore in Cherry Creek this evening at 7:30, and another one in the LoDo branch on Friday.

Perfect.

Her website had lots of pictures of her.

She was very nice.

Definitely someone he could spend some quality time with.

She looked tall, though.

And strong.

He'd have to be careful.

THAT EVENING THERE WERE ALREADY forty or so people at the author event when he got there. The lights were off and the author, Janelle Parker, was showing slides of the photos from her book, explaining their back-stories and occasionally answering technical questions from the audience regarding F-stops, lengths of exposure, and equally mysterious things that were way beyond Wickersham's particular knowledge or expertise.

There were a few things he did know, however.

He knew that he liked her voice.

And he knew that he liked the way the light from the projector played on her face whenever she walked in front of the screen to point something out.

He left before the lights came on.

That night, after dark, he parked the Camry on Williams Street and then walked over two blocks to Race, where the woman lived. He wore dark clothes, a baseball cap, black frames and the fake moustache. Although the neighborhood was older, the houses were beautifully maintained and sat on spacious grounds, a rarity for Denver. Washington Park was just a stone's throw to the west. Judging by the cars in the driveways, the area was a trendy place that attracted people of money.

He got the feeling there were plenty of security cameras around, even though he couldn't see any, at least not right now in the dark.

Janelle Parker's particular house was one of the smaller ones. A blue Toyota Tacoma extended-cab pickup sat in the driveway, an outdated body style, maybe five years old or thereabouts. The license plate said FOTOG.

Perfect.

Easy to remember.

At a quarter to ten, all the lights were out in the house except for two rooms upstairs, which clearly had to be a bedroom and bathroom. He continued walking, to all intents and purposes just one more guy from the neighborhood out for a stroll in the night when it wasn't so hot.

When he got back to the Camry he swung by her house.

All the lights were out now.

He headed back to the farm, deep in thought. Who could possibly want her dead? She wasn't married. She seemed like a nice person.

Weird.

Chapter Fifty-Four

THEY WERE ON THAT STRETCH of nothing-but-highway in northern New Mexico, just south of the Colorado border, cruising at 78 with country-western on the radio, when Coventry's cell phone rang. The desert topography surrounded them with an untamable aura. To the left a distant mountain range squatted under a black thunderstorm.

"It's me," Coventry said, one eye on the road and one on the storm.

"How do you know it's you?"

He recognized the voice as Jena Vernon's.

"You're calling to tell me you got another letter today," he said. "Our friend's going to strike again this weekend. Am I right?"

"You are, but then again, even a monkey at a typewriter is going to spell a word every now and then," she said.

He chuckled.

"Is that how you think of me? A monkey at a typewriter?"

"No, you're twice that, any day of the week."

"Twice, huh?"

"At least, maybe thrice. Is that a word?"

"I don't know," he said, and then switched gears. "How's Darien doing? Behaving herself?"

"Darien tells me you've been a bad boy."

He had a pretty good idea what she was talking about but feigned ignorance.

"Me? Bad?"

"She tells me you tied her up and teased her into a orgasmic frenzy," Jena added. "How come you never did that to me?"

Before he could answer, the windshield exploded and glass blasted into the car.

SHALIFA SCREAMED AND HE INSTINCTIVELY SLAMMED on the brakes. By the time he got the vehicle off the road and to a stop he figured out what happened.

They hit a bird.

Any not just any bird.

One of those gigantic black vulture-like birds.

They hit it so hard that it actually came through the windshield and landed in the back seat. Blood and feathers were everywhere. He got out, shook glass out of his hair, and surveyed the damage. The windshield had a hole in it the size of a basketball and what was left was shattered so badly that you couldn't see through it. He decided that the safest course of action was to take it all the way out so glass chips wouldn't fly in their eyes. He set about kicking it out while Shalifa picked the bird up by a foot and threw it into the brush.

"It's going to be one of those days," he said.

She looked at him. "Nothing's ever normal with you Coventry, do you know that?"

He chuckled. "What, this is my fault?"

She shook her head as if in wonder. "I'm not saying it's your fault, all I'm saying is that stuff like this just seems to find you."

He thought about it.

"I see your point," he said.

Wearing sunglasses to keep the wind out of their eyes, and afraid to go any slower than fifty-five for fear of being run over from behind, they ended up driving all the way to Pueblo before they could find an Avis and exchange the vehicle for a new one.

When they pulled in Coventry said, "I'm not going to need lunch. The three pounds of bugs filled me up."

Shalifa couldn't help but laugh.

"You should see your hair," she said.

WHEN THEY FINALLY MADE IT BACK TO DENVER, Coventry went straight to the sixth floor to meet with Paul Kubiak, who was munching on a carrot when he walked in.

"What's with the rabbit food?" Coventry asked.

Kubiak made a sour face. "The wife says I'm getting fat."

"Getting?"

"Not even funny."

Kubiak gave him an update regarding the blindfold, whips and other items retrieved from Paradise's basement. They'd been able to lift quite a few good prints. So far, though, none of them were drawing any database matches.

"Okay," Coventry said. "But let's exhaust that before we call it quits. Here's the latest emergency. You probably heard that this same guy struck in Santa Fe."

Kubiak nodded.

"The word's floating around."

Coventry handed him a DVD. "This is a copy of footage from a Channel 9 news report, taken when the crime scene investigation was underway at the gallery. Some of the crowd shows up in the background. We need to correlate this to the videotape of the crowd at the 6th and Federal scene, to see if the same face shows up in both places."

Kubiak frowned.

"That's a tall drink of water," he said.

Coventry nodded and walked towards the door. "Use it to wash down those carrots," he said.

THAT NIGHT, HE AND DARIEN KICKED BACK on his couch and watched *Casablanca*, which Coventry hadn't seen in over ten years and now wondered why.

Most of his thoughts, however, were focused on whether they were doing everything possible to prevent another attack this weekend. Police visibility would be unprecedented, starting at 6:00 on Friday night. Every cop on the payroll would be on duty all weekend. If they could suppress an attack on Friday night, the guy would be under a lot more pressure Saturday. Maybe enough to force him into a mistake.

He looked at Darien, who was engrossed in the movie.

"You told Jena about our little adventure at Paradise's," he said.

She nodded. "Yep, I did." She turned and looked at him: "Why, you want to do it again?"

Before he could answer his cell phone rang. He sensed trouble, given the late hour of the evening.

It turned out to be Kate Katona.

"Hey, Bryson," she said. "I just remembered, I forgot to tell you that we got Nick Trotter coming in again to talk to you, like you wanted. He'll be in at one-thirty tomorrow."

"Great."

"You don't sound excited," she said.

"Oh, I'm excited all right. Just not in a good way."

Chapter Fifty-Five

Day Ten - July 20
Thursday

WITH AN IMPENDING SENSE that time was running out, Taylor Sutton rescheduled her morning appointment and headed back to farm county, on the hunt for a van and black glasses. Whoever it was that picked up her business card from Bob still hadn't called, maybe because he was stalking her instead.

While the hunt became increasingly frustrating as the hours passed, the topography never got tiring. The farmers around here must have some serious water rights because the corn was thick and the fields were green, quite the opposite of dying-of-thirst Denver.

The Porsche ran great.

She even opened it up once.

Unlike yesterday, when she was out here with Nick, she had binoculars this time. Every farm she came to got looked at good and she made notes on a map. Places with evidence of kids got a big red X; same for old-fart farmers. Places with no evidence of a van got a black X. She also took digital pictures and kept a log of where they were taken.

She had to.

Everything was starting to look the same.

She gassed up at Bob's and chatted with him for a few minutes. He couldn't remember much about the guy who took her business card, other than he seemed to be about thirty and strong looking, not in a heavy muscular way, but more in a sinewy toned way.

"No black glasses, though," he reminded her.

"Right. I understand."

By noon she needed to stretch her legs and ended up parking the Porsche under a tree on a gravel road and then taking a walk under a bright summer sky. She ate a sandwich on the way and washed it down with a warm diet Coke.

She looked around, saw no one, crinkled the can and almost threw it into the terrain. Instead she stuffed it in her back pocket.

She walked a good mile and was just about to turn around when Nick Trotter called her with some very interesting news.

IT TURNED OUT THAT HE WAS GOING IN this afternoon for another interview with Bryson Coventry.

She was shocked.

"Take me with you."

He paused. "Why?"

"Because he knows stuff about your mystery client that we don't," she said. "This is an opportunity for me to get inside."

He paused.

"He'd never fall for that."

"He doesn't know we're looking for anyone," Taylor insisted. "He'll just think I'm there as your attorney and won't have his guard up."

A pause.

"All right," he said. "But it's scheduled for 1:30. Can you make it in time?"

She looked at her watch.

12:45 p.m.

She ran towards the Porsche.

"No, but don't start until I get there."

Chapter Fifty-Six

Day Ten - July 20
Thursday Morning

NATHAN WICKERSHAM WOKE UP TIRED Thursday morning, the victim of pitching and flipping half the night, wondering what the hell he should do. No one came for him in the darkness, though.

No police.

No blackmailer.

No angry mob carrying torches.

That was encouraging.

Then he checked on Ashley Conner and was amazed at what he found. She was in a different position. She didn't respond to shaking, or pinching, but had definitely moved of her own accord at some point during the night. He was sure of it. He checked the fridge and found no missing food. The glass of water sitting on the bathroom counter was still there, untouched. So, she hadn't actually gotten out of bed, but she must have slipped out of her coma at least long enough to move her body. That was encouraging because he wanted her awake and attentive when he killed her.

It wouldn't be any fun to kill someone who was already

dead.

If she was awake by supper, he'd kill her then.

And dump her body tonight.

That way the dungeon would be free for Janelle Parker tomorrow. True, he could also kill Ashley Conner in front of the Parker woman, to get her attention. But the more he thought about it, the more he liked the idea of not having any overlap between the two women.

Play it safe.

Things were already getting squirrelly enough without further compounding the matter.

IN A PERFECT WORLD, he'd take the Janelle Parker woman on Friday night. She had a book signing scheduled to start at 8:30 at the Tattered Page Bookstore in Historic LoDo. He might have an opportunity to take her after the event when she walked to her car. The problem, though, is that the area would probably be crowded, plus the event might be over before it got dark. If that didn't work, he would probably have to take her at her house. That presented a very different set of problems.

Neither option was all that good.

On the other hand, maybe she'd surprise him and go out with friends after the signing and get drunk in a bar.

The first order of business was to scope out the area around the bookstore. So he drove down there in the afternoon, parked the Camry at Union Station and then hoofed it up Wynkoop. He found the Tattered Page Bookstore, browsed around inside for a few minutes, then walked the surrounding area thoroughly over a two hour period, until he knew every nook and cranny. The whole thing would hinge on where she parked.

While he was downtown, just for grins, he decided to walk down the 16th Street Mall and check out the ladies. One in particular attracted him, a young woman with a punk hairdo, wearing a tight white T-shirt with black lettering stenciled across huge boobs. He stared at it as he approached, wanting to read it and not caring that he was obvious. It said "You Better Make More Money Than I Can Spend."

He chuckled.

She smiled as she walked by. "You like that?"

"Very cute," he said.

Then she was gone.

From there, he drove to Janelle Parker's house and criss-crossed the neighborhood to get a better feel for it. The more familiar it became, the less anxious he was.

Then he headed back to the farm.

Excited.

If Ashley Conner was out of the coma, he'd kill her as soon as he got home. In fact, even if she wasn't, he'd still kill her. It wouldn't be as much fun, but it was time to be done with her and move on.

Daddy's coming.

Hold on.

He already knew where to dump the body.

Coventry would shit.

Wickersham wished he could be there to see his face.

Chapter Fifty-Seven

Day Ten - July 20
Thursday

DARIEN JADE DIDN'T HAVE A DRIVER'S LICENSE but Coventry let her take the 4Runner anyway so she could move some of the things from her apartment to his house. There was no way he'd let her stay anywhere alone until this whole thing was over. He had a patrol car meet her over there, just to be extra careful.

The morning turned into a flurry of motion, but only time would tell whether any of it was forward. He met with the chief and the mayor for more than an hour. In fact, he was the one who called the meeting. He wanted them in on the hunt so they couldn't second-guess things if it all went to hell. They authorized unlimited overtime for every cop in the city through Monday morning, at a minimum.

They told him that more national news teams were checking into hotels in anticipation of the weekend, even as they spoke.

More spotlights.

More scrutiny.

"If this guy hits again," the mayor said, "we can kiss a whole lot of convention business goodbye. And I'm talking about the stuff that's already booked, much less future events."

After that meeting Coventry checked in with Kubiak, who had a Ziploc bag of celery sticks on his desk.

"These are negative calories," Kubiak said. "You actually burn more calories eating them than you get."

"Just be careful you don't disappear altogether," Coventry warned.

Other than the celery information, Kubiak had nothing new to bring to the party. His team was still trying to cross-reference the faces from the two crime scene crowds, but it was turning out to be a lot harder than it looked. They had no matches so far—in fact, nothing even close.

"Concentrate on everyone," Coventry said, "even the men without glasses. It turned out that the black glasses concept was off base. Darien did see the man before, like she said, but it turns out he was legit—part of a TV crew. So the guy may or may not wear glasses."

TWO HOURS LATER, COVENTRY WAS AT HIS DESK staring at the snake plant when Kate Katona walked over. She was, as usual, dressed for the job below, wearing her weapon on a belt. "Nick Trotter's here," she said.

Shit.

He'd forgotten all about that.

He stood up, tired.

"He has a lawyer with him this time," she added.

Coventry nodded. "I would too, if I was him. I want you to sit in on this with me. You got time?"

She did.

When they walked in, Nick Trotter sat at the conference table, with a female to his left. She didn't wear lawyer clothes but did have that lawyer look of intensity in her eyes. He'd seen her somewhere before but couldn't place her. Kate seemed to recognize her too.

Then he remembered.

She was the woman from 6th and Federal who overheard the conversation about the van and black glasses.

He shook her hand.

"You still forgot all that stuff you heard, I hope."

"What stuff?"

"Exactly," Coventry said.

Nick Trotter was taken aback. "You two know each other?"

"Sort of but not really," Coventry said. Then to the woman: "I'm Bryson Coventry and this is Kate Katona."

"Taylor Sutton," the woman said. "Mr. Trotter's attorney."

Coventry stood up, leaned against the wall, looked at Nick Trotter and said: "I'm not going to read you your rights because we're not going to use anything you say against you. There are no hidden cameras or tape recorders. This is all off the record. Unless you want it recorded."

"No, that's fine."

Coventry nodded.

"Okay then," he said. "I'm just going to be honest with you. The reason you're here is because I'm getting pressure from above to make headway on this case. So I needed to do something to appease the Gods and the best thing I could think of was to call you in and make it look like I'm asking you more questions. The problem is, I don't have any more questions."

Both Nick Trotter and his attorney looked dumbfounded.

"This is harassment," Taylor Sutton said.

Coventry agreed.

"That it is," he said. "To be honest, that's why I don't want it documented."

"We could sue," Taylor added. She had a book of matches in her hand and twisted them around in her fingers.

Coventry shrugged.

"I wouldn't blame you if you did," he said. "And if you put me on the stand I'll admit it. So that's it. That's all I have. Now at least it'll look like I did something and I can get back to real work."

"Meaning the man terrorizing Denver," Taylor Sutton said.

"Exactly."

"How's that coming, by the way? Is it safe for me to start bar hopping again?"

Coventry chuckled.

"I'd hold off for a while, at least for this weekend."

"So are you getting close, or what?"

Coventry put his hands up in surrender. "It's hard to say," he said. "You do things and sit back and hope. Sometimes they work and sometimes they don't."

"That doesn't sound like anything too solid," Taylor said.

"Like I said, don't go bar hopping this weekend." He looked at Kate, didn't detect that she wanted to add anything, then looked back at Nick Trotter and his attorney.

"That's all I have," he said.

THE TWO STOOD UP AND THEY ALL SHOOK HANDS. Nick Trotter almost had his hand on the doorknob when Coventry said, "Oh, there is one more thing."

They stopped.

"I've been going back and forth in my mind as to whether you killed her or not," he said. "For a long time it wasn't sitting right in my gut one way or the other. But it's funny how things work. As I got up from my desk five minutes ago to walk back here, my gut said you did it. So here's the deal. You can tell me right now, before you walk out of this room, what happened. If you do, I'll be sure the D.A. doesn't charge you with the death penalty."

He put on a serious face.

"But if you don't," he added, "if you walk out of here and make me hunt you down, then I'll be sure you never get this opportunity again."

The woman—Taylor Sutton—stared at him.

"Screw you," she said. "You don't know anything about this man."

Then they stormed out.

And slammed the door so hard that Coventry jumped.

AFTERWARDS, FILLING UP THEIR COFFEE CUPS, Katona said: "That went well."

Coventry shrugged.

"That's the only card I had," he said. "Try to rattle him."

"Well, I don't think it worked."

He chuckled. "Apparently not."

"*Screw you,*" she added.

He laughed. "Right, screw me."

She put on an inquisitive face. "What about all that talk about your gut knowing he's guilty? Was that just smoke and mirrors?"

Good question.

"That lawyer, Taylor Sutton," he said, "followed me and Darien to Colfax Avenue last Saturday night."

Katona was shocked.

"She did?"

"Yep," he said. "Darien saw her there and then recognized her in the crowd photos that we got at 6th and Federal. She saw her hanging out down the street while we were interviewing hookers. She was leaning against a building and lighting matches, apparently. I didn't personally see her, myself."

"Why would she follow you?"

"I don't have a clue," Coventry said. "But she's up to something, and now that I know she's Nick Trotter's lawyer, I know that Nick's up to something, which means he's guilty."

"Wow."

"Major wow."

"So what are you going to do, to find out what she's up to? Get her in the sheets and make her scream out her dirty little secrets?"

Coventry considered it.

Actually, it wasn't a bad idea.

"I don't know if I'll go that far," he said. "But maybe I'll take her out for a drink."

Chapter Fifty-Eight

Day Ten - July 20
Thursday Night

LARIMER STREET AFTER DARK is a trendy mix of nightclubs, restaurants, coffee shops and chance encounters. Tonight the temperature was pretty damn nice. The scorching heat had dissipated into the thin Rocky Mountain air. Taylor Sutton meandered down the sidewalk, watching the lovers, and letting the energy of the night wash over her. Two riders on crotch-rockets popped wheelies and disappeared around the corner. She walked into a bar and found it half full, mostly with younger upwardly mobile types. More than enough guys checked her out as she came in. Vivid music spilled from high quality speakers hidden somewhere in the ceiling. She walked past a number of empty bar stools and found a cozy table for two near the back corner.

Then ordered a screwdriver.

And another.

The second one was half gone when Bryson Coventry walked in. The man was more than attractive in daylight, but now, in the dim lighting and with liquor in her gut, she found him absolutely stunning. If he asked her to stand up and take her clothes off she'd do it.

"Hey there," he said, sitting down. He raked his hair back with his fingers. It hung in place for a moment and then fell down.

A waitress appeared.

Already.

Coventry ordered a Bud Light. The waitress beamed as if that was a stroke of genius and scurried off to fetch it for him.

"You didn't dress up for me," he said. "I like that. It shows self-confidence."

He was right.

She wore shorts and a green blouse.

Nothing fancy.

She held his eyes with hers, took a sip of the screwdriver, and leaned towards him. "I know why you wanted to meet," she said. "You want to get to Nick through me. That won't happen."

The waitress showed up with the Bud Light and said, "Three-fifty." Coventry handed her a five and told her to keep the change. Then he raised the bottle and clanked Taylor's glass.

As if they were buddies.

Or lovers.

He took a long swallow, about a third of the bottle, then set it down. He looked around the room and back at her. "Do you ever get in the mood to just get seriously drunk out of your mind?"

She laughed.

"Me? Never."

"That's sort of how I feel tonight." He leaned closer to her. "You're right. I came here to pump you for information and try to get something on Nick. But now that I'm here, it seems like a low trick and I really don't care about it anymore."

Then he stared at her.

With one blue eye and one green one.

"Tell me a secret," he said. "Tell me something about you that no one else knows."

She thought about it.

Half tempted to play along.

"And then you'll do the same?" she asked.

He nodded.

"Absolutely. Fair is fair."

SHE DRAINED THE REST OF THE SCREWDRIVER, then waved the empty glass over her head until she caught the attention of the waitress. She pulled out a book of matches, lit one and watched it burn, thinking.

He watched the fire.

Waiting patiently.

"If I tell you a secret, does it stay a secret?"

"Absolutely," he said.

"So you won't tell anyone?"

"That's a promise," he said. "And you too."

"Okay," she said. "I had a client once. He was a big-shot at a brokerage house and got screwed big time. He had a legitimate claim for a lot of damages. The more I was around him the more I realized what a jerk he was. He was divorced for a couple of years. A friend of mine happened to know his former wife. It turned out he used to beat her up pretty bad, which is why she left."

The waitress returned with another screwdriver. Taylor said, "Run a tab," and sipped it.

Then lit a match.

"The bottom line is that I settled the case for a pittance," she said. "I knew I could get ten times more, but told him to take it, that he was getting a good deal. I screwed him over because he was an asshole."

Coventry clinked her glass again and drained the bottle. The waitress was back at the table before he could even set it down.

"Another one?" she asked.

"Absolutely," Coventry said. "Thanks."

Then he looked at Taylor.

"Armchair justice," he said. "It's everywhere."

"Yeah but lawyers are supposed to be above that," she said, which was true. "It undermines the entire justice system. We're supposed to be the advocates, not the judge and jury."

Coventry cocked his head.

"So would you do it again, if the same situation presented itself?"

She shrugged.

"I don't know," she said. "I'd like to think that I'd kick him out of the office and tell him I'm not interested in breathing the same air as him, instead of screwing him behind his back."

Coventry cocked his head.

"But you're not sure."

"No, I'm not," Taylor said. "Your turn."

HE GOT A DISTANT LOOK IN HIS EYE, as if going deep in thought. The waitress set another beer in front of him, smiled and left. "Okay, but remember, you can't tell anyone."

She promised.

"All right," he said. "You know Jena Vernon, the TV reporter?"

She did.

"Well," he said, "back in my high school days in Fort Collins, she was the younger sister of Matt Vernon, my best friend. She was sort of a tomboy and hung around all the time. I always had kind of a crush on her but she was three years younger so nothing ever happed, other than we'd tickle her now and then. Anyway, another one of my friends, a guy named Travis, lived on this farm that had a mountain lion in a cage, one they'd raised since it was a little cub. It was real friendly and Travis and Jena and me used to go into the cage with it and hang out, just to see how long we could stay in there before freaking out."

He took a swig of beer.

"Cool," she said.

"That's not the story though," he said. "One day Travis dares me to spend the whole night in the cage. No one had ever done that before. Jena's with me and I said I would if she would. Being the tomboy that she was, she said she would if I would. So we go there one evening just before dark. Travis opens the lock and Jena and me get in the cage. Travis locks us in and leaves. After a couple of hours the mountain lion starts to get freaked out with us being in there so long. That freaks Jena out and she's hiding behind me, wanting more than anything in the world to be out of there. Somehow we survive all the way to morning. It was the longest night of Jena's life, mine too for that matter."

She thought about it.

"So what's the secret?"

Coventry smiled.

"The secret is that I had another key to the lock in my

pocket the whole time."

"You never told her, afterwards?"

He shook his head. "She still doesn't know, to this day."

"Awesome."

Chapter Fifty-Nine

Day Ten - July 20
Thursday Afternoon

THE DRIVE FROM THE TATTERED PAGE BOOKSTORE to the farm was taking Nathan Wickersham forever. He had the radio off, concentrating on the details of the upcoming events. As soon as he got home he'd kill Ashley Conner, using his signature technique. Then he'd put her in the tub and scrub every possible trace of DNA off her lifeless little body, especially her stomach and mouth. Then, under cover of darkness later tonight, he'd dump her on Green Mountain, on the ridge above Coventry's house, right where the rattlesnake bit the lady in the face.

It would definitely be a lot of work to carry the body that far. But luckily little Ashley wasn't more than a hundred pounds soaking wet. The effort would be worth it, just to picture the look on Coventry's face.

CNN would appreciate the irony too.

As soon as he got home he took a long piss on one of the junipers in the front yard. He could have waited another ten seconds and done it in the house, but for some reason he always enjoyed pissing outside.

It brought out the caveman in him.

ONCE INSIDE HE HEADED STRAIGHT FOR THE DUNGEON to see if Ashley Conner had come out of her coma. Then something strange happened. The key wouldn't go all the way into the door lock. It went in about halfway and then seemed to hit something.

He checked to be sure he had the right key.

Yes, he did.

He tried again.

Same thing.

It wouldn't go in. It was almost as if someone had jammed something in the lock from the other side, a paper clip or splinter of wood or something.

Had Ashley Conner jammed the lock?

He pounded on the door.

No sound came from the other side.

He checked the key.

It looked okay. It didn't seem like he bent it by mistake or anything like that. He pounded on the door again. More silence.

"Ashley," he called.

No response.

He studied the door. The hinges were on the inside of the room. There was no way he could take the door off from this side.

HE RAN UPSTAIRS AND TURNED ON the dungeon monitor. Rather than getting a picture, the screen stayed black. He had a vision of Ashley Conner smashing the camera lens.

Damn it!

He should have never left her down there unchained.

Even in a coma.

He stormed back downstairs.

"Ashley," he shouted. "You want me to use a gun instead of the bag. I'm still willing to do that if you un-jam the lock right now. You can't go anywhere. You can't escape. This stupid little trick won't do anything except get me mad."

Silence.

He wasn't sure whether she heard him or not.

Maybe not.

He went out to the garage and came back with a sledge-hammer, then gave the door three solid blows.

Then he heard something.

"Go away!"

The words were barely audible.

But they were definitely words.

He pounded on the door with the sledgehammer, swinging it with all his might, not stopping until his shoulder hurt.

Breathing hard.

Out of control.

"Un-jam that lock right now!" he shouted.

"Screw you, asshole!"

Chapter Sixty

Day Eleven - July 21
Friday Morning

———————

COVENTRY SLEPT IN, WITH THE ALARM CLOCK OFF, until his body actually wanted to get up on its own accord. When he looked at the time he was shocked: 9:52 a.m. He rolled over on his back and kept his eyes closed. At first he was pissed that he slept so long and wasted so much of the day. Then he remembered he did it so he could rest up from the drinking with Taylor Sutton last night, and be in good enough shape to be on the streets until the wee hours tonight when Mr. Wacko would be out stalking his next victim.

Instead of showering he decided to run first.

Darien intercepted him in the kitchen. She looked fantastic.

"Sorry I was asleep when you got back last night," she said. "How'd it go, with the lawyer?"

Coventry cocked his head.

Good question.

"She knew what I was up to," he said, "so it took me some time to get her off guard. I'm pretty sure that she and Nick Trotter are somehow tied into this guy who's terrorizing Denver."

Darien looked shocked.

"Really?"

Coventry nodded.

"Don't ask me how I know," he said, "or even why I think it, but I do." She wore one of his long-sleeved shirts. He lifted it up, squeezed her ass and headed for the front door. "I'll be back in a half hour."

THE JOG MADE HIM REALIZE that he hadn't had a good workout in over a week. There was a time, at one point in his life, when he got to the gym five days a week, no matter what. He really needed to get back into that routine before he got soft. He needed to improve his eating habits too.

He let his legs stretch and his lungs burn.

The sun felt good and so did the sweat.

When he passed Kyffin Elementary the playground was empty. So he did three sets of pull-ups on the monkey bars and then did pushups and sit-ups in the sand.

When he got back he smelled pancakes and heard Darien moving around in the kitchen. "You're going to undo everything I just did," he shouted from the next room, heading to the shower.

"I'll work it off you later," she hollered back.

HE DROPPED DARIEN OFF with Jena Vernon and went straight to headquarters. When he got there he couldn't believe his eyes. The FBI profiler—Dr. Leanne Sanders—sat at his desk going through files.

She looked at her watch as he walked over.

"Rough night?" she asked.

He ignored it and gave her a huge bear hug, actually lifting her a full foot off the ground. "You came," he said.

She looked exactly as he remembered her from the David Hallenbeck case: about fifty, dressed to intimidate, step-master legs encased in nylons, and a diamond on her left hand the size of a small planet. Definitely not in the crime game because she needed the money.

She put on a serious look.

"Don't get too excited," she said. "I don't have any brilliant ideas."

"You will," Coventry said.

"One thing I did note," she added, "relates to the work that Paul Kubiak's doing, trying to match the two crime scene crowds to see if the same face is in both places."

"Right."

"We have a software program where we can take an off-center shot of a face and rotate it to the front—all the way around, actually—so you can see it from whatever angle you want. If Paul takes all the faces from the crowds and converts them to front shots, it might be easier to find a match."

Coventry grinned.

"See," he said, "you already earned lunch."

UNFORTUNATELY, THE SOFTWARE PROGRAM not only worked well, it also worked fast. Within three hours they had their answer.

The same face wasn't in both crowds.

Another dead end.

"This guy's giving me a headache," he told Leanne.

Chapter Sixty-One

Day Eleven - July 21
Friday

———————————

TAYLOR SUTTON DEVOTED ALL FRIDAY to her neglected law practice, shoring up the cases that were in the most danger of washing away. It almost killed her to sit in a chair that long but she had no choice.

At seven o'clock, long after Claudia left, she opened the safe and pulled out the Smith & Wesson handgun, together with the concealed weapon permit and a box of bullets.

She checked the clip.

It was full.

She checked the action.

The gun seemed to be in perfect condition.

She shoved everything in her purse and locked the office behind her. She went home, ate a few pieces of fruit, worked out at 24 Hour Fitness and went back home to shower. As twilight set in, she hopped in the Porsche, threw her purse on the passenger seat and headed downtown.

On the hunt for a killer.

THE MEETING WITH COVENTRY LAST NIGHT at the bar had been productive, well worth the effort. It took her a while to get him off guard, but his tongue loosened up after a few beers.

From what she could tell, Coventry had no idea that the man terrorizing Denver lived on a farm, much less the general location of it. So Sarah's body seemed safe from discovery, at least for the time being. In fact, Coventry's hunt overall didn't appear to be going very well.

He confirmed that the man was driving a van.

But told her that the information she overheard about the black glasses was, in hindsight, misplaced. The man may or may not wear glasses.

BY THE TIME SHE ARRIVED AT LARIMER SQUARE the street-lights were on. With no Rockies game tonight, parking places weren't as scarce as normal and she managed to find an empty space in a lot on Blake Street.

She wore the shortest shorts she could find, showing plenty of leg. Up top she had a skimpy tank top. She also wore tennis shoes, laced tight, in case she needed to run. A long blond wig completed the picture. She looked young and sexy.

Perfect bait.

With the purse over her shoulder, she headed to the darker areas, where clubbers were forced to park after all the good places were taken.

Her plan was to draw in the van.

Get a look at the guy.

And get a license plate number.

Chapter Sixty-Two

AFTER CIRCLING AROUND FOR A LONG TIME, Nathan Wickersham finally spotted Janelle Parker's blue Tacoma—FOTOG—in a lot on Blake Street. By some miracle the space next to her car was actually open. He stepped on the gas to get there two seconds before a red Porsche, then looked around for surveillance cameras as he went to the box to pay.

There were none.

Then he hoofed it over to the Tattered Page Bookstore.

At 9:10 the sky still had some light in it but not much. In fact, half the streetlights had already kicked on.

When he got to the bookstore, as before, Janelle Parker was already into her slide presentation. She wore expensive black pants, leather pumps and a white short-sleeve shirt. She talked energetically, in a good mood, and had the audience hanging on every word.

Photography nuts.

She looked great.

It almost amazed him that she would be his.

Life could definitely be worth living at times.

In a perfect world, though, Ashley Conner would be dead. This afternoon he drilled through the keyhole with a ½" carbon drill bit in hopes of freeing the lock mechanism. That didn't work and a phone call to the door manufacturer confirmed that drilling couldn't defeat the lock.

"It's a security door," they reminded him. "Our very best."

So he decided that the best way to break into the dungeon would be to rent or buy a powerful enough torch to cut a hole in the door. He didn't want to do that, however, until he had a replacement door. So he ordered one this morning and it would be delivered on Monday. Then Ashley Conner would die, but not before he taught her a lesson.

HE WENT BACK TO BLAKE STREET with his hands in his pockets and wandered around the fringes of the parking lot, just to be absolutely sure there were no surveillance cameras. In the dark it was hard to tell, but it didn't seem like there was much in the area that anyone would want to keep an eye on.

He had mixed emotions about bringing the van instead of the Camry. The integrity of the van may have been compromised last week when Coventry's woman seemed to recognize him on Speer Boulevard. She must have remembered his face from the encounter in the stairwell of the apartment building, when he walked down with Alicia Beach's news crew and she walked up with a bag of groceries.

Coventry might be on the lookout for a van.

But not a Camry.

Still, the van offered greater security. All he had to do was get the woman inside and get the door shut. She could be totally conscious and screaming like a madman after that but it wouldn't make any difference.

She couldn't get out.

No one would hear her.

But with the Camry, he would probably have to knock her out. Then either get her in the trunk or into the back seat and put a blanket over her. In the process of knocking her out there was a chance he'd kill her.

And he needed her alive.

HE WAITED IN THE SHADOWS ACROSS THE STREET. He wore a dark blue, loose-fitting Abercrombie & Fitch sweatshirt and jeans. An eight-inch serrated knife lay hidden under the A&F.

His heart pounded.

He had to be careful with the woman.

She had to be every bit of five-nine, maybe even five-ten, and had the body of a surfer or a volleyball player. If they ended up in a wrestling match or a physical struggle, she'd be able to fend him off for a while.

And make lots of noise in the meantime.

His watch said 9:52.

She shouldn't be much longer.

The conditions were right.

There were no lights in the parking lot.

The surrounding lights were minimal.

Not many people around.

He saw her a block off, walking towards the parking lot, carrying an oversized briefcase, probably filled with books or literature.

He scooted over to the van and opened the side door a

crack, just enough so that he could slide it back effortlessly and throw her in. Then he went around to the rear and crouched in the dark, with his heart racing.

He slipped on latex gloves and then pulled out the knife and held it in his right hand.

Her footsteps became audible.

He swallowed hard.

Then looked around one last time and saw no one.

When he heard her keys rattle, he jumped.

HE HAD THE KNIFE IN FRONT OF HER FACE before she even knew he was there. "Don't make a sound!" he warned.

She froze.

Perfectly quiet.

Then her body jerked and a terrible pain exploded in his groin. The bitch kneed him!

She screamed and turned to run, but he got a handful of hair and pulled as hard as he could. Her head snapped back and she fell to the ground.

He punched her face.

Then again.

And again.

Unable to stop.

The little bitch!

Then he heard a man's voice, not far away, coming fast in his direction: "Hey, what's going on?"

Wickersham stood up.

"Help," he said. "This woman had a seizure or something."

When the man bent down to take a look, Wickersham stuck the knife in his back and twisted. The man made an awful sound, twitched for a few seconds and then stopped moving. Wickersham grabbed the man's wallet, wedding ring and watch. Then he picked up the woman, threw her in the back of the van and got the hell out of there.

Chapter Sixty-Three

Day Eleven - July 21
Friday Night

AS THE DESERT SHOT BY at over a hundred miles an hour, the man went back to running a finger ever so teasingly up and down the inside of the woman's thigh. Then finally, after an eternity, he touched her where it counted, with that magic rhythm of his.

The road went on, perfectly straight.

The heat built up between her thighs and her hips gyrated with a mind of their own, getting the most from his contact.

They crested a hill. Then . . .

Shit!

They were on the wrong side of the road.

Headlights came directly at them.

Another car.

There was no time to get back in their lane.

They were going to crash head-on.

She clenched the steering wheel with all her might and stared at the lights. Then, just before impact, she shut her eyes as tight as they would go and screamed . . .

THE ONCOMING VEHICLE VEERED AND SWEPT BY so close that the woman actually felt their car get sucked over towards the vacuum. It was at that exact nanosecond that she realized that they hadn't crashed and that they wouldn't. She opened her eyes and saw that she was even farther on the wrong side of the road and now veering onto the shoulder.

She slammed on the brakes and brought every muscle in her leg to bear down. Her body immediately lunged towards the windshield and then abruptly jolted when the seatbelt snagged her. The man flew into the dashboard, shouting. The cooler pounded into the back of her seat and things flew through the air. Somehow she fixed her eyes on the rearview mirror and saw the red taillights of the other car rolling over and over, in the process of a violent crash even as she watched.

The vehicle eventually muscled itself to a stop.

It took her several seconds to process the fact that the movement had actually ceased and that she could lighten up on the brake pedal.

The man pushed himself off the dash, opened the door, and fell outside, as if wanting to be anywhere in the world except inside that car. He smacked the ground and shouted, "Goddamn it!"

The CD still played as if nothing had happened. The woman fumbled with the controls, turning the sound up even louder before she managed to turn it off.

The smell of spilled wine and beer permeated the interior. Outside, a cloud of desert dust rose up around the car, looking like smoke where the headlights cut through it.

She turned the engine off and stepped outside.

"Are you okay?" the man asked.

Her neck felt a little weird, as if it might have been whiplashed, and she rolled it around to test the motion. When she turned it to the left, the muscles on the right side felt like they were being pulled overly tight. That wasn't normal, but wasn't serious.

"Yeah, I'm fine. You?"

He had a minor cut on his forehead that he was padding dry with his shirtsleeve. Otherwise, he was fine.

Their vehicle didn't have a scratch.

The man walked off the road and took a few steps into the darkness. A few seconds later, she heard him urinating on the ground.

"That scared the piss right out of me," he said.

THE WOMAN FELT THE SAME WAY. For whatever reason, the wine was suddenly going right through her. She staggered into the desert. The attempt at movement, after having been stuck in a seat for more than an hour, made her realize just how much the wine and pot had screwed her up. She squatted down, feet wide, and pissed in the dirt, looking back down the road for evidence of the other car. It wasn't visible, hiding behind the crest of the road.

The man was calling her now, standing impatiently by the passenger door, his voice intense. "Come on," he said. "We got to get the hell out of here."

"What do you mean? Just leave?"

"Hell yes, just leave. Before the cops show up or something."

There was no way she could do that.

"We got to go back, they got to be hurt."

"We screwed up, in case you didn't notice. If we get busted, we're in some serious shit. We need to get our asses out of here, right this second."

"No, we're not leaving. Get in the car," she said.

He slammed the fender with his hand.

"Bad idea. You mark my words."

DISORIENTED, SHE FUMBLED AROUND to find the ignition, then remembered it was located to the left of the steering wheel, not the right, found it and cranked the engine over while the man shoved the cooler back into place.

She turned the vehicle around and doubled back.

As soon as they reached the crest in the road, she expected to see the red taillights of the other vehicle. Instead, the other car faced them, with one headlight pointing at them and the other one not working. The vehicle was stationary, about a half mile or more down the road.

She continued driving in that direction with a queasy feeling in her stomach, the kind she got when she was a kid standing in the roller-coaster line as it got shorter and shorter.

The other car had flipped over more than once, but landed right-side up, in the dirt not more than ten feet off the road. She pulled up about thirty feet short, shifted the vehicle into neutral, put the emergency brake on, and left the engine running, just in case they had to get out of there in a hurry.

They stepped out and walked hesitantly towards the other vehicle. Everything was cemetery quiet.

"BMW," the man said. His long hair looked like a mane, backlit by the headlights.

"Yeah," she said, recognizing the signatory double ovals in

the front end.

As they walked past the headlight of the other car, to where it didn't blind them anymore, they saw a female, on the passenger side of the vehicle, hanging halfway through the windshield with her head and torso on the hood of the car and her legs still inside. She was alive and staring straight at them, in obvious pain. Her eyes followed them as they moved. Every part of her looked dead, except her eyes.

The sight forced the driver's stomach into her mouth. She turned and ran ten or twenty steps, then dropped to her knees and vomited in the dirt. It was one those violent uncontrolled regurgitations, a merciless one that shot out of her mouth and nose at the same time. She gasped for air, then wretched again. The whole world smelled like putrid wine.

When she finally got herself together and came back to the wreck, the man had the driver's door of the BMW open.

"You don't want to see this," he warned her.

But he was wrong.

She did.

She had to.

A MAN, NO DOUBT THE FATHER, WAS BLOODIED and dead in the driver's seat. Airbags had deployed from numerous locations but now hung flat and empty. In the back seat, three girls—two with blond hair and one with raven black hair—lay in a heap of flesh. The woman guessed that none of them were older than ten.

"The driver's dead and so are the kids," the man told her.

She trembled. "You checked?"

He nodded.

"Yeah, there's no question," he added.

They turned their attention to the mother. She was staring at them and they could tell that she was trying to say something but couldn't.

The woman could read her thoughts though.

Tears filled her eyes.

This couldn't really be happening.

Ten minutes ago everything was perfect.

SHE RAN OVER TO THE CAR, rummaged around until she found her purse, pulled her cell phone out and opened it.

No signal.

"Damn it!"

There was no way they could call for help.

She pulled her blouse up to wipe her eyes, realizing that she was smearing mascara all over it and wondering if she could really be so petty to even let a thought like that enter her mind at a time like this.

She disgusted herself.

She looked at the man. "What do we do?" she asked, desperate for an answer.

He shook his head, uncertain.

Seconds went by and neither of them said anything.

"Should we put her in the car?"

The man answered immediately. "No. She's too messed up to move. She could have a broken back for all we know."

That was true.

There was only one other thing she could think of. "You drive to a phone. I'll stay here with her."

The man shifted feet.

"And then what?" he questioned.

"Call for help. What do you think?"

"Bad idea, very bad idea."

"Why?"

"Because first of all, it won't do any good. She's going to die, anyway. Look at her. And, if she does live by some miracle, then what?"

"What do you mean?"

"Think about it," he said. "She lives in a world that has no husband or kids. She lives in a world with a body that's all messed up, maybe even paralyzed or something. Do you really think she wants that?"

The woman screamed in frustration and pounded her fists on her legs.

Shit!

"If I was her, I'd just want to get it over with, right here, right now. I'd just want to be out of my stinking misery."

Oh my God.

Then, before she knew it, he was out in the desert, walking around, looking for something. She saw him bend down and pick something up. When he got back he was holding a rock the size of a softball.

He grabbed her by the arm, just above the elbow, and squeezed. "One good blow," he said. "Right on the top of the head. She'll never feel a thing. It's the most merciful thing we can do."

She backed away from him.

"No," she said. "We need to get help."

The man kicked the dirt.

"She's seen our faces," he said.

SUDDENLY HEADLIGHTS FLICKERED in the desert, still a long way off, small and dim, but definitely heading in their direction. The man walked towards the wreck.

Rock in hand.

"Get in the car and turn it around," he said over his shoulder. "Hurry!"

SOMETHING SHOOK THE WOMAN VIOLENTLY. She woke up enough to tell she was in a dark bedroom and that someone was frantically trying to wake her from a nightmare.

The man.

"Same dream again?" he asked.

She rolled onto her back and breathed heavily. "Yes." She rested her hands on her stomach and realized she was drenched in sweat.

"It'll be over soon," the man said. "Go back to sleep."

She closed her eyes.

If only it had been just a dream.

Instead of a memory.

Chapter Sixty-Four

Day Twelve - July 22
Saturday Morning

BRYSON COVENTRY CUT HIS SHOWER down to three minutes, popped in his contacts, threw on jeans and a button-down
cotton shirt, and dashed past Darien's sleeping body with his
hair so wet that it still dripped.

No time for cereal or coffee.

He threw the morning paper, three granola bars, a banana
and an empty thermos in the passenger seat of the 4Runner and
then squealed out of Green Mountain to the 6th Avenue freeway.

Heading directly east, the sun broke over the horizon just as
he came to Wadsworth and set about blinding him as best it
could. He put the visor all the way down but still had to squint
from the glare off the hood. There were no sunglasses in the
vehicle, of course, because there was some kind of law that he
had to either sit on them or lose them within twenty-four hours.
In fact, the more expensive they were, the faster he was obli-
gated to do something stupid to them. Cars shot past him doing
eighty, reminding Coventry how he was going to die.

He knew Shalifa Netherwood was asleep but called her any-

317

way.

She didn't answer.

He called Dr. Leanne Sanders, the FBI profiler.

She didn't answer either.

The radio spit out the voice of an incredibly awake morning disc jockey who talked faster than Coventry's brain was working. He listened for a few moments, decided that if the guy was a dog he would be French Poodle, and punched him off.

He turned his attention back to the traffic just in time to see that he was about to rear-end the last vehicle in a string of cars that had come to a stop in front of him.

Shit!

He slammed on the brakes and braced himself while the antilocks grinded and mashed, trying to see how many people were in the car ahead.

The 4Runner miraculously managed to bring its bulk to an uneventful stop and still have two or thee inches to spare. He immediately thanked Toyota for equipping the vehicle with sticky tires. The person in the car in front of him, an African American man, powered down his window, stuck his arm all the way out and gave him the finger.

Coventry waved apologetically and said, "Sorry, it's one of those mornings," just in case the man was a lip reader.

JUST THEN DR. LEANNE SANDERS PHONED HIM. "You called me," she said.

She sounded asleep.

"Right."

She must have detected something in his voice because she asked, "What's wrong?"

"Nothing," he said. "Except I just got the bird and deserved it."

"The bird?"

"Yeah, you know, the finger."

"Oh, that bird," she said.

"Yeah, the Colorado State Bird. Listen, can you meet me at Blake and 19th?"

"When?"

"Now."

He stopped at the 7-Eleven on Broadway. Inside, "Don't Worry Baby" spilled out of speakers with more treble than bass. Coventry filled the thermos, grabbed two Styrofoam cups and pulled into the Blake Street parking lot seven minutes later. As he suspected, the blue Tacoma pickup was still there and, in fact, was the only vehicle in the lot besides one other parked about fifteen spaces down, an older model Chevy sedan. Coventry just finished running the plates when Leanne Sanders showed up, looking confused.

"What are we doing here?" she asked.

He filled one of the Styrofoam cups with coffee and handed it to her.

"Hunting," he said.

HE TOLD HER HIS THEORY. An unidentified man was stabbed in the back here last night. Detective Richardson drew the case and conducted the initial investigation. Every indication pointed to a garden-variety robbery gone bad. Coventry swung by the scene near midnight just to see what was going on, didn't stay for more than thirty minutes, and concurred with Richardson's assessment.

"They found a briefcase here. Inside were eight copies of a book called *Denver After Dark*. I couldn't get it out of my head," he told her. "Why would the dead guy have ten copies of the same book? So I came down this morning to see what cars were still in the lot, found these two, and ran the plates." He sipped the coffee. "That Chevy over there is registered to one David Poindexter. My guess is that he's the dead guy."

Leanne nodded.

Starting to get interested.

"This car here," Coventry said, kicking the tire of the Tacoma, "is registered to one Janelle Parker. Coincidentally, she's the author of the book. Her picture's on the back of it and guess what?"

"What?"

"She's hot."

He paused as Leanne retreated in thought.

"So," he continued, "I could see how she'd have ten copies of her book with her, but the dead guy wouldn't. Meaning she was here. She was the one carrying the briefcase. But her car's still here, meaning she made it to this spot, but never made it into her car."

"So you think our friend took her?"

Coventry nodded.

"She's gone and there's a dead guy on the ground. My guess, a Good Samaritan who came over to help."

Leanne looked doubtful. "That doesn't fit the profile," she said. "This place isn't secluded enough for his taste. It's too risky. Think about it. Ashley Conner was a dark alley. Jennifer Holland was a breakdown on an offbeat road."

Coventry shrugged.

"Maybe he knows that's where we were looking for him. So

he shifted over to where we weren't."

SUDDENLY HIS CELL PHONE RANG. A man's voice came through, disguised, the same voice that called last week. "Do you want to know her name?"

"No thanks," Coventry said, and hung up.

He must have had a look on his face because Leanne stared at him.

"Tell me that wasn't him," she said.

He shifted feet.

"It was," he told her.

"And you hung up on him."

He nodded. "I did."

She frowned. "We talked about this. I thought we were on the same page."

He looked at her, hard, understanding her point of view, but wanting her to understand his as well. "I'm not going to play games with this guy," he said. "I won't give him the satisfaction."

Chapter Sixty-Five

Day Twelve - July 22
Saturday

THIS TIME, WHEN NICK TROTTER FIRED HER ASS, Taylor
Sutton knew deep down that that was that. The decision was
irreversible. In hindsight, she shouldn't have told him about
going out last night dressed as bait. He didn't understand that
she was actually safe and could take care of herself.

"This is too much, Taylor," he said. "Even for you. I don't
even know who you are anymore."

She didn't blame him.

Maybe he was right.

Maybe she'd turned herself into a crime junkie.

Maybe the whole thing was a way to pump excitement into
her life.

If Nick didn't know who she was anymore, she wasn't sure
she did either.

She worked at the office all day.

Then went home and slept.

She woke up at eight, threw supper in the microwave, and
then got herself looking all soft and feminine. Now it was Saturday night, time to forget everything and get laid.

SHE STARTED WITH SCREWDRIVERS at The Supreme Court, got bored, and headed over to an insanely upbeat nightclub in LoDo where the music was louder and the bodies were sweatier.

Much better.

She ordered a drink, downed it, and headed straight for the dance floor. The music controlled her. She was nothing more than a slave, twisting at its whim, unable to remember if another reality even existed. She went with it, letting it wash over her, taking her. A body came behind her, grinding on her from behind, moving with her. She didn't turn around, not caring who it was, just enjoying the touch. A hand reached from behind and held her stomach, directly on her skin, caressing her abdomen as she gyrated. She looked down and saw it was a woman's hand. She guided it up to her breast, never missing a beat, and bit her lower lip.

She hadn't had a woman in years.

And now wondered why.

She turned around, looked into mysterious green eyes, immediately fell in love, and kissed soft full lips, as if it was the last kiss she'd ever give.

Deep and sensuous.

THREE ORGASMS LATER, TIRED AS HELL and nearly asleep at the wheel, she drove down her street, almost ready to turn into her driveway, when a yellow light popped out of the darkness up ahead. It looked like a single firecracker, no more than four or five feet off the ground, appearing from out of nowhere and then gone just as fast.

By the time she registered it as gunfire the windshield of the Porsche exploded.

Chapter Sixty-Six

ASLEEP ON THE GROUND in the barn, Wickersham woke when his nervous system detected something wrong with his face. His brain slowly came to life, enough to realize that his lips tickled. He reached up to scratch them and felt a rough object, something that shifted when he touched it. Something alive. He instinctively brushed it with his hand. It moved, but not all the way off, and curled up. A snake! He wrapped his fingers around it and threw. A piece of flesh broke away from his index finger as the reptile shot through the air.

He jumped up.

He was in the barn. The snake was ten feet away, curled up in a defensive posture, waving its head in the air and hissing at him. A rattlesnake! He chopped it in half with a shovel and watched both halves twist until they stopped. On closer examination he found it was a bull snake.

Shit.

He opened the door of the van and confirmed that Janelle Parker was still there, as she should be, chained and drugged. Last night he decided that was the safest place to keep her. He slept next to the van, on the ground, just to be absolutely sure she didn't escape.

He threw the snake in the woods and then went to the house for a shower and coffee as the sun broke over the tree line to the east.

WHEN HE CAME BACK THE WOMAN WAS AWAKE. He had removed her pants, panties, socks and shoes last night but she still wore the white shirt.

"I need to use the facilities," she said. "Bad."

"Shut up."

He cuffed her hands behind her back, put on leg shackles, and walked her into the house. He didn't care if she saw the place because she wasn't going to live to tell anyone. In the master bathroom he let her use the toilet as he stood there and watched. Because of Ashley Conner, no one would ever get any leniency again.

"Is that better?" he asked.

"Yes, thanks."

He smiled.

"Good. Come on, let's get some food."

He walked her into the kitchen and had her sit on a bar stool at the island while he made scrambled eggs. Then, with her hands still cuffed behind her back, he fed her and gave her coffee. They chatted, almost as if old friends. Wickersham knew she was trying to get information to help her escape, or at least figure out how to ingratiate herself so he wouldn't kill her.

He didn't give a shit.

Let her try.

He pulled the other bar stool next to hers, so close that they almost touched, and sat down. Then he put his arm around her shoulders. They were full of muscles and reminded him to be careful.

"The reason you're here," he said, "is that someone wants you dead. I have nothing against you. I don't want to hurt you in any way and, so long as you cooperate, I won't. What I need you to do is tell me who wants you dead."

She looked at him.

Mystified.

"Me? Someone wants me dead?"

Wickersham nodded.

"No one," she said. "I don't have an enemy in the world. You have the wrong person."

Wickersham shook his head, sadly, as if contemplating what he'd be forced to do if she didn't cooperate. "You need to help me," he said, "so I can help you."

THEY TALKED FOR A LONG TIME before finally, together, figuring it out. It related to what she saw in the desert last month.

She camped about a quarter mile off the road, up on a ridge, in a primitive Nevada topography east of Las Vegas. Three cameras sat on tripods, pointed at different parts of the valley, set to continuous exposure to capture the movement of the starlight above the desert floor. They'd be great shots for her upcoming book, *Secrets of the Desert.*

At some point during the night, squealing tires woke her from a deep sleep.

She looked over just in time to see a vehicle roll several times and coast to a stop. Then it sat there, motionless, with one headlight and both taillights still on.

Not a sound came from it.

Or a movement.

She grabbed the binoculars.

Another car doubled back. A man and woman got out. She could see the woman clearly through the binoculars, but the man never had his face to her. All she could tell about him was that he had extremely long hair, down his back, and moved like he was young.

He bashed the passenger's head in with a rock.

Then they took off.

She went down to the scene and found everyone dead. Then drove to the nearest town and filed a police report. The police had her work with a sketch artist and she was able give them a very good composite of the female.

She actually saw the female on the 16th Street Mall last week. She even followed her to see where she went, to get an address or license plate number or something, but lost her.

Wickersham smiled.

"Now we're getting somewhere," he said.

Chapter Sixty-Seven

Day Thirteen - July 23
Sunday

BRYSON COVENTRY PUT THE ARMRESTS into a death grip as the Learjet pushed him back in the seat with serious G's and then shot up into a black sky at an incredibly steep angle.

"You should see your face," Leanne said.

Coventry didn't even respond.

Sweat dripped into his eyes.

After a few seconds he craned his neck and looked out the window. The night lights of Denver were disappearing at an alarming rate. Then they vanished altogether as the aircraft pushed west over the Rocky Mountains.

Darien, sitting in the window seat, leaned around Coventry and said to Leanne: "He's such a baby sometimes."

Leanne chuckled.

"You have no idea," she said.

Coventry looked first at Darien, then at Leanne and said, "Hey, guys, I'm right here. I can hear what you're saying." Then he concentrated on the sounds and movement of the plane, searching for that inevitable telltale sign of a malfunction that would plunge them to their death at any second.

But minutes passed and they still didn't fall out of the sky.

"Next time we're driving," he said.

Darien leaned around him again and said to Leanne: "I was hoping to join the Mile High Club, but I think the little guy's too scared to come out and play."

"Hey, I'm right here. Remember? And so is the little guy."

Fifteen minutes went by and he started to calm down, at least enough to communicate. "I talked to the chief yesterday about our idea," he told Leanne. He was referring to the plan that he and Leanne came up with to draw the killer out. "He nixed it," Coventry added. "I knew he would. He's too conservative. We should have just done it and asked for forgiveness afterwards."

Leanne nodded.

"That doesn't surprise me."

They were the only three people in the aircraft, an FBI charter. Coventry sat with Darien on one side of the aisle. He wouldn't leave her in Denver alone. The FBI profiler, Dr. Leanne Sanders, sat on the other side of the aisle. On the seat next to her sat yesterday's edition of the San Francisco Chronicle.

Page 8 of that newspaper had a short story about a body that washed up on the beach. The head of that body had a plastic bag over it, duct taped at the neck.

BY THE TIME THEY LANDED IN SAN FRANCISCO dawn was breaking. Coming back down to earth wasn't nearly as frightening as leaving it, until they entered a fogbank so thick that Coventry tightened his seatbelt six or seven times.

After they landed without dying, they took a cab to the

homicide department of the SFPD and met with a detective by the name of Merle Brown.

Merle reminded them it was Sunday.

He usually didn't work on Sundays.

Since the body just washed up recently, a positive identification hadn't been made yet. The body had suffered serious decomposition and it looked as if every small fish this side of Hawaii had taken a nibble out of it. At this point they'd need to review dental records to get a solid identification. But a bracelet still present on the left wrist of the body matched the description of the one worn by a young woman named Tess Singer, who disappeared on March 18th.

So Coventry and Leanne went through her missing person's file, a thin manila folder that didn't tell much of a story. The woman was finishing up her senior year at Berkeley, majoring in mathematics. She walked out of her apartment one evening to buy a few snacks at a convenience store two blocks down the street and never made it there.

She had no enemies.

No one saw anything.

She was never seen or heard from again.

Very baffling indeed.

THEY VIEWED THE BODY, ate lunch in China Town and then wandered over to Fisherman's Wharf and watched seagulls fight each other for scraps of food. The minute one of them got something in its mouth it would fly off. Three or four others would give immediate chase, trying to steal it in mid flight.

"Survival of the fittest," Coventry said.

On the flight back to Denver, Coventry told Leanne: "We

need to get airline manifests from Denver to San Francisco, particularly roundtrips that include March 18th."

She nodded. "I already have it in motion."

He scratched his head.

"I'm confused," he said. "Are you one step ahead of me or am I one step behind?"

Chapter Sixty-Eight

Day Thirteen - July 23
Sunday

TAYLOR SUTTON STAYED AWAKE ALL NIGHT looking out the front window, gun in hand, waiting for the shooter to show back up.

Hoping he would.

He was a bad shot and she was still alive. Sitting there alone in the dark and thinking about it, she found it incredible that her entire existence hinged on such a little fact.

He didn't show back up.

And she finally fell asleep on the floor of her living room just as sunrise broke.

She woke at noon, her body achy from the hard carpet, and went to the garage to survey the Porsche by the light of day. The bullet had entered the windshield on the passenger side and exited through the back glass. The shooter must have used a handgun because it would be hard to miss with a rifle at that distance.

How long had he waited for her out there in the darkness?

A long time apparently.

Plus there'd been no assurance she would even come home,

especially on a Saturday night. Obviously the guy didn't know her very well.

She fired up the coffee machine and opened the Sunday paper. The front-page news startled her. Apparently the story about the man killed in the Blake Street parking lot on Friday night was deeper than it first appeared. Now, it seems, the police believed that the next victim had been abducted from the parking lot. The dead man, they theorized, tried to stop it and got killed in the process.

She set the paper down.

Her hands shook.

That's the same parking lot where she parked on Friday night.

She came back to the Porsche about 9:40 to get a couple of more books of matches. The man got killed shortly after that.

Had she been followed?

Had she been the intended target?

Had someone come to get her and ended up taking the other woman by default?

SHE TOOK A CAB TO THE BUDGET ON COLFAX AVENUE, rented a Mustang and then headed over to Nick Trotter's place. He had a right to know about the gunshot last night.

If she was in imminent danger then he probably was too.

Chapter Sixty-Nine

Day Thirteen - July 23
Sunday Night

AFTER DARK, WITH JANELLE PARKER safely pumped full of sleeping pills and securely chained inside the van, Nathan Wickersham hopped in the Camry to pay a little visit to the lovely photographer's house. If she told the truth, she had her own personal copy of the composite sketch of the driver that she helped the Nevada cops create. Also, if she told the truth, that composite sketch was folded in thirds and holding a place in a novel. That novel sat on a shelf in her bedroom, sandwiched between other books that he could care less about.

When he drove by her house he saw yellow police tape on the front door. Good. That meant the cops had already been there and wouldn't be walking in on him.

He parked the car four streets away and doubled back on foot, dressed in all things black. From the sidewalk he snuck into the bushes at the side of the house and hung there, looking and listening.

He slipped on the latex gloves.

And took the knife out of the sheath.

Just in case.

Then he walked briskly to the back door, used her key to enter, and stepped inside.

There were no sounds.

No movements.

No lights.

He locked the door behind him, waited for over a minute while his eyes adjusted to the darkness, and then headed deeper into the house.

IN THE LIVING ROOM a copy of the woman's book sat on the coffee table in front of the couch. Lots of loose eight-by-ten color photos were scattered on the table as well. They were nighttime desert scenes, probably taken during her Nevada shoot last month.

Then he had a neat idea.

Take something that the cops would later recognize as gone.

Just to screw with them.

Rub their faces in the fact that he was here.

Suddenly he had an even better idea and switched the positions of a white chair and a black one. He danced in the middle of it all—a rock star on stage—as he pictured the look on their faces the next time they came in. If only he could be there to watch.

In the kitchen he found a bowl of fruit. He grabbed a few grapes and then headed over to the stairs that led to the upper level. They creaked as he walked up.

The novel was right where it was supposed to be. Inside was a piece of paper folded in thirds. He stepped into the closet, closed the door and then looked at it with a small flashlight.

Bingo.

A composite sketch of a woman.

She looked vaguely familiar but he couldn't place her.

When he stepped out of the closet he heard a noise downstairs and froze.

Shit!

Someone was in the house!

HE SLIPPED UNDER THE BED as quietly as he could. The fit was coffin tight with hardly any breathing room. He already knew that staying there too long would drive him nuts.

Voices came from downstairs.

A man and a woman.

He recognized the man's voice.

Bryson Coventry.

He must have come back to have another look around.

Don't panic.

Just stay calm.

You can take him in a fight.

Plus you'll have the element of surprise.

He could make out their conversation now. Hey, what are you doing?—we're here on business. *Maybe you are.* Stop that. *I'm going to be a bad girl tonight.* Oh, really, how bad? *You'll see.* Why, what are you going to do? *You'll see, just be ready for it. And don't let me down.* Have I ever? *Don't even go there.* Name one time I ever let you down. *Am I in the Mile High Club? Hah! Gotcha!* Yeah, well, there wasn't any place to do it anyway. *Leanne would have closed her eyes. Hell, she might have even joined in. Would that have bothered you?* I don't know, maybe yes, maybe no. What are those? *What do they look like?* They look like scarves. *There you go, five scarves.* What are they for? *Let me put it this way, only one is for a blindfold.* Are you getting kinky on me? *I told you, I'm going to be a bad girl tonight, and don't disappoint me.*

A few minutes later they walked into the bedroom.

"Leave the lights off," the woman said.

They kissed.

The woman's clothes dropped to the floor one garment at a time. Then she sat on the bed, raised her feet off the floor and fussed with something. When her feet came back down she had scarves tied around her ankles. Then more fussing, and Wickersham pictured her tying scarves on her wrists.

She got on the bed.

"Okay, fasten me down," she said.

Coventry swallowed.

"This is nuts. You are being bad, aren't you?"

"Totally. Blindfold me too."

There was lots of motion on the bed, then Coventry said: "Okay you bad girl. Try to escape."

The bed wiggled.

"I can't."

"Such a predicament," Coventry said. "I think I've created a monster."

"Yes you have."

"Let's see how much I can turn this monster on using just one finger."

WICKERSHAM LAY THERE, UNDER THE BED, as quiet as he could, while Coventry slowly worked on the woman's body above him, not more than two feet away. He could actually sense the woman moving to increasingly deeper levels of arousal.

They didn't talk.

Their breathing filled the room.

Wickersham hung on every sound.

In his pants a raging hard-on sprung to life.

Then Coventry said, "Ah, crap. I left my wallet in the car."

"So?"

"So that's where the condom is, sweetie. You want a happy ending, right?" He hopped off the bed and headed out of the room. "Be back in a jiffy," he said. "Don't do anything without me."

"Real funny."

Wickersham slid out from under the bed and stood up, quieter than a cemetery. He tiptoed to the corner, unplugged a small lamp and took off the shade. When Coventry walked back into the room, Wickersham hit him so hard on the back of the head that he fell to the ground before he could even say anything, and then lay there motionless.

Wickersham sat on the edge of the bed and studied the panicked woman, who was now talking a mile a minute and pulling at her bonds. He put the knife to her throat and said, "Shhhhhh." Then it was time to let the fun begin. He played with her nipples and ran his hands up and down her body, in every sensitive nook and cranny, until he had her memorized.

He was her new lover.

Her rock star lover.

If he had a bigger cock, this is when he'd stick it in.

Instead he used his fingers.

Chapter Seventy

Day Fourteen - July 24
Monday Morning

FOLLOWING A TANGLED SUCCESSION of bizarre dreams, Bryson Coventry woke, realized the room was still pitch-black, and shifted around to see what time it was. With any luck he still had a full night of sleep ahead of him. The familiar red digital numbers of his alarm clock said 4:32.

Ordinarily, this is where he would turn to the other side and go back to sleep. But the events of last night wouldn't leave him alone and, after ten minutes of tossing under the covers, he climbed out. The cut on the back of his head must have opened last night because his hair was matted with dried blood. He showered on the lower level, so as to not wake Darien, popped three Tylenol for the headache and then started the coffee machine and watched it gurgle.

An animal desire gripped him.

The desire to kill.

He wondered, if the opportunity arose, whether he'd have the strength to not give in to it.

He poured skim milk directly into the coffee pot, stirred it with a spoon until it was a solid cream color, then poured a cup into his favorite mug and sat outside on the front steps in the dark.

Crickets chirped.

Lots of 'em.

And the pine trees in his yard filled the air with scent.

Suddenly the door opened behind him, Darien sat down and put her arm around his shoulders.

He kissed her.

"I'm thinking I could kill this guy," he admitted. "I want to see his eyes roll back into his head and feel his heart stop pumping."

"Don't."

"I'm not sure it's my choice."

She looked at him. "Something like that is always a choice. He's not worth screwing your life up for."

"Yeah, but . . ."

She cut him off. "Enough," she said. "I'm okay. It wasn't that big a deal."

"What he did is rape," Coventry said. "Any kind of penetration qualifies."

"Like I said, I'm okay. Just forget about it. And remember, I can't have the cops involved."

He chuckled.

"I'm a cop," he reminded her.

"You know what I mean."

He did indeed. Last night, she talked him out of filing a report. She couldn't be involved in any official police business. She couldn't be fingerprinted. She couldn't have her DNA taken.

Darien Jade wasn't her real name.

"Should I just walk down the street and get out of your life?"

she asked.

"No. Absolutely not."

HE GOT TO WORK BEFORE EVERYONE ELSE and tapped into every system he could think of to find out if Darien Jade was wanted and what for. Whatever it was it wouldn't make a difference. But he wanted to know.

He got one dead end after another.

The FBI profiler, Dr. Leanne Sanders, walked into the room shortly before seven in an expensive outfit, looked around, saw only Coventry and headed over to the coffee machine.

Coventry met her there to refill.

"Where is everyone?" she asked.

"They think they have lives," he said.

She chuckled.

"Having a life just gets in your way."

"Yeah," he agreed. "Lives are overrated."

They ended up at his desk. He almost propped his feet up out of habit but caught himself at the last moment. Leanne opened a tan leather briefcase and pushed a stack of papers across the desk.

"Airline manifests," she said. "Between Denver and San Francisco."

Coventry was impressed.

"That was quick."

"I called in some favors and now officially owe three blow-jobs," she said. "I was wondering last night why our guy—assuming he lives in Denver—would fly out to California to kill someone."

Coventry cocked his head. "He probably didn't want to pee

in his own backyard—same thing regarding the woman in Santa Fe, assuming they're all connected."

"Maybe," Leanne said. "I mean, he's peeing in his own backyard now, big time. So why not in March? That's only four months ago."

Coventry shrugged.

"He's mutating," he said. "You know how these guys are. Now that he has a few notches on his belt he's suddenly bullet-proof. The dumb-ass cops will never catch him, so why waste all the time and money traveling? Plus, you can't create a media frenzy if you spread yourself thin."

She nodded.

"Maybe."

Coventry looked at her. "You keep saying that."

She sipped coffee.

"Or maybe the out-of-state women were specifically on his radar screen," she said. "People he had a grudge against for some reason or another. We need to take a closer look at whether they had any enemies. I'm also wondering if it would make any sense to see if the Santa Fe woman and the San Francisco woman have anything or anyone in common."

Coventry shrugged. He didn't see it as a priority, but had to agree that it wouldn't hurt. "Yeah. Maybe they both dated the guy."

He studied the airline manifests.

There were pages and pages of names, from several airlines.

"Do we know who any of these people are?" he asked.

"Not yet. That's why we got up early."

He chuckled. "And I thought it was to drink coffee."

Chapter Seventy-One

Day Fourteen - July 24
Monday Morning

YESTERDAY, SUNDAY, TAYLOR SUTTON RESOLVED once and for all to get out of the case. Nick Trotter had fired her anyway and wouldn't ever change his mind. So there was no gratitude or money coming her way. Plus, whoever it was she was chasing tried to kill her Saturday night. Her sister was right. It was time to get her ass back to lawyering and out of the sleuth business.

That was yesterday.

Today she saw it differently.

The problem being, however, she didn't have much to go on. About the only thing she hadn't run to ground, to the extent that she wanted, was the phone call to Nick Trotter from the Texaco station on May 5th at 10:42. According to her notes, two gas purchases were made in that approximate timeframe, one by John S. Martin and another by someone using the card of a company called Seven Circles. Maybe one of those people placed the call to Nick when they stopped for gas.

According to Google, though, John S. Martin was sixty-five and the president of a local chapter of a model railroad club.

Not exactly the kind of guy to send chills up your spine.

Claudia walked in just as Taylor lit her first match of the day.

"What are you doing here?" she asked. "Did your hearing get cancelled?"

Shit!

That's right.

She was supposed to be in Denver District Court for a motions hearing at nine. Her watch said 8:51. She ran to the closet and got dressed in the middle of the room while Claudia poured her first cup of coffee and watched with amusement.

As she ran for the door Claudia said, "Third time this year."

"Call 'em and tell 'em I'm on the way!"

"Sure. Lucky I have them on speed dial."

"Not funny."

THAT NIGHT AFTER DARK SHE DROVE THE MUSTANG to County Road 6 in the heart of farmland, parked on the side of the road in the gravel and killed the engine while a cloud of dust kicked up.

She got out, locked the door and—dressed in black—headed up the road with a queasy feeling in her gut and the gun holstered under her sweatshirt. Binoculars hung from her neck and a medium-sized flashlight was wedged in her back pants pocket. Crickets sang in droves but other than that the night lie still and quiet.

She swallowed.

According to the continuing research conducted earlier today, Seven Circles was a Colorado Corporation. It was also a limited partner in a Colorado Limited Partnership called Dusty Dirt, L.P. Public records indicated that Dusty Dirt owned 350 acres of land with a mailing address known as 9861 County Road 6. That property, in turn, wasn't too far from Bob's gas station, the place where Bob gave Taylor's business card to the driver of a van.

Someone with a Seven Circles credit card bought gas from the Texaco station in Westminster on May 5th, about the same time the mysterious Northwest phoned Nick Trotter from the station's phone.

Taylor's gut told her this was the north forty she'd been looking for, the place where Northwest lived.

In twenty or so minutes she came to an asphalt driveway that snaked into a fairly flat field for about two hundred yards and ended at a large house that appeared to be a fairly modern ranch. Hiding behind a tree she pointed the binoculars at the house. The lights were on but she didn't see anyone home, even after watching it for two or three minutes.

She walked up the asphalt, hugging the shadows, to get a closer look.

As she got near the house she spotted a large auxiliary building of metal construction, something in the nature of an oversized modern barn. No lights came from it.

She walked over and found a man-door next to the large overhead door. She tried the doorknob, found it unlocked, quietly opened it and stuck her head inside.

All quiet.

No one was there.

She went in and looked around.

Inside, she saw a number of vehicles.

Including a van.

Her heart pounded.

She came back out and now saw movement inside the house.

Taking a position in the shadows behind a tree, she focused the binoculars on the activity.

She saw a man, about six feet tall, who looked to be in incredibly good shape. He was in the kitchen, holding up a wineglass and dancing, almost as if he was twirling with a partner.

Except he wasn't.

Suddenly he looked right at her.

She gasped and dropped the binoculars.

Chapter Seventy-Two

Day Fourteen - July 24
Monday

USING THE COMPOSITE SKETCH AS A REFERENCE, Nathan Wickersham hung around the 16th Street Mall in that part of downtown where Janelle Parker thought she actually saw the woman once. It was a long shot, he had to admit, but he absolutely had to find her one way or another. She was the driver who ran the other car off the road in the desert. The man with her at the time, the one who bashed mommy's head in with a rock, was the same person who blackmailed Wickersham. Together they wanted Janelle Parker dead because she was a witness who could put them away. Except they were too chicken-shit to do it themselves so they somehow found out who he was and set him up to do the dirty work. No doubt they were out of town this last weekend in a public place, with plenty of witnesses to back them up.

He hung around for hours.

Sweating up a storm.

Even in the shade.

Then, just as he was about to give up, he spotted a young lady with a remarkable resemblance to the person in the sketch, walking out of a building near Glenarm. He snapped a couple of pictures of her with the digital camera when she wasn't paying attention and then followed her all the way to a parking lot on 20th Street. There she got in a tan colored Honda Accord— license plate number DTM-337—and drove off.

BACK AT THE FARM HE WENT STRAIGHT TO THE VAN, pulled the door open with a loud clang and shook Janelle Parker's drugged body until she woke up. "Is this the woman?" he asked, showing her the digital pictures.

He could tell by the expression on her face that it was.

"My God! Yes! I can't believe you found her." Then: "Now you'll let me go, right?"

"Not quite yet," he said.

He checked her chains, found them solid, and slammed the door.

USING THE WOMAN'S LICENSE PLATE NUMBER, he found out her name and address. Snapping his fingers to the oldies station, in a damn good mood, he drove by her house in the Camry after dark. She lived in Arvada, in a so-so place on a large wooded lot.

Taking her wouldn't be a problem.

Yeah, baby.

Oh yeah.

Get yourself ready.

Chapter Seventy-Three

PAUL KUBIAK HARDLY EVER CAME DOWN to homicide because when he did everyone wanted to know if he had their
stuff done yet. So when he walked into the room Coventry
raised an eyebrow.

"Got something to show you," he said.

"Celery sticks?" Coventry asked.

"No, I'm off that crap. Come on."

Coventry followed him, realized he left his coffee on the
desk, ran back to get it, then followed the man to the elevators
where he stopped and pressed the down button. "Parking garage," Kubiak said. Coventry took the stairs and actually beat
him down.

"This way," Kubiak said.

Coventry followed him until he stopped in front of a yellow
1963 Split-Window Corvette. "So what do you think?" Kubiak
asked.

"Is this yours?"

Kubiak grinned and nodded. "All original, numbers match-
ing, Second Flight," he said. "A friend of my dad's bought it

new. I don't even remember the guy, but apparently I used to play with his son back in my diaper days. I'm the second owner."

"You're kidding."

No he wasn't.

They checked it from bumper to bumper. Coventry couldn't believe the condition.

"Want to drive it?" Kubiak asked.

He seriously considered it but shook his head. "If I crack it up I'll have to hear you whine about it for the rest of my life," he said. "So I better not."

So Kubiak drove instead.

With no AC and no way for the air to escape out the back, it was without a doubt the warmest, stuffiest, most unbearable car ever built. Within three minutes Coventry said, "I'm getting one. That's all there is to it."

KUBIAK WANTED TO KNOW THE LATEST on the case so Coventry filled him in while they drove around the city and made heads turn. Now, more convinced than ever that the San Francisco case was related to theirs, they were telephoning everyone on the airline manifests and recording the conversations. Then they were playing them for the Santa Fe woman who swore she'd recognize her attacker's voice if she ever heard it.

"Any matches so far?"

"Let's put it this way," Coventry said. "We're having lots of luck. Unfortunately it's all bad."

"I hear you," Kubiak said.

"I mean it," Coventry said. "If we don't catch this guy soon I'm going to end up directing traffic in Waddle Worm, Nebraska."

Kubiak laughed.

"Waddle Worm? Is that what you just said?"

Coventry grinned. "I think so."

"Waddle Worm," Kubiak repeated.

"Waddle Worm, Nebraska."

"That's the stupidest name I ever heard."

Coventry chuckled.

"Waddle Worm," Kubiak went on. "It doesn't even make any sense."

"It's not supposed to," Coventry said.

"Good, because it doesn't."

"Anyway, that's where I'm going to end up."

"In Waddle Worm."

"Right. Waddle Worm, Nebraska."

WHEN COVENTRY GOT BACK TO HIS DESK he looked around for his coffee cup and then remembered he set it on the ground in the parking garage so he wouldn't spill anything on the 'Vette.

So he got another cup.

Then he had a wild idea and called Jena Vernon.

"Listen I got a favor to ask you. Do you remember after the body showed up in my truck and you ended up doing a news coverage of the CSI up at my house?"

She did.

"The helicopter up above that day, that was from your station, right?"

It was.

"That was the day the woman got bit in the face by the rattlesnake and died, up on the ridge. Do you remember that?"

She did.

"Good," he said. "There was a guy up there that day, who flagged the chopper over. Do me a favor and see if your helicopter friends picked up any footage of that guy."

"Why?"

"No reason," he said. "Just curious. By the way, have you ever heard of Waddle Worm, Nebraska?"

She laughed.

"That's the stupidest name I ever heard," she said. "When do you want to know about the footage?"

"Let me put it this way. Do you have it yet?"

A pause: "He's the one, isn't he?"

"No," Coventry said. "And don't tell anyone."

Chapter Seventy-Four

Day Fifteen - July 25
Tuesday Afternoon

IN HER LEFT HAND TAYLOR SUTTON CARRIED a paperback book called *Native Birds of Colorado.* Around her neck hung light-weight bird-watching binoculars. She wore a large brown hat that gave good protection from the sun, a brown T-shirt, light-weight earth-green cotton shorts, and oversized black sunglasses. She wore a fanny pack on her stomach. Inside that she had the gun, the concealed gun permit, two granola bars and a plastic bottle of water.

She blended in with her surroundings on this beautiful Tuesday afternoon.

If anyone happened to spot her, she was nothing more than a curious observer of nature, out on a stroll in the open lands of Colorado to see what she could see.

She entered the farm property all the way across the field from the house, parking on a gravel road about a hundred yards from a metal building.

She watched for people.

And so far saw none.

Every so often she brought the binoculars to her eyes and

scouted the trees. If she saw a bird she watched it for a few moments. Every once in a while she opened the book and looked at a picture.

Then she walked some more.

As she did she kept her eyes on the ground. She never walked over the same spot twice. More than an hour into her stroll, in the field at the north edge of the property, not far from the trees, she saw something that might actually be what she came to find.

A possible grave.

She stood ten feet from it, brought the binoculars to her eyes, pointed them at the trees, and then shifted her vision down to study the ground.

The earth mounded up slightly in the approximate size of a body. While the grasses surrounding the area were of uniform thickness, the mounded area had spotty patches. You could actually see dirt in some places, unlike most of the rest of the field. Also on one side of the mound, there was a pile of dirt, possibly thrown there while digging and then never raked or shoveled back in.

WHEN SHE BROUGHT THE BINOCULARS DOWN and looked around just to be sure she was still alone, she couldn't believe her eyes. Across the terrain a man raced directly towards her on a dirt bike, still a long ways off, but definitely coming right at her.

She immediately hit the ground.

As the sound of the engine got closer she frantically pulled the handgun out of the fanny-pack and took off the safety. Holding it in two hands she pointed it in the direction of the bike.

She could actually see the motorcycle now through the weeds, even while lying flat.

It was bright green.

But strangely quiet.

The man riding it was the same man from the farmhouse.

He wore a medium sized backpack but no helmet or eye protection.

He looked intense.

Almost insane.

She tightened her finger on the trigger.

Then peed in her pants just before he got to her.

Chapter Seventy-Five

SNATCHING THE WOMAN from her house turned out to be easier than Nathan Wickersham expected. The heavy trees provided all the privacy he needed. The sizzling summer day kept her windows beautifully open. The knife put more than enough fear in her heart. He tied her hands behind her back, fastened a ball gag in her mouth, and then marched her out the front door in her pajamas, straight into the trunk of the Camry.

Piece-of-cake.

He got caught at a red light at Ward Road. Headlights approached from behind and another vehicle pulled up and stopped—a cop car with two cops inside. One of them looked at Wickersham's license plate.

Shit!

He had the plate lights off.

He reached under the dash and flipped the toggle switch. The cops talked to each other. The light turned green and Wickersham took off, not too fast or too slow. The cops followed him.

They stayed on his ass, tailgating, trying to get him to speed so they'd have a reason to pull him over. He kept it two under the limit until they finally thought of more important things to do and turned around. He exhaled, got safely to I-25 and headed north, finally relaxed enough to power the radio back on. "Smells Like Teen Spirit" came out of the speakers. He sang along with the words he knew and faked the rest, which were most of them.

WHEN THEY GOT TO THE FARM HE TOOK THE WOMAN to the metal building at the far end of the property, where he kept the getaway car. He brought her inside, strapped her to a chair and then sliced a chunk of flesh from the end of her baby finger while she screamed through the ball gag.

Now that he had her attention he said, "Tell me your boyfriend's phone number. Right now!"

She did.

He dialed it.

A man answered.

"Listen carefully, otherwise your little lady friend here is going to die a horrible death," he said. "You want Janelle Parker dead? Well fine, but you're going to do it yourself and I'm going to videotape you doing it. After you do it then I'll have as much on you as you have on me. That's the only way I'll ever be sure that I'm free of you. After you do it I'll let the woman go. You have my word on that. Then you two go your way and I go mine. That's the deal and that's the only deal. I'll call you tomorrow with instructions. In the meantime don't do anything stupid. I have the woman where you'll never find her so don't even think about a rescue. Just follow the plan and we'll all get through this alive."

He hung up.

The woman watched him with wide eyes. He ran his fingers through her hair, and said, "We're about to find out if he really loves you or not." He cocked his head. "What do you think? Will he kill for you?"

The look on her face told him she didn't know.

"Well, he better," he warned. "It looks like you two black-mailed the wrong person, doesn't it?"

Chapter Seventy-Six

Day Sixteen - July 26
Wednesday

COVENTRY COULDN'T SLEEP. He got up at four in the morning and went to work. Two hours later—wired on coffee—he paced back and forth so fast that he knocked over the snake plant and spilled a load of dirt onto the carpet. He muscled the stupid thing upright then scooped up the soil with his hands and threw it back in the pot.

Good as new.

An hour later Kate Katona walked in needing coffee in the worst way.

"What would it take for you to get on a plane to San Francisco?" Coventry questioned.

She ignored him and filled a coffee cup.

"Here's the thing," she said. "You've had coffee, I haven't."

He waited while she took a swallow.

"I'm serious," he said.

"But you were just there," she noted.

He nodded.

"Yeah, but we didn't get into the victim's background all that much," Coventry said. "I'm starting to give more and more credence to Leanne's theory that the guy flew there specifically to kill her. So we need to dig into her background, find out who has a motive, and maybe that's the guy we're looking for."

"Wouldn't San Francisco have already done that, when she disappeared?"

Coventry nodded. "They did to an extent. I want you to find out if they went far enough."

WHEN SHALIFA NETHERWOOD SHOWED UP thirty minutes later he intercepted her at the coffee pot.

"Here's my idea," he said. "You go down to Santa Fe and see Jacquelyn Davis-Wade again," he said. "Hypnotize her, get her drunk, I don't care how you do it, but find out something we don't already know. Maybe go over the police file again too. See if there's any more news coverage with crowd scenes that we don't already have, or amateur video, or whatever. Bring me back something."

She wrinkled her forehead.

And gave it ample consideration before responding.

"Bryson," she said. "That seems like a long shot. We were already more than thorough."

He slumped in his chair and closed his eyes.

She was right.

It would be more productive to think of something new instead of plowing the same tired ground.

The morning turned into a flurry of motion: task force meetings, placating the chief and the mayor, phone tips, cross-referencing data, developing press conference strategies, continuing work on the airline manifests.

Shortly after 10:00 Jena Vernon called with two updates.

Another letter arrived in today's mail. The next strike was scheduled for this weekend, meaning two days from now. Also, the
helicopter had no footage of the man on the ridge, the one who
was with the woman when she got bit by the rattlesnake. By the
time the aircraft was landing the guy was already leaving. They
never talked to him or got a good look at him, or even a bad
look for that matter.

"Figures," Coventry said. "Thanks for checking."

BY NOON COVENTRY COULDN'T EVEN THINK STRAIGHT.
So he left the building, headed down to the South Platte River
and found a shady spot on the bank, about twenty feet away
from a couple of homeless guys who were sleeping next to overflowing shopping carts.

The guy lived north of Denver.

Coventry was pretty sure of that because the guy came upon
the woman with the flat tire at three in the morning. His hunt
was done for the night and he was headed home.

That road was a back street way to get from LoDo to I-25.

The guy also lived in a place where he could hold people
captive. Coventry pictured a place that had space between the
houses. Or better yet, a remote place where no other houses
were even visible.

He stood up and headed back to the office.

Chapter Seventy-Seven

Day Sixteen - July 26
Wednesday Night

THE MOON SHINED SO BRIGHT that it threw shadows. In the distance a coyote barked, then another, and within seconds a whole frenzied pack yelped and yapped. Taylor Sutton paused briefly, shivered, and pictured something lower in the food chain scrambling desperately for ten more seconds of life.

Carrying a shovel through the darkness, she felt like anything but a lawyer.

She felt more like a grave robber.

Or a Voodoo woman.

She wasn't sure yet what she'd do if the place she spotted yesterday actually turned out to be Sarah Trotter's grave. She did know, however, that she had to find out, one way or the other.

She continued walking.

Just her and her night shadow.

The place reminded her of yesterday, when she pissed in her pants. It still surprised her that the man on the dirt bike didn't see her. He ended up at the metal building, where he parked the bike and then went inside for thirty minutes. Then he headed back across the field to the house.

363

She didn't turn the flashlight on until she was pretty sure she was at the right place. As soon as she confirmed she was, she turned it off again.

THEN SHE DUG. The soil was loose, as if it had already been turned up before, and the shovel went in easily. She put the dirt in one pile so she'd be able to find it all again afterwards. Even though the thin Rocky Mountain air had cooled the night considerably, she still worked up a sweat.

She concentrated in the middle of the mound. After getting down a good foot or so, she found nothing and sat down to rest. The silence seemed so strange. It was as if the rest of the world didn't exist.

She pushed to her feet and continued digging.

Now she was down two feet and still nothing.

She rested again.

When she got down three feet she hit something. Not something hard like a root or a rock, but more like a rubbery object. She got down on her knees, shined the flashlight in the hole, and pulled dirt out with her hands.

A stench filled the air.

She uncovered a bellybutton and gasped.

Shit.

This was real.

This whole thing was actually real.

She removed more dirt and saw even more of an abdomen. The putrid smell almost made her vomit, but she forced herself to stay there and threw dirt back in the hole.

But she wasn't done yet. She had to see the face. She had to be sure this was the body of Sarah Trotter. So now she dug where the face would be. Her body ached but she didn't slow down. She was almost finished. She just needed to verify this one thing. Then she could get the hell out of there. Be home by midnight. Three feet down she hit rubber again.

She pulled dirt out with her hands.

And uncovered Sarah Trotter's face.

Staring up at her.

The eyes were open but filled with dirt.

Looking so strange.

Still, it was her.

There was no doubt.

Vomit shot up into her mouth but she managed to gag it back down. Then she covered the body up as fast as she could and ran.

Chapter Seventy-Eight

Day Sixteen - July 26
Wednesday Night

WITH THE POINT OF THE KNIFE pressed against the small of Janelle Parker's back, Nathan Wickersham walked her through the dark into a remote field more than twenty miles from his house. She sobbed through the ball gag, which was sort of neat. When they got a hundred yards or so from the road, he found the perfect spot and told her to stop her ass right there. He spread a blanket on the ground at the base of a small tree and laid the woman on her back with her head near the trunk and her feet pointed away. He pulled her arms above her head and handcuffed them around the tree. Then he stretched her legs down as far as they would go and staked them. She looked like she was on a medieval torture rack except she was on the ground.

There.

Perfect.

She couldn't escape in a hundred years.

Then he got the tripod and camera situated and hoofed it back to the car to wait. The man showed up thirty minutes later, right on time, pulled next to Wickersham's car and killed the engine, exactly as he had been instructed to do. Wickersham stayed in the shadows and let him sit there for five minutes, until he was reasonably sure that the police weren't coming, and then snuck over and pounded on the driver's side window with the butt of his weapon.

The man jumped.

"Step out of the car," Wickersham said. "I have a gun."

He patted the man down, found no weapons, and led him into the darkness, all the way to Janelle Parker. When they got there he turned on the flashlight—one of those powerful ones with six batteries—and shined it on her.

She narrowed her eyes against the intrusion and pulled against her bonds.

Frantic.

Sensing the end.

"Make your peace," Wickersham told her, then put the light on the man's face. "Are you ready?"

"I'm ready," the man said. The tone of his voice sounded sincere. "If you screw me over you'll wish you hadn't."

"No one's going to screw anyone over," Wickersham reassured him. "This is a win-win deal, except for her."

Wickersham started the video camera, made sure it was filming properly, and said: "Do it."

As Wickersham shined the flashlight, the man picked up the plastic bag, slipped it over the woman's head while she resisted as much as she could, then sealed it on her neck with three wraps of duct tape. They watched her twitch and struggle until she stopped moving.

"Take the bag off," Wickersham ordered.

The man did.

"Now step back."

Wickersham zoomed in on the woman's head. Her lifeless eyes were frozen open. The sheer terror of her last breath was still etched on her face.

"You did good," Wickersham said.

He put the cuffs, the plastic bag, the duct tape, the stakes, the video camera and the tripod into a pillowcase and slung it over his shoulder.

"Dump her somewhere at least ten miles from here," he said. "Someplace semi-public where she'll be found in the morning. Tomorrow you get your girlfriend back unless you do something stupid in the meantime."

The man walked towards Wickersham.

Dangerously close.

Wickersham shined the flashlight directly into his eyes and pointed the gun at him. "Not another step," he said.

The man stopped.

But the intensity in his eyes was unmistakable.

"Remember what I said," the man warned.

"Don't worry," Wickersham assured him. "You did your part, I'll do mine. Then we all walk away."

"Tomorrow," the man said.

WHEN WICKERSHAM GOT HOME HE WATCHED THE VIDEO.

It came out perfect.

He locked it in the safe, next to the plastic bag—that wonderful piece of evidence that had the man's fingerprints on the outside and Janelle Parker's saliva on the inside.

Then he checked on Ashley Conner. Nothing had changed. He pounded on the dungeon door with the sledgehammer until she screamed for him to go away.

The new door hadn't come on Monday as originally scheduled, but was definitely supposed to arrive tomorrow.

Wound up, he kicked back with a couple of glasses of wine and flicked the TV channels until he got bored. Then he went to bed. He couldn't have been asleep for more than ten minutes when his phone rang.

Chapter Seventy-Nine

Day Seventeen - July 27
Thursday Morning

AT FOUR IN THE MORNING Coventry woke up on the couch
and remembered falling asleep there last night with his head in
Darien's lap, watching a Nicholas Cage movie called *8mm*. He
wandered into the bedroom, found Darien sleeping in the middle of the bed, then went back to the couch rather than wake
her.

A flicker of light suddenly appeared on the wall and then
disappeared.

Curious, he walked to the front window and pulled the curtains back a touch. Headlights came up the street. For some
reason he sensed that a body was about to be dumped in his
front yard.

He ran to the bedroom, grabbed his weapon, deactivated the
alarm system and walked straight out the front door. The cool
night air sent a chill up his spine. The vehicle was at the end of
the street now, turning around, heading back down.

It slowed suspiciously at his house.

Someone suddenly threw something at him.

He almost shot before he realized it was a newspaper.

He shook his head, picked it up and walked back inside.

FULLY AWAKE NOW, WITH A BEATING HEART, he knew that going back to sleep wasn't an option. Rather than lie there like a sack of potatoes for an hour he decided to cut his losses and head to work. When he got there he kick-started the coffee machine and then waited for it to do it's magic while he propped his feet up on the desk and watched. He closed his eyes just to rest them for a second.

When he opened them Shalifa Netherwood was at the coffee machine, singing something in that terrible voice of hers. Coventry put his feet down, stood up and then fell over. Shalifa laughed while he figured out that she had tied his shoelaces together.

"You should see your face," she said.

"I'm glad I amuse you so much."

The oversized industrial clock on the wall, the one with the twitchy second hand, said 7:28. He must have really been out cold to sleep that long.

Shalifa brought a cup of coffee over, a peace offering.

"I had a brainstorm," she said.

The sound of her voice told him she was serious now. He untied the shoelaces but kept most of his attention on her. "Go on."

"Well," she said, "it relates to the San Francisco airline manifests. So far, we've been concentrating on getting voices recorded to see if the Santa Fe woman recognizes anyone."

Coventry nodded.

That was true.

"The woman said she could identify the man's voice if she

heard it again and I believe her," he said.

"So do I," Shalifa said. "That's not the point. These people have faces too. We can pull their licenses and see if any of their faces match anyone in the crowd scenes."

Coventry stared at her.

"I'm going to say something, but if you ever repeat it, I'll deny it."

"Oh? And what might that be."

"Brilliant," he said.

THEY GOT BUSY ON THEIR COMPUTERS, pulling up the licenses of the men listed on the airline manifests, and downloading them into a central file.

Pounding down coffee as they went.

"Brilliant," Shalifa shouted every now and then.

Every once in a while Coventry found a face that looked familiar and printed a black-and-white hardcopy of the man's license. In the end he had three photos of interest, but had no idea where he had seen any of them before, or even if he had. One of the guys seemed vaguely familiar to Shalifa, but she couldn't place him either.

They transferred all of the downloaded licenses onto a CD.

"Okay," he said. "Let's go up and talk to Kubiak and see how long it's going to take him to compare all these photos to the crowd scenes."

Shalifa looked at the wall clock.

"It's only 9:05," she said. "He won't be in for another ten minutes."

Coventry disagreed.

"Actually he gets here by eight when there's important stuff going on."

"No way."

"Way."

They bypassed the elevators and walked up the stairs.

"What do you want to bet?" Shalifa asked.

Coventry considered it.

Then they made a bet and shook.

When they pushed through the door on the sixth floor, Kubiak was at his desk, eating a donut.

Coventry looked at Shalifa and grinned.

"Sweet," he said.

Chapter Eighty

UNABLE TO CONCENTRATE, Taylor Sutton left her office and walked down the 16th Street Mall. She passed a homeless guy begging for money outside the Hard Rock Café and ignored him. A block later a homeless woman sat on the sidewalk in the shade. Taylor leaned down and asked her name, which was Mary. She reached in her pocket, pulled out five twenties, and put them in the woman's hand, making sure she had a good grip on them before she walked away.

"Don't let anyone take that from you," she said.

Ten minutes later she sat in a Starbucks sipping coffee. It felt good to be around people. The buzz helped to squeeze Sarah Trotter's dead face out of her thoughts.

What to do?

She could call Bryson Coventry and tell him where to find his man.

Put an end to the killing.

Stop the maniac dead in his tracks, before tomorrow came.

But the cops would search the man's property, to try to determine how many others he may have killed that they didn't know about.

They'd find Sarah Trotter's body.

Then they'd connect Nick to the scene, as the man's attorney. And, she had to admit, Nick was right. The cops would think there had been a conspiracy, at the least.

Nick—her client—would go down.

She couldn't take the maniac down without taking Nick down.

So which was more important?

Stopping a killer?

Or protecting her client?

She walked outside, sat down and leaned against a building. Then dialed Nick Trotter. When he answered, she said: "Your client's real name is Nathan Wickersham. Note his initials are NW, which just happens to be the abbreviation for Northwest. He lives about thirty miles north of Denver on a large tract of land, 350 acres to be precise. I found Sarah's grave on the property. I dug it up and saw her face."

She expected Nick to be emotional.

He was quite the opposite.

He concentrated on the facts and asked her a hundred questions, until he knew as much as she did.

"So now what?" she asked.

Nick didn't hesitate.

"I have to get Sarah's body out of there. Then, even if this guy—what'd you say his name is? Wickersham?—even if he lies to the police and tells them that I asked him to kill Sarah, or tells them I went along with his offer to kill her, there won't be a body to back his story up. Without a body, even if the police believe him, they won't have anything solid enough to bring a case against me."

She agreed.

"Then what?"

"What do you mean?"

"I mean, after we get Sarah's body out of there."

"First of all, there's no *we*. You're not involved."

"But I'll help you," she said.

"No, absolutely not."

"At least let me show you where it is."

"No," he said. "Just tell me how to find it."

"But," she said, "either way. What happens next? Do we call the police?"

"Call the police?" The tone of his voice registered the question as an absurdity. "Of course not."

She stood up, suddenly too agitated to sit, and rocked on her feet. "But the guy's a killer and he's not going to stop," she said.

"The guy's also my client," Nick said. "We're lawyers, Taylor. We don't turn in our own clients. That's Rule Number One."

"Yeah we're lawyers," she said. "But we're people too. And I was a person a long time before I was ever a lawyer. I'm thinking that the best course of action is for you to get Sarah's body out of there, then I'm going to make an anonymous call to Bryson Coventry and get the killing stopped."

"No," Nick said. "That's wrong."

"I don't care if I get disbarred," she added, which was true.

"That's not the issue," Nick said. "The issue is loyalty."

She paused.

"Don't do anything until we talk some more," he added. "I'll get Sarah's body out of there tonight. Then we'll talk. The guy won't strike until the weekend, so we have time to think things through."

Chapter Eighty-One

Day Seventeen - July 27
Thursday Afternoon

TAYLOR SUTTON FOUGHT THE URGE to pick up the phone and call Bryson Coventry. Nick Trotter's words kept ringing in her ear: "We're lawyers, Taylor. We don't turn in our own clients. That's Rule Number One."

He was right.

Rule Number One.

And it wasn't just a rule.

It was a founding pillar of the entire judicial system. Clients had to be able to trust their lawyers. They had to be able to tell the truth to their lawyers without having it bite them in the ass.

But the fact that she could stop the killing with just one simple phone call was too important to dismiss so easily, rules or no rules.

As far as any fallout to herself, she couldn't give a shit about that. She didn't care if she ended up disbarred.

She could live with that.

That wasn't the issue.

Her sister Brooke dropped by in the afternoon to pick up some more employment policies for Image. She looked stressed

and had a bandaged finger. Taylor told her that she found out
who was terrorizing Denver.

"My dilemma is whether to call the police," she said.

Brooke responded emphatically and immediately. "No. You
can't do that."

Taylor felt grim.

Trapped, even.

"You're a lawyer," Brooke added.

That was true.

But it seemed to take on less and less significance.

"If this guy kills again, and I could have stopped it but did-
n't, I'm not sure I could live with myself anymore," she said.
"The hell with being a lawyer."

Brooke slumped into a chair.

Her face serious.

"Okay," she said. "I need to tell you a few things. Get ready
to hate me."

"Hate you?"

Brooke nodded.

Tears welled up in her eyes.

"I'm not the person you think I am," she added.

WITH THAT, BROOKE TOLD A STORY that Taylor could hardly
believe. It started last month, when Brooke and Aaron bor-
rowed Taylor's Porsche to drive to Las Vegas to meet with potential investors for Image. They were driving at night, drunk,
smoking pot, doing over a hundred, and ran another car off the
road. When they doubled back to see what they'd done, they
found three kids and a man—presumably the father—dead. A
woman, the mother, came through the windshield but was still

alive. Aaron bashed her in the head with a rock.

"We talked about it being a mercy kill," Brooke said. "But deep down there was more to it. She was a witness."

They came back to Denver without incident and thought it was all behind them, except for having to live with what they had done.

Then Aaron discovered there was a witness. "In fact, you were with me the day he told me," Brooke said. "Remember? When we were walking through the construction site at Image?"

Taylor remembered.

Brooke got a call from Aaron, something that clearly upset her. Taylor asked if Brooke was having relationship problems but Brooke said no, it was something else.

"Yes, I remember," Taylor said.

BROOKE CONTINUED.

"The witness was a photographer who had been camping out in the desert and saw the whole thing. She gave the police a good composite sketch of me."

Taylor lit a match and watched it burn.

Okay.

"I threw up at the scene," Brooke added. "So the police had my DNA and blood alcohol count. If they ever tied me to the crash, I was screwed. Once they found me it would just be a matter of time until they found Aaron. He'd go down for murder. Hell, we'd both go down for murder."

Brooke swallowed.

And fidgeted with a pencil.

"We found out the name of the witness: Janelle Parker. It turned out that she actually lives in Denver. Since you and me look a lot alike, and since you get on the news so much, we were scared that it was only a matter of time before she saw you, thought you were me and called the police."

SUDDENLY TAYLOR FLASHED BACK.

"So the woman who followed me on the 16th Street Mall, the one who disappeared into Nick Trotter's building, that was . . ."

"Right."

". . . Janelle Parker."

"Right. She thought you were me," Brooke said.

Another flashback.

"I was in the Tattered Page Bookstore after that," she said. "I remember picking up a book, it had photographs of Denver in it. The author's picture was on the back cover. I knew I recognized her from somewhere but couldn't place her."

"That was Janelle Parker."

BROOKE STOOD UP AND PACED.

"Then things got worse," she said. "Nick Trotter hired you to find out who his mystery client is. I came by your office one day to drop off some draft employment policies. Aaron was with me. You played us the latest conversation between Nick and his mystery client. You said that both you and Nick believed that Nick's client was the same person who was terrorizing Denver."

Taylor nodded.

"I remember that," she said.

"Well," Brooke said, "Aaron recognized the guy's voice. He was a professor from Berkeley who stopped at CU the summer before last during some kind of national tour, talking about recent mathematical breakthroughs or some such stuff. Anyway, Aaron recognized his voice. He'd forgotten the professor's name, but we dug around a little and found an archived listing of events. Aaron recognized the guy's name when he saw it—Nathan Wickersham."

"That's the guy," Taylor confirmed.

BROOKE BOWED HER HEAD.

"Then it got even worse," she said. "We figured this guy was going to kill someone anyway, so why not Janelle Parker? We smashed a window in his house and broke in, just to rattle him up. Then we blackmailed him. We called him up and told him we knew who he was. We told him to take out Janelle Parker. That's why Aaron and me went out of town last weekend, so we'd be somewhere far away, in public and with plenty of witnesses. That way if the police ever figured out that we had a motive to kill Janelle Parker, we'd have an alibi."

"Wow."

"Right, wow."

Brooke dabbed at her eyes.

"So Wickersham actually took her just like he was supposed to," Brooke said. "Aaron and me heard about it and thought it was all over. Except it wasn't. Instead of killing her he interrogated her to find out who would want her dead, figuring that's who was blackmailing him. He found out that she witnessed the crash in the desert. He found that out she gave a composite sketch to the police. He got a copy of that sketch from her house. Janelle Parker told him she saw the woman, me, on the 16th Street Mall. Actually, of course, she saw you and thought it was me. Anyway, he hung around in the area looking for the person in the sketch and saw me one day when I came out of your office building. He followed me and got my license plate number. He used that to get my name and address. Then he kidnapped me."

Taylor was shocked.

"He kidnapped you?"

Brooke nodded. "He told me the whole story while he had me captive. That's how I know it. Then he made Aaron kill Janelle Parker, while he videotaped it," Brooke said.

"Aaron killed Janelle Parker?"

"To save me," Brooke said. "That's the only reason the guy let me go. Now he thinks we're at a standoff and it's all over. But he's wrong."

"What do you mean, he's wrong?"

BROOKE PACED EVEN FASTER.

"Sooner or later the police are going to catch him," she said. "They'll find the tape of Aaron killing Janelle Parker. So tonight, Aaron's going to pay this asshole a visit and get that tape. Then he's going to kill him."

"Aaron's going to kill Nathan Wickersham?"

Brooke nodded.

"Yes. Tonight."

"Tell me you're not going with him."

She hesitated, then said, "He won't let me. He's going alone. But you can't call the police. We can't have the police anywhere near that guy's house until we get that videotape back. After Aaron kills him, there won't be a need to call the police any-way."

Chapter Eighty-Two

Day Seventeen - July 27
Thursday Evening

NATHAN WICKERSHAM SET THE TORCH down to rest for a few moments while he surveyed his handiwork. With another twelve inches of cutting he'd have a hole in the dungeon door big enough to step through.

"Daddy's coming, Ashley," he shouted.

"Go away!"

"You've been a bad girl," he added.

"Screw you!"

"Ten more minutes," he said.

It was then that he felt something poke him in the back. When he turned, Aaron Cavanaugh had a gun pointed in his face. Behind him stood Brooke Sutton.

His heart raced.

And he tried to think of a way to kill him.

Right here right now.

In the next two seconds.

But nothing came to mind.

"No games," Aaron said. "We want that videotape. Now!"

He held his hands up as if in surrender, and said, "Sure. No problem. It's in the barn."

Aaron waved the gun at him.

"Let's go," he said.

They walked to the barn, then through it all the way to the far end. A ladder led up to an elevated storage area. Wickersham leaned against a workbench, and nodded to the area. "It's up there," he said.

He watched Aaron Cavanaugh think deep, as if deciding whether he should climb up himself, send Brooke, or make Wickersham go up.

Wickersham reached behind his back, as if steadying himself, picked up a circular saw blade lying on the bench and threw it as hard as he could.

The blade hit Aaron Cavanaugh directly in the forehead.

It sank into his skull and stuck there.

So deep that it didn't even fall out when the man hit the ground.

The woman screamed and ran.

Wickersham bounded after her.

"Come here, bitch!"

Chapter Eighty-Three

Day Seventeen - July 27
Thursday

―――――――――――

BY FIVE O'CLOCK NEITHER BRYSON COVENTRY nor Shalifa Netherwood could figure out why they both seemed to recognize the picture of one of the men from the airline manifest, Nathan Wickersham. When the lobby phoned him and said Darien Jade was waiting downstairs for him, instead of taking her out to supper he brought her up to the office.

"Where do I know him from?" he asked.

She shrugged but continued to stare at the picture.

Finally she said, "I don't know, but he does look familiar somehow."

Coventry folded it up and stuck it in his shirt pocket. "I'm starved," he said. "Let's get some food."

They ate burgers and drank beer at the Outback.

Then took a long walk.

They were back at his house, just before dark, when he walked into the kitchen and found Darien sitting at the table, drawing glasses and a moustache on the printout.

"I'm not sure," she said, "but this could be the guy I saw in the van, down on Speer."

"The guy we chased?"

She nodded.

"I thought you said you recognized that guy as one of the TV crew who was at the apartment building."

"Right," she said. "Him. He was walking down the stairwell when I was coming up. I got the feeling he turned around and stared at my ass." She drew the moustache darker. "In fact, that's probably why he seems familiar to you and Shalifa—you must have seen him there that day."

Coventry thought about it.

Then he called Alicia Beach, the news reporter, to ask her if she had someone named Nathan Wickersham on her TV crew that day at Ashley Conner's apartment building.

She didn't answer.

He left a message and then called and left six more.

She didn't return his calls, maybe because she had already gone to bed.

Finally he said, "Come on, let's take a ride."

Two minutes later they were in the 4Runner heading to Nathan Wickersham's house with a pair of binoculars in the back seat.

Chapter Eighty-Four

TAYLOR SUTTON FREAKED OUT when the night came and Brooke no longer answered her phone. Brooke's promise that she wouldn't go to Wickersham's with Aaron tonight was beginning to seem more and more like a lie.

Taylor pictured her dead.

Or dying.

Then Nick Trotter called her. He said he was leaving in a few minutes to dig up Sarah's body. He wanted to be absolutely sure everything was still safe and that she hadn't told the cops anything.

"I'm heading out there too," she said.

"Why?"

"It's too complicated."

"No. You can't."

"I have to."

"You're going to blow it for me," he warned.

"I'm sorry about that but I don't have a choice."

"Damn it!"

"I'm sorry."

"All right," he said. "At least let's drive out together."

That made sense.

If wouldn't hurt to have a strong man at her side. Plus she could show him exactly where Sarah's grave was.

She holstered the gun under a loose fitting sweatshirt and paced frantically waiting for Nick to show up. She dialed Brooke's number every sixty seconds and got nothing but the stupid voice mailbox.

Nick finally swung by in a Ford F-150 pickup truck—which he would use to transport Sarah's body—and she followed him in the Mustang, heading north on I-25 at five miles over the speed limit.

THEY GOT OFF THE FREEWAY and headed towards Wickersham's place down a deserted road. The night was black and the road was bumpy. Without warning Nick pulled over to the side and killed the engine.

She pulled in behind him, confused.

"Got to piss like a madman," he said.

She did too, actually.

They each headed to different sides of the road and disappeared into the darkness. She squatted and peed in the weeds. Just as she pulled her pants back up Nick stuck a gun in her back.

"Taylor, you screwed up," he said.

WITH THE GUN IN HER SPINE and a handful of her hair in his fist, he made her walk a long way into the darkness.

"At least tell me what I did," she said as they walked.

"You're going to tell the police about Wickersham," Nick said. "You think it's your moral duty. You think it's important enough to violate attorney-client confidentiality."

That was true.

But only to a point.

"Not until you get Sarah's body out of there," she said. "I'm no threat to you, Nick. You'll end up okay."

He pushed the gun into her back and kept her walking.

"Here's the problem," he said. "Sooner or later you're going to find out the truth. If you're the kind of person who'd turn Wickersham in, you'd turn me in too. And we can't have that."

Her mind raced.

What did he mean, The Truth?"

"What truth?" she asked.

"SURE, WHY NOT," HE SAID. "I guess you have a right to know why you're going to die. Nathan Wickersham did in fact start out as a mystery client, just like I said. But then I found out who he was. I killed Sarah and buried her on Wickersham's property. That way, if the police ever found her, they'd think he did it. After all, he is a killer."

"You killed Sarah?"

"Of course," he said. "She was a bitch. Trust me, she deserved it."

She fell to the ground and he pulled her up.

"Tell me you're kidding," she said.

He laughed. "Then, after the fact, I figured out that my little plan wasn't as foolproof as I thought. I started to worry about the police making the connection between Wickersham and me, and thinking that I asked him to kill Sarah, in exchange for

---

money or legal representation or something. I worried that Wickersham might even go along with it and take me down to get a deal for himself."

"I can't believe you killed Sarah," Taylor said.

"So," Nick continued, "I needed to shore up my story somehow. So I hired you, told you about a mystery client, and the fact that the client killed Sarah. I had you investigate it. Then, later, if the need ever arose, I would waive the attorney-client privilege and have you talk about all our conversations where I said that the mystery client killed Sarah, and even paid you big money to find him. I'd have you talk to the police, the press, and maybe even get your testimony in at trial. You were my alibi, in effect."

HE YANKED ON HER HAIR AND BROUGHT HER TO A STOP.

"Far enough," he said. "You weren't supposed to actually find anything. But you were too good for your own britches. I fired you twice but you still wouldn't stop. Then I put a gunshot through the window of your Porsche to scare you off."

"That was you?"

"Of course it was me," he said. "That still didn't get you to back off. Then you not only found Wickersham but also found Sarah's body. Now you want to go to the police."

"Nick," she said. "I would have never figured this out."

He disagreed.

"Yes you would have," he said. "You never stop. But even if you didn't, I still can't have you making a call to Coventry and stirring everything up. The last straw for me was finding out that you'd turn in Wickersham. If you'd turn him in, you'd turn me in too."

He paused.

"The police will look for me," she warned. "They'll connect me to you."

"Wrong," he said. "They'll connect you to Wickersham, because that's where your body will be buried, if it's ever found. You were getting too close to him—passing out your business card to all those gas stations, going out into the night dressed as bait, sucking up to Bryson Coventry, and all the rest—so he had to take you out."

"Nick. You won't kill me," she said. "We're friends."

Silence.

"Just say you won't kill me," she said. "Let's just go back to Denver and forget that any of this ever happened. We can still make all this work out."

More silence.

"The time for talking is over," he said. "I'll give you a moment to make your peace."

She already had her gun in hand.

Out of the holster.

Hidden under her sweatshirt.

Instead of making her peace she fired at his chest.

He fell to the ground and she ran.

Chapter Eighty-Five

Day Seventeen - July 27
Thursday Night

NATHAN WICKERSHAM MADE BROOKE SUTTON sit on the toilet and watch as he filled the bathtub with cold water. He didn't say a word to her.

He didn't need to.

She knew what was coming.

She was stripped down to her panties.

Her hands were tied behind her back with the belt from his bathrobe.

He walked over and pulled her to her feet by her hair.

"We're going to take our time and have a lot of fun," he said.

Then he threw her in the tub on her back and held her head under water. She kicked her legs like a maniac, splashing water all the way to the ceiling. When it seemed like she was about to give up he yanked her head up.

"Having fun?" he asked.

Then he pushed her under again.

The legs kicked.

So beautiful.

So helpless.

Suddenly he saw something out of the corner of his eye. Someone ran into the room pointing a gun at his head. A woman.

"Die you asshole!" she screamed.

She shot.

Just as her feet went out from under her on the wet tile.

The bullet came so close that it brushed through Wickersham's hair.

She hit her head on the floor, and crawled disoriented, but still had the gun in her hand. Her face was insane.

She fired again.

And again.

The woman in the tub had her head out of the water, gasping for air, sensing a rescue and kicking at him.

He ran.

All the way through the house.

Then out the front door.

And headed for the barn.

Chapter Eighty-Six

Day Seventeen - July 27
Thursday Night

BRYSON COVENTRY KILLED THE ENGINE of the 4Runner on County Road 6, about a hundred feet down from Nathan Wickersham's driveway, just as Kate Katona called from San Francisco.

"Big news," she said.

He sensed urgency in her voice.

"How big?"

"It turns out that our San Francisco victim had an enemy after all," she said.

"Really?"

"Oh, yeah," Katona said. "Apparently she filed claims against one of her professors at Berkeley, alleging sexual harassment and stalking. The guy denied everything, but the school removed him with pay pending an investigation. Then she withdrew the claims contingent upon him never teaching there or anywhere else again. Everyone signed confidentiality agreements, including the school. So the whole thing was buried pretty deep."

Coventry scratched his head.

"Very interesting," he said. "What's the professor's name?"

"Someone called Nathan Wickersham."

"Did you say Nathan Wickersham?"

"Yeah, why? Does that ring a bell?"

Before he could answer gunfire came from the house.

HE JUMPED OUT OF THE CAR, told Darien to call for backup, and ran to the house. He got there just in time to see a man run into a metal building. A woman bolted out of the front door of the house, holding a gun, chasing the man.

Coventry pointed his gun at her.

"Stop!" he shouted. "Throw down the gun."

She did.

"Get him!" she screamed. "He's getting away!"

Coventry ran into the structure just in time to find a man riding out the other end on a dirt bike.

He looked around.

He spotted a jeep.

And a pickup truck.

He ran for the jeep hoping the keys were in the ignition. They were. He fired it up, put it in first gear and took off so fast that he stalled. He started it again and shot out the back of the building. He looked for a red taillight and found none.

"Shit!"

Then he headed into the field.

Hoping against hope that he was going the right way.

As his headlights bounced up and down they lit a red reflector up ahead.

"Got you," Coventry said.

But he didn't.

The bike was pulling away.

Headlights came from behind him. It must be the woman. She must be in the pickup truck.

Coventry stepped on the gas and the jeep bucked ferociously and threatened to roll. He realized he never put his seatbelt on and didn't care.

This was the man.

The man who had Denver on its knees.

The man who put his hands on Darien.

A METAL BUILDING APPEARED AHEAD in the far distance. The bike headed that way. Coventry stepped on the gas even harder, desperate to catch up. This time the jeep shot into the air and landed with a violent crash, rolling over.

He flew out.

And landed on his back with a spine-compressing jolt.

He couldn't tell up from down.

He felt for his gun and realized it was gone.

Headlights came at him dangerously fast. A vehicle ground to a stop two feet before it ran him over.

"Come on!" someone said.

A woman's voice.

He opened her door, pushed her into the passenger seat and took off.

"He's a killer," she said. "He's the one terrorizing Denver. His name's Nathan Wickersham. Don't let him get away!"

"I know!"

Coventry bounced over the terrain as fast as he could without rolling again. They got to the metal shed just as another car was coming out. Coventry rammed him, their wheels locked and both vehicles flipped.

The pickup landed on the roof. The door wouldn't open and Coventry climbed out the window just in time to see the other man run. Coventry ran as fast as he could and tackled him. They twisted on the ground and pounded each other. Coventry felt his flesh rip and blood spill out.

Then a gun fired.

Flesh ripped in Coventry's thigh.

He'd been shot.

The other man twisted away.

And almost got loose.

But Coventry got him from behind and put him in a head-lock. Then he twisted his weight. The man's neck snapped and he immediately went limp. Coventry stayed there gasping for breath, and then finally rolled over and concentrated on the pain in his thigh, not knowing if he'd killed the man on purpose or not.

Chapter Eighty-Seven

Day Twenty-One - July 31
Monday Morning

WITH A CUP OF COFFEE IN HAND, Bryson Coventry opened
the door of Taylor Sutton's law office and hobbled in with a
heavily bandaged right thigh. She was alone in the room, lighting matches and throwing them into an ashtray.

"You need better security," Coventry said. "Anyone can just
walk in."

She frowned.

Fearing the worst.

"I don't know if you heard," he said, "but your client Nick
Trotter's body was found last night. Someone shot him in the
heart."

Taylor tried to look surprised.

"Someone shot Nick?"

Coventry nodded.

"Who?"

He shrugged. "I don't know and I don't really care. It wasn't
in our jurisdiction so it's not my problem."

"That's so sad," she said. "Poor Nick."

Coventry cocked his head. "Not really, after what he did to

his wife. It's almost sort of like that armchair justice that you and me were talking about. Whoever did it ought to pat himself, *or herself*, on the back."

She had no idea what to say.

So she just looked at him and said nothing.

He was draining the last drop of coffee from the cup. She took it from him, walked over to the coffee pot, filled it up and brought it back over

"How's your sister?" he asked.

"Brooke's fine. I hear Ashley Conner's doing good too."

Coventry nodded. "We have her in counseling but she's nineteen. She'll be painting up a storm by the end of the week. Everyone in the department chipped in and bought her a ton of brand new supplies."

Taylor smiled.

"She'll probably end up with a seven figure book deal."

As AN APPARENT AFTERTHOUGHT Coventry reached into his shirt pocket, pulled out a piece of paper and handed it to her. It was a composite sketch of a woman—Brooke—folded into thirds.

"Thought you might want that," he said.

She looked at him.

"I found it at Wickersham's," he added. "I didn't see it as relevant to anything. It was just cluttering up the place."

"Is this the only copy?" she asked.

He nodded

She hugged him.

Then put her head on his chest and fought the urge to cry. As he held her she said, "Sorry about the leg."

He chuckled.

"No big deal. That's why we have two."

A few minutes later he shuffled to the door, then turned and said: "Someday maybe you'll buy me a drink, off the record, and tell me a story."

She nodded.

"Count on it."

WHEN HE WALKED OUTSIDE HE COULDN'T BELIEVE IT. Rain poured out of the sky. More rain than he had ever seen in his life. Darien Jade twirled around on the sidewalk, her arms stretched out and her face to the sky, totally soaked. He hobbled over and was drenched from head to heels by the time he reached her.

She hugged him.

"It's raining," she said.

He looked at the sky.

"Of course it is," he said. "I just washed the car."

"My real name's Amanda Kathleen Jones," she said. "So now you know who to investigate to find out about my past."

Coventry cocked his head. "I like the name Darien better," he said. "Let's just stick with that."

"I killed a man," she said. "But he had it coming. I'd do it again in the same circumstances." A week ago Coventry wouldn't have understood that concept as well as he did today. "It happened in England," she added. "I had to tell you, to be fair. It wasn't right of me to keep it from you any longer. So now you know. If you want me gone I don't blame you, not a bit."

He kissed her and said, "I can't believe it's actually raining."

Darien.

ABOUT THE AUTHOR

Jim Michael Hansen, Esq., is a Colorado attorney. With over twenty years of high quality legal experience, he represents a wide variety of corporate and individual clients in civil matters, with an emphasis on civil litigation, employment law and OSHA.

www.JimHansenLawFirm.com.

For information on the other novels in the *Laws* series, please visit Jim's website.

www.JimHansenBooks.com
Jim@JimHansenBooks.com